*Happy 7
Ann*

WHEN THE FOREST BLEEDS

Hope You Enjoy!

Phil

WHEN THE FOREST BLEEDS

David Bailey

Writers Club Press
New York Lincoln Shanghai

When The Forest Bleeds

Writers Club Press
an imprint of iUniverse, Inc.

For information address:
iUniverse, Inc.
2021 Pine Lake Road, Suite 100
Lincoln, NE 68512
www.iuniverse.com

ISBN: 0-595-26400-X

Printed in the United States of America

Justine and Carmen, thank you both for the never fading smiles and words of encouragement when I seemed to need them the most. You two are awesome.

Larry thank you, for taking the time to sit down and help me, when I know you were trying to juggle your busy life to fit me in.

To everyone else, do not think that in any way I do not appreciate what you all did. I shall not forget. I hope you enjoy the reading of this book, as much as I enjoyed writing it.

"A man should first be happy with the power within himself, before he attempts to have power over others."

—P.E.

CHAPTER 1

❀

As he opened his eyes, the pain flooded in like a tidal wave. The night before was about to make him pay for allowing himself the freedom to enjoy life. Tony Parkins' life had come to a sudden halt after his marriage abruptly ended over three years ago. Having had time to reflect, he realized that it had ended a long time before that. The pain still stung him that he had caught his wife having affairs. His work, at the *Garibaldi Daily Newspaper*, and relationships with friends were hurting. None of it seemed to matter; all he wanted to do was to be left alone to grovel in his self-pity for awhile.

Making his legs swing out from under the covers, he fought to control the spinning. He had been down this road so many times lately, that it almost seemed natural. He had been only putting in a half-hearted effort at work, and after many meetings with the top brass, it had been brought to his attention that it was time to shape up or ship out. Even before his feet hit the floor, the dreaded sound of the phone ringing pierced his brain. If a gun had been handy, he would have blown it right off the nightstand. He laid back down wishing that the irritating sound would mysteriously stop, even though he knew it wasn't going to happen. Shakily, he reached over and picked up the receiver.

"Yeah, it's your dime," He answered in a dry croaking voice.

"Jesus, Tony, you sound like shit." It was Cathy Montgomery. She was the only person at the newspaper that he even remotely associated with. He had even tried to have a brief relationship with her. It didn't take long before he realized that he was not close to being ready to commit, and she was far too sweet to be leading her on. She, on the other hand, had fallen in love with him. She always seemed to be there for him, and on many occasions, had said she was willing to wait until he was ready.

"And your point being?" he moaned.

"Listen, something big is going down here. Jason has been locked in his office for hours and there is a lot of yelling going on."

Jason Burke was the man, and he always made sure everybody else knew it. Tony thought this was a good thing for the little shit. Tony and Jason had always butted heads right from the time Jason had taken over running the newspaper. The thought of him having a bad day, gave Tony a great deal of pleasure.

"So, you just called to make my day, or what?"

"Oh, quit with the sarcasm. Something big has happened. I can only get bits and pieces of what all the fuss is about, but sounds like a mass murder some place. From what I can gather, Jason's arguing with TNT over who's going to cover the story. Now hang on to your shorts, the old boy wants you to do it."

Terrance Neil Tibbet, or TNT as most of his friends and enemies called him, liked Tony because, as TNT put it, "The man comes from the old school of reporting, and doesn't pussy foot around." Tony knew that if it weren't for old TNT, he probably wouldn't be working as a reporter today. He had covered and backed Tony's ass more times than he could recall. He had hired Tony as a young boy right out of school. He hired him as an errand runner and over the years groomed him to become one of the top reporters at the paper. After he retired and handed the reins over to Jason, the problems started. First it was the changes in procedure Jason wanted to implement; saying it would help streamline the operations of the paper. Why screw with something that's working just fine, was Tony's thinking. Then after that his marriage had fallen to pieces and that just seemed to compound his distaste for Jason and his changes. It didn't just stop at Jason though; he wasn't much in the mood to put up with anyone much lately. The thought of old TNT chewing Jason a new butt, brought some relief to the pain he was reeling from.

"Bet that's making his day," he laughed, "I'll be down there after I grab a shower and clear out the cobwebs. Give me an hour, and see if you can scoop out any more details on this story they're all fired up about."

"Ok, will do. You know you really should slow down on the drinking a bit. I don't mean to sound like your mother, but…"

"Well, then don't." He said sharply. He really didn't mean to be so blunt to her, but the last thing he needed at this point, the way he was feeling, was a lecture.

"Sorry, Cats, just a little on the edge this morning." He had been calling her Cats for as long as he could remember. She reminded him of a cat. She had a sleek, firm body that would turn men's heads when she entered a room. He had always smiled at those poor souls when she would accompany him into a room. She had long, toned legs that formed into a smoothly rounded ass. Her mid section was hard and flat, and he had always joked with her that her breasts were like two perfectly rounded apples. Her long neck seemed to constantly call to him, inviting him to dive in like Dracula and her hair was an auburn colour that hung down just past her shoulders. He remembered how it used to feel, brushing against his bare chest and the way her hazel eyes sparkled as they made love. How he wished he would have held off, trying to start a relationship with her, until he was ready. Oh well, you never know, stranger things have happened, he thought to himself.

"Hey, no problem, it's just that I care what happens to you." She replied, with that voice that had a way of creeping into him, whether he wanted it to or not.

"I know, I'll be there as fast as I can." He almost whispered and hung the receiver up before she could say anymore.

As he sat on the edge of the bed, curiosity was mounting as to what kind of story would bring the two main men of the paper into a confrontation on who would cover it. What was so special about this story, that TNT would be fighting so hard for him to cover it? The more he let his mind dwell on it, the worse the pounding in his head became. He pulled his way up off the bed and staggered for the bathroom, hoping some pills and a shower would help him make it through another day.

The Firebird jumped to life without hesitation. Tony loved this car and the feeling he would get when the countryside was flying by. Whenever he needed time for himself, he would turn up the music and take her for a run. It was as if he could out run anything bad, and leave it behind him. This particular morning, he was in the need for some speed. He pulled out from the underground parking lot, of his apartment building, and headed for the freeway. As the Firebird merged into the freeway traffic, he pressed down hard on the accelerator and at the same time reached over and turned up the stereo. The sound of AC/DC filled the interior. As he watched the West Coast Mountains pass by, he couldn't help but smile. This had always felt like a dream world to him. The towering snow capped mountains on one side of the highway, and the calming deep blue of the Pacific Ocean on the other. His favorite times, were when he could escape down a lonely winding stretch of highway, with majestic red cedars bordering either side and the soft light green carpet of the moss, that covered the forest floor, crept up their trunks. He had always likened it to some child's fairy tale story.

As the car raced along, dodging in and out of traffic, Tony found his thoughts heading back to the morning phone call and what it could all mean. The words "sounds like a mass murder…" kept flashing through his mind. Was it another one of those doomsday cults, that hardly required this much hoopla? Nowadays, it seemed like that was happening on a regular basis. It was a mystery to him, how some people needed something to believe in, no matter what the cost.

"Crazy assholes. What ever happened to just believing in yourself." He murmured.

No, this had to be something more involved than that. Pressing even further down on the accelerator he raced for The Garibaldi Building. Soon the glass monolith of the *Garibaldi Daily Newspaper* was looming large in his vision. He could remember when it was a small personable paper, with an office downtown and a small group of reporters who were like family to each other. Now it had become a dog eat dog business, with everybody trying to place their noses a little further up Jason's butt. All he wanted to do was kick that butt as hard and as far as he could.

Turning into the staff parking lot, he saw Cats pacing in front of the doors that led into the employee's entrance. When she saw him, he noticed a huge sigh escape from her. She immediately stepped into the lot and quickly made her way toward him. He pulled the Firebird into his assigned parking stall, at the back of the lot. It used to be next to the entrance door, the spot reserved for the main reporter. Jason had taken it upon himself to reassign parking stalls, and seeing as how he wasn't ready to kiss Jason's ass, he got put to the back of the bus. The stall next to the door, now belonged to a reporter by the name of Randy Watson. Randy was one of those people that just seemed to grate on your nerves, by just being in the same room. It wasn't that he was a bad person, it was just that he had that know it all attitude, and if he didn't know it then he knew somebody who did.

Climbing out of the Firebird he was met by Cats. She was fidgeting and had a hurry up expression on her face.

"Well, this could be big," she exclaimed, "Seems that a crew of loggers were killed, no let me rephrase that, were butchered I think would be a more appropriate way of putting it."

"Ok, slow down." He had his hands on her forearms trying to calm her down. "Have you got any details?"

"All I know, is that it happened at a logging camp north of here. Other than that, everything is fairly sketchy. From what I've heard, who ever did it really did a number on them."

"No idea who did it or why?"

"Not that I've heard. Jason wants to see you right away, and he is some pissed. Even threw his coffee mug against the wall in his office."

"This day just keeps getting better." Tony said with a smile. "The old man must have won this one. Christ, I wonder what's up?"

They both knew that usually TNT would put in his opinion on how a story should go, but for the most part he stayed out of the everyday running of the paper. His philosophy had always been, "If you don't trust the people you got working for you, then they shouldn't be there." TNT had always run the newspaper like that and even Tony had to agree with it. Even with his dislike for Jason, there also came a strange bit of respect for the way he had made the newspaper prosper, since taking over. He just didn't like the way he treated people. Or maybe he just didn't like the way he treated him.

"Well, we're never going to find out standing around out here." Cats said impatiently.

"Alright, already. Shall we?" Tony bowed and waved his arm in an elegant manner toward the building.

They turned and walked toward the entrance door. Tony noticed that he had a certain spring in his steps as he got closer to the doors. This should be beautiful, he thought to himself, as he held the door open for Cats and gave her a big smile. Being able to watch Jason squirm, as he assigned him a real newsworthy story, was going to be so enjoyable. Lately, it seemed as though all he was getting assigned were the boring community interest ones, that no one else wanted. Cats stopped in the doorway and looked up at him.

"Now you try to be nice in there." She said with a stern face, knowing perfectly well that there was no way, on God's green earth, that was going to happen. She had watched over time, as the man she loved slowly unraveled before her eyes, and there was nothing she could do to help. He had to get through this himself, with nobody's help. All she could do was to stand by and be there for him when he needed her.

"I must be stupid." She mumbled, as she turned and continued through the door.

"What was that?"

"Nothing."

They showed their badges to the security guard and crossed the lobby to the elevators at the far side. As they waited for the elevator, Tony remembered a time when a security guard was not needed. Nowadays though, threats came in on a regular basis in response to many of their stories. As the elevator doors opened, Randy Watson stood in the middle of the tiny lift, like a guard. He was dressed in his usual professional attire, as Jason always referred to it. He had a gray tweed sports jacket, with patches on the elbows and a white shirt with a black tie. His pants were black and perfectly pressed. His shoes looked like he was getting ready for inspection, they were so spit and polished. To Tony's delight, Randy looked as uncomfortable as hell. Major suck hole, was the only thought that ran through Tony's head.

"Hi, guys." Randy greeted them. Before they could answer, he was off on his usual rambling. "I hear there's a big story breaking upstairs. Jason has been on the phone all morning with Mr. Tibbet." The smug look on his face, as if he had an exclusive story, made Tony want to burst his bubble big time. Cats looked at Tony, smiled and with a wink turned to Randy.

"No kidding. Any ideas as to what's going on?" she asked, looking up into Randy's eyes making him take a deep swallow.

"Well, I probably shouldn't be saying anything, confidentiality and all, but if you promise it won't go any further than here." Randy was looking at the two of them as if the next words out of his mouth could destroy human kind, as they knew it.

"Not a word." Cats whispered.

"My lips are sealed." Replied Tony, trying hard not to smile.

Staring at them for a moment longer, Randy decided to continue. "Ok, from what I have found out, they found four loggers cut to pieces with a chain saw. It happened just north of Newport."

Newport, was a small, beautiful town on the coast with a post card view of the mountains standing guard over it, and the blue Pacific Ocean dotted with islands spread out in front of it. Its main industry was logging and had been for decades. Over the last few years, it had started to embrace tourism as a viable commodity. Newport had been in the news headlines the past few months, due to a confrontation between logging companies and an environmental group. The group was trying to stop logging in and around the area. The environmentalists were saying that logging was destroying century old forests and habitats for rare animal species. The logging companies countered, that it was a renewable resource and provided jobs for thousands of people and kept the economy of Newport alive. For the most part, the community was totally behind the logging companies.

"That's about all I know right at this point. I haven't had an opportunity to consult with Jason yet." Randy finished, in a smug, almost dismissive manner.

You arrogant prick, Tony thought. I could wipe that smug attitude of yours all over the inside of this elevator. Almost as if on queue, Cats slid closer to Watson.

"Come on Randy, there must be more to it than that. Does anyone have any idea who might be behind it?"

Tony smiled at how smooth she was. As he looked at Randy, he knew that he was going to spill more about what he knew. But then if anyone knew that you couldn't keep anything from Cats, it was him. He had tried many times and every time she was able, and without too much difficulty, to pull any info out of him at will. Tony knew, that by the time she was through with Randy, he would tell all and not even realize he'd done it. This would be fun to watch, he mused to himself. Randy was already well into telling all, looking straight into Cats eyes as if hypnotized.

"...had told me that one of the environmentalist's vans was seen heading that way the night before. No one has seen them since. From what I understand, the police are up the Whallington Valley looking for them right now. I think they have a suspect in particular that they're looking for, but I'm not really positive on who."

"Is the Whallington Valley where the killings took place?" queried Cats, still working her magic on him.

"That's where they found the bodies, around mile eighteen."

The Whallington Valley, was where the majority of the logging had always taken place. It was also where most of the confrontations had taken place between the two groups. It was a very pristine area and the local natives claimed to have many sacred areas in the region. Their ancestors had used many of these areas for ceremonial purposes and burial grounds. About two months ago, the environmental group, Nature's Select, set up a roadblock to prevent any logging companies from proceeding into the valley to log. After a long court battle, the logging companies won a court injunction that was to prevent the environmentalists from setting up any more blockades. The environmental group was ordered to take the barricade down. The protesters declared that the roadblock would stay, until the government protected more areas from logging. In the past few years, the government had declared huge blocks of crown land as reserve and felt that it would leave it at this state, until they had time to study whether there was enough areas left for the logging industry to survive.

The logging companies were putting great pressure on the police to remove the blockade, so that they could get back to work. However, things seemed to be getting tangled up in the red tape and moving very slowly. The justice minister had held off using any force, as it was coming up to election time, and the government was trying to portray themselves as environmentally friendly.

After much discussion and several beers in the Ocean Port Hotel, one of the local pubs in Newport, a few of the loggers decided to clear the Nature's Select blockade themselves. After all, they rationalized, they had the law behind them. That night they parked about a mile from the blockade and stealthily approached it through the forest. As these men made their living in the woods, they covered the ground with great ease. They could hear the voices of the protesters and smell the smoke from their fires. The plan was to charge the camp and scare the "pussies" off. As they stood invisible in the woods, watching the unsuspecting group in front of them, they couldn't help but to get wrapped up in the moment. With adrenaline levels boosted by alcohol, they charged from the trees screaming like wild animals. They caught the protesters so totally off guard, that it took only a few minutes and the encampment was torn to the ground. Cooking utensils were scattered all over and tents were ripped down then thrown on the fires. Some resistance was shown, but only greeted with punches and kicks. Cameras were smashed and tossed on the flames. The loggers forced the protesters into the center of the camp and surrounded them holding pieces of wood.

"Are you people crazy?" Sherri Maider screamed. She was one of the organizers of the blockade for the Nature's Select. She had been in confrontations before, but never involving violence of this magnitude. As she looked into the eyes of the men surrounding them, she became very frightened.

"No, not crazy. Just fed up with you people coming around here and disrupting our lives and stealing a life from our families." Frank Cotis snarled. Frank was one of those men that other men always looked up to and wanted to be around. He was a tall man, with a very defined muscular body. After years of climbing up and down mountainsides, carrying chainsaws and axes, his body was chiseled to a god like state. As he looked at the people cowering in front of him, he suddenly realized what an explosive situation he was in.

"Yeah, and it's time you learnt that you can't come in here and do what ever the hell you want. This is our home and we won't stand for it!" George Ruber was and always had been a firecracker ready to go off at any time, and this seemed like a very good time, to him, to let it go. He was a short man but like Frank, very solid from many years of hard work.

"Schools in." one of the other men snarled, as the loggers started to move in toward the confused and frightened protesters. Whimpers and silent prayers could be heard from the small group, huddling ever closer to each other.

"Please, don't do anything you're going to regret later. We'll move out immediately, but please, many of these people have families." Sherri was pleading and praying for sanity to prevail. She knew that this situation could turn more violent at any moment. Being one of the organizers for the Nature's Select, she would be called in whenever it had been determined that all other options to draw attention to a certain cause had failed. One of the other organizers or herself, would step in to organize a protest of some kind to draw attention, especially media attention. She believed strongly in what she was standing for, but tonight she was wishing that she had accepted that invitation from friends to go camping this week.

"Oh, we should worry about their families, when they don't give a damn about ours. All you care about is getting your names in the paper and looking like heroes, when you don't really give a shit about anything!" George was screaming and his eyes were on fire. He was tapping a piece of wood in his hand and stepping from one foot to the other, as if ready to spring at any moment. "Well, after tonight your wish will come true. Your names will be in the paper alright, but not for the reasons you want."

Frank heard the mumbled agreements from a few of the other men, and knew he better do something fast. This whole situation was escalating and would get out of hand in a hurry. The other men would be ok, he could calm them down, but it had been a long time since he saw George this wound up. With the way the loggers' emotions had been stretched, over all the protesting against them and their profession, it was only a matter of time before something was going to snap.

"Give it a rest." Frank jumped in. "No one is going to hurt you, just get out and don't come back. You see if you push men too hard, they will eventually retaliate." He was looking into Sherri's eyes, almost pleading her to keep her mouth shut and just leave.

"Are you nuts?" George yelled, grabbing Frank by the arm and spinning him around. "These bastards will be back even before we get home. We have to make sure we get the point across." With surprising speed he sprung forward and swung the piece of wood hard across one of the protesters ribs. The wind escaping from the man, could be heard as he dropped to his knees. George raised the wood above his head and was about to bring it down, on the fallen man's back, when it stopped suddenly in mid air. Frank had reached out and grabbed it at the last second. George swung around to see who had interfered with the lesson, that was about to be administered. As their eyes met, Frank could feel the anger and hate emanating from George. He knew at that moment, that things had changed in a big way. A line had been drawn and they both had chosen a side of it to stand on.

"We came here to scare these people, not hurt anyone or maybe even kill someone. Use your head man, we're trying to save our jobs, not become some kind of vigilantes." Before George could answer, Frank turned to the protesters. "Now get your sorry asses out of here and listen very carefully. Do not come back, cause next time you may not be so lucky."

As the group held on to each other and started to walk away, some thanked Frank quietly as they passed by. Others looked in fear, as they cowered past George, which seemed to bring a smirk to his lips.

Sherri stopped in front of Frank and looked into his face. No words were spoken, but the gratitude and respect that showed from this small lady, made him realize that he had definitely done the right thing. As he watched the little group walk away into the night, he could feel the eyes behind him boring into his back.

"Never figured you to be a chicken shit." George spat.

As Frank turned around, George was standing so close, that he could feel and smell the foul stench of George's beer breath. Frank braced himself for the confrontation that was about to happen. He hadn't planned on things going this way. It was suppose to be just a mission to scare these free loaders off. Now he had to deal with men that felt like they had been cheated from the opportunity to vent all the frustration they had been collecting over the years, from people messing with their lives. People had been accusing them of doing things without knowing the facts. Quite frankly, for a short moment when he saw those people huddled and scared, he felt like he would have liked to hurt these so called friends of the environment. What a laugh. All they knew about the environment was what they were taught in school, or what some environment group with money, was able to get them to believe through their propaganda. It was the loggers who lived and worked all their lives in the woods. They had nothing but the highest respect for the forests, because it was their livelihood.

"No, not a chicken shit, just using my brain not my brawn. If we end up in jail, then they win. This way, we can stay on top of them, in jail they can carry on however they feel like and we look bad in everyone's eyes."

"Yeah, that may be all fine and dandy, but I'm telling you right now, if they come back, you stay out of my way Frank, cause I will go through you too." George snarled sticking his chest out as if to challenge. Even in the dark of the night, Frank could see the steely glare from George. They stood, not moving, just letting each other know that neither one would be intimidated by the other.

"Come on guys, we're suppose to be on the same side here, remember. Now let's get the hell outta here," Billy Pacster cut in, "The cops may be coming out and we sure as hell don't want to be standing here."

That was enough to convince them, the men turned and disappeared into the night as quickly as they had appeared. Lives changed that night, in ways that none of them could imagine. If any of them could have seen the future and what was waiting, none of them would have been out there. None of them, loggers or protesters.

CHAPTER 2

$Even before the elevator doors opened, Tony was already getting himself mentally prepared for Jason. He wasn't going to take any unnecessary crap from him, but he was very interested in what Jason had to say. He figured he would take a little sacrificial verbal diarrhea, to get what he wanted. He held the door open while Cats stepped out, then followed her out into the main office area. Randy was going to the main research floor. He had a deadline to make and needed to know more about the effects of working around power lines for any length of time. There was a lawsuit against the hydro company. One of the power line employees was claiming that he had developed severe headaches, due to being forced to work long hours around live power lines.

As the doors closed behind them, Tony looked around the oak walled reception area. The walls had gold-framed pictures of peaceful scenery from different world locations. There were eight desks lined up in two neat rows of four, and each desk had a gold desk lamp, with a green lampshade. On the back wall behind the desks, was the name of the newspaper in individual raised letters with a brushed gold finish. Neon lights had been placed behind the letters so that they glowed with a halo effect. Every time he had to come up here, he always thought this belonged in a lawyer's office and looked out of place here. However, Jason had insisted on doing the renovations. He said it would give it a more professional atmosphere to work in, and would be more appealing to visitors. To the right was a hallway with three offices on either side and the copying and coffee room at the end. To the left it was exactly the same, with the exception of Jason's office at the end of the hall.

Cats grabbed his elbow and leaned over to whisper in his ear. "I'll see you later. Give me a call on my cell and we can meet for a drink. I'm dying to hear what this is all about."

"Ok, sounds good. Later." Tony looked at her and smiled, then turned and started the march down the hall toward Jason's office.

"Hey."

Tony stopped and turned to look at Cats. He could see the grin on her face and the wink. "You be nice in there now." she chuckled and headed for the elevator. He was so happy to have her around. She never pressured him for anything and always had a way of calming him, making him feel good about himself.

He stopped in front of Jason's office door, took a deep steadying breath and knocked. He grabbed the doorknob with the other hand and proceeded to open it before Jason had the opportunity to invite him in. This bugged Jason and Tony loved doing it.

"So, you always barge in without being invited?" Jason snarled.

"But I was invited, remember. You're the one who wanted to see me." Shit, thought Tony, this is starting well, better calm down and play the game a bit. He stood in the doorway waiting for Jason to ask him to sit down. That might appease the arrogant jerk. As Jason looked up from the desk, Tony was taken by the look on his face. He was red in the face and his mouth was set in a hard firm line. He looked angry and yet there was a touch of fear in his eyes.

"What the hell's with you? You going to stand there in the doorway all day, or you going to sit down? It really doesn't matter to me."

Tony gently closed the door and moved over to a round coffee table situated in front of the desk. The top was glass and sat on a beautiful wood burl. He pulled out one of the black leather chairs and sat down. Jason kept on reading the document on his desk, and seemed to ignore Tony completely. After what seemed like an eternity of silence, Jason finally looked up at him.

"Do you know why I asked to see you?"

"No." Tony lied.

"I find that hard to believe. A building full of reporters and you don't know what the scoop is. Especially someone like you, who thinks he's Gods gift to the reporting world. Thought everyone would have known by now. There was a butcher job done on some loggers up at the Whallington Valley."

"I did hear rumors about that."

"Yeah well, it's not just a rumor. These men had their bodies cut up by chain saws and axes. How soon can you get up there?"

Oh no, you're not getting off that easy, Tony thought to himself. "You want me to go?" he asked, deliberately putting a little extra emphasis on me.

"No, I don't," Jason replied, without hesitation, "but Mr. Tibbet is insisting on you. As far as I'm concerned, we have far better reporters for this story. Reporters that have their heads out of their asses and still want to report. He seems to think that they're too soft and will miss the real story about what happened up there. Besides, I owe him one, so this is pay off for me. Don't screw this up Parkins. Then again, if you make the old man look bad, you won't have anyone covering for you anymore. Now, we have reservations for you at the Travelers Eight Motel, in Newport. Can you be there by tonight?"

Sitting there coldly staring at Jason, Tony didn't answer for a few seconds. "Yeah, I guess I could. Are you sending a photographer with me?" he finally replied, after getting his anger under control.

"Well, I hadn't thought about it. Why, do you think you need one?" Jason asked, in a tone that made Tony's hair stand up at the base of his skull. His tone had made it sound like he was not capable of handling this assignment on his own, but needed someone to baby sit him.

"Have no problem handling this on my own, but we both know that this is going to be a big story and that there is less of a chance of missing anything with two people there. For someone who is so worried about the old man looking bad on this, I would think you would have figured that out." The biggest problem for Tony, was that he was a reporter not a picture taker. That's why there were photographers in the world. They take the pictures and he writes the stories.

"I guess I could send Paul Pratt up with you." Jason said, without any hint that Tony's last remark even fazed him. Tony knew he had gotten to him though. Jason's hands had formed into fists resting on his desk.

Tony liked the thought of doing this assignment with Paul. He was a good photographer and was a good partner to travel with. Paul was thirty years old, black hair combed straight back, which really made his sky blue eyes shine. His smile was always big and seemed like it was especially for you. When you were on the road with him, you also knew that pretty ladies would always be around.

"Paul sounds good to me. Will you get a hold of him, or would you like me to?"

"No, you can, I've got other things to deal with right now."

Jason put his attention back to the task he was doing, when Tony had entered the room. Tony stood up and started out the door. Stopping in the doorway, Tony turned back towards Jason.

"Hey, Jason"

"Yeah, what is it?" Jason looked up.

"It must have been some big favor you owed him, huh." Tony turned and walked out closing the door behind him.

Considering all, that didn't go too bad, Tony thought to himself. He still didn't understand why TNT wanted him so bad on this story. What did he mean that the other reporters were too soft and wouldn't get the true story? What was up with that? He decided to give the old man a call later and see if he could get an answer right from the horse's mouth. He stepped into the elevator and pushed the fourth floor button. The fourth floor was often referred to as the maze. It was where all the reporters worked and was a maze of cubicles and aisles. Tony hated it because he felt like it sucked a person's personality right out of them. You could sit there in a cubicle not doing a thing, and by the end of the day you felt drained and depressed. After years of being in his cubicle there were times when he felt very much like a walking zombie. He thought about the loggers, outside working in the outdoors, life all around them. Now that's the way a man was meant to live. Fresh air, the room and freedom to move. Shit, he wouldn't even last five minutes out there, he chuckled to himself. Those guys worked harder in one morning, than he probably did in a whole week.

As the elevator doors opened, it hit him. The noise of telephones ringing, the clattering of keyboards being punched and a background noise of mingled voices, that seemed to all converge into one loud murmur. People were hustling about amongst the aisles. He wondered how many of them really knew where they were heading. Most had deadlines they had to meet, but some were totally lost. They were easy to pick out by the panic on there face. These were the unfortunate souls that got a bad case of writer's block or had partied a little too much and didn't even have a start on their story. Then there were the situations that seemed to be happening to him over and over again. They were given stories to cover that didn't even justify wasting any time on them. He figured Jason usually had something to do with him being handed those assignments. Many a day he had wandered around this same floor lost, trying to come up with something to bail his ass out. Surprisingly enough he had always managed to do it. Even though most of his solutions were far from award winning articles, at least he always had a story ready to go to print. To him that was one of the many things that made a reporter, being able to make deadlines with something for the readers to ponder about over their morning coffee.

"Jesus, I've got to clean this up one day." he muttered to himself, as he stood in front of his desk. He had pictures and little out dated reminder notes pinned on the walls. Papers, books and manila envelopes covered the desktop to the point that you couldn't see the top. The shelves had all kinds of knick-knacks that he had been meaning to throw out but just couldn't get himself to. Not yet anyways. Most of them he had acquired while he was married and they still reminded him of a happier time. They were also a constant reminder of his past twenty-two years and kept a certain pain deep inside so that he would always keep his guard up in the future.

As he picked up the folders from his chair and placed them on the floor, he noticed the note stuck to his computer keyboard. It was from Cats; she was going to be down at the Rail. The Rail was a great bar downtown. It had a nice casual atmosphere during the day and, in his humble opinion, the best strip joint by night. The note said three o'clock so he had a couple hours to kill. He decided to try and get a hold of Paul and maybe come up with a game plan to get to Newport tonight. As he reached for the phone to dial Paul's number, it rang making him jump.

"Hello, Tony Parkins here. How may I help?"

"Tony, how are things these days? Very long time no see. You over that nasty bit of business with your marriage yet?" It was TNT.

"Wow, and to what do I owe this unexpected pleasure?" joked Tony, deliberately avoiding the question about his marriage.

"Well, I figured by now Jason and you have had your meeting. Hope it wasn't too nasty. I know how much love you two share for each other," he chuckled, "Anyway I thought maybe we could get together this afternoon. Knowing you, there must be a ton of questions running through that head of yours."

It had always impressed Tony how this man seemed to know exactly how he thought all the time. TNT, on many occasions, would answer a question before Tony even had a chance to ask it.

"What time were you thinking of? I've got an appointment at three."

"We can do it later, but I think it would be a good idea to get together before you head up to Newport. Is anyone going up with you?"

"Yeah, Paul Pratt."

"Good choice. I always liked that boy. Any chance you could cancel this other appointment or schedule it for later?"

"No, I don't think so. I really should make this one." Tony didn't want to cancel his meeting with Cats. He loved getting together with her. It was one of the few things that brought him real pleasure. "What are you doing for dinner? Maybe we could get together for a bite and a few drinks. I didn't figure on heading up to Newport till around nine tonight."

"Sounds good to me. I think Laurie is making meat loaf tonight anyways, and that's one meal I really don't mind missing." Tony caught the smile in TNT's voice. Laurie and TNT had been married for over thirty-six years, and Tony loved seeing them together. It struck Tony that the two of them were actual soul mates. They would still gaze into each other's eyes, walk holding hands and were not afraid or ashamed to share an intimate kiss in public.

"All right, how about we meet at Alfredo's Roof?" Tony knew there would be no argument with that suggestion. It was a great seafood restaurant on the top floor of a mall and one of TNT's favorites.

"Now you see that sounds way better than meat loaf. Ok, see you there around seven?"

"Sounds good to me. See you then."

As Tony hung up the phone, his reporter instincts were going crazy. It was as if he could feel the start of something big happening and he was about to be thrust into the core of it. Why would TNT just call out of the blue like that? Why did he want him on the story so bad? If it was such a big story to them, why didn't they already have someone up there? Why was TNT involved at all and what kind of favor could Jason owe that would make him back down and allow Tony to cover it? Yes there were a lot of questions and he was hoping that tonight was going to be the start of getting a few of them answered. For the first time in a long while, he was getting excited about reporting again. Instead of feeling like it was just a job, the fire of knowing that there was a story to be told burned at his senses. He picked up the phone and quickly dialed Paul's number with slightly shaky hands.

"Hello." Paul answered.

"Hey, Paul, it's Tony."

"Hey, buddy how are ya? So what is it, pleasure or business? I'm kinda hoping it's pleasure. Was thinking of going partying tonight."

"Well, my friend I hate to break it to you but it's business."

"I figured as much. So what's up?"

"Well, there's been a killing up in Newport and we've been assigned to go cover it."

"Newport? Is this about those loggers getting the hack job done on them?"

"Yeah. You heard about that already?"

"There was a short blurb on the news tonight."

"Damn, news travels fast. I was thinking of heading up around nine tonight. I could pick you up shortly before."

"Ok, you got it. Any idea how long we'll be up there?"

"No, not really sure. I'm thinking maybe four days at the very most. My gut is telling me this could be a big one."

"Right on, lets do it. See you around nine then. I'll be waiting with bells on." Paul laughed which made Tony smile. Yeah, he was real glad to have this man work with him on this one. Considering the nature of what they were about to investigate, it was good to have someone along that could keep your spirits up. He placed the receiver back in its cradle and sat staring around his cubicle. Yeah, one day he would have to straighten this place up and get organized.

That would have to wait for now though, he had a meeting that nothing would keep him from.

Man he loved this place. The Rail was just one of those places where you could kick back, have as much or as little fun as you wanted and no one gave a damn. It was not a bad sized place. Entering through the front doors the bar sat at the far end with bar stools lined up along the front of it. In the centre of the room a stage with tables surrounding it waited for the dancers at night. The décor was done in a railroad theme. Behind the bar, looking as though it was coming through the wall, was a replica of the front end from some old historic steamer. He had been told so many different tales as to which train it was suppose to represent, that he just gave up trying to figure it out. Hell I'm a reporter maybe I should do a story on that, he mused to himself. The walls were lined with old photos of trains and their crews. Old implements that were used in the construction of the rail lines and on board the trains themselves hung on the walls and ceiling. Lamps resembling the old oil lanterns that conductors used to use were spaced along the walls, to give the room a warm glow. Set at the back of the room were two raised areas with a chain railing around them to look like the platform of a caboose. Each platform had a table and chairs that were usually occupied by people from out of town who found this charming.

He arrived before Cats and chose a table close to the bar but set close to the wall so they could have some privacy. He ordered himself a Crown Royal on the rocks. He was sitting and people watching when he saw Cats come through the doorway. She immediately saw him and waved. As she headed toward the table, he couldn't help but feel a sense of pride that it was him, who she would be sitting with.

"Well, I don't see any bruises or blood on your clothing, guess things didn't go too bad with Jason. What did you find out? When are you going to Newport? Come on tell me everything." She slid her chair closer to Tony's.

"Hello to you too. I would love to tell you but your going to have to put a cap on it long enough so that I can get a word in." he said and they both broke out in laughter.

The waitress came over and took Cats order, vodka and cranberry, and Tony ordered another Crown Royal. As they watched the waitress walk away, Cats turned to him with a, lets have it, look on her face.

He went over his meeting with Jason and the phone call from TNT. This in itself took a while as Cats continued to interrupt with questions, not wanting to miss anything. They discussed all the possibilities of the why, what and where's. They were both enjoying coming up with all types of possible explanations as to why he had been chosen for this story. When Tony suggested that maybe it was just because he was a great reporter, Cats ribbed him about having his head in the clouds and that this was a plot to get him out of town for awhile so that nobody had to look at his sorry face. They drank and laughed for a couple of hours just enjoying the time together. Tony didn't get much of that lately and Cats would take anytime she could get with him.

"Well, I better get my ass in gear." Tony said.

"Aw, already?"

"Yeah. I've still got to throw some clothes in a suitcase, shower and meet TNT for dinner yet. Then I have to blast over and pick Paul up."

"I understand. Give me a call when you get to Newport will ya?" Cats asked with a longing in her voice.

"You know I will. Hell, Newport isn't that far away, drive on up one day if you get a chance. I'm thinking that maybe we'll be up there four or five days at the most. Should be able to get all the details by then and if not, like I said it's not that long a drive, I can always blast back here."

Cats was now looking at him in that way that made him feel like running before he said or did something that he would regret or maybe even embrace. He knew how she felt and that made it even worse because he knew there was no other woman for him but he just wasn't ready to commit himself yet. After twenty-two years of being with someone, he really needed to be by himself and just enjoy doing what he wanted, when he wanted. He caught the waitress's attention and indicated that he would like the bill.

He walked Cats to her car and stood there as she unlocked the door. Opening the door she suddenly turned and gave him a kiss on the lips, which made him place a hand on the roof of the car to steady himself. God, she could make him melt.

"Sorry, Tony, couldn't help myself."

"Nothing to be sorry for. Believe me, it was all my pleasure." He replied, with a smile. "You drive home safe and I'll call you from Newport. Think about driving up there one day."

"Yeah, maybe I will." She said, as she climbed into the car.

"Hey, Cathy." He said, still standing there holding the door open while she placed the keys into the ignition.

She looked up with a startled look. It had been a very long time since he had called her by her real name. Flashes of the last time came to her mind. He would always call her Cathy when they were making love, and right now she wanted to do just that in the worst way.

"Thanks and you do know that you are very special to me, don't you? It's just that I need some time."

"Yes, I do. I'll wait for your call tonight. Say hi to Paul for me."

"Will do. Later." And with that, he closed the door and she drove out of the parking lot, leaving him standing there thinking, "I must be out of my mind."

He raced home and quickly threw some clothes into a couple of suitcases. As he pulled into Alfredo's Roof parking lot, TNT was climbing out of his car. He was impressive for a man in his late sixties. His hair was a silver gray and there was never a strand out of place. He carried himself straight and walked with a flair that just flowed with confidence. His broad shoulders and well toned body made a lot of men of lesser years, including Tony, envious. As he looked up and saw Tony pull in, he smiled and nodded an acknowledgement. Tony got out and walked toward the restaurant where TNT stepped in beside him and they headed toward the building.

"So, how did your meeting go this afternoon?" TNT asked.

"Not bad." Answered Tony, hoping that would be the end of that line of questioning. He liked to keep his personal life to himself.

"Good, good."

When they entered, the maitre d' immediately recognized TNT and came straight over with a smile and hand extended.

"Mr. Tibbet how good to see you again. Will it just be the two of you?"

"Yes."

"Follow me then." He led them to a table in the center of the room. The décor was done very Italian with paintings showing Rome, Sicily and gondolas being maneuvered by men in striped shirts and wide brimmed hats. The tables had white laced covers and silver candle holders with a large red rose floating in a small round vase placed in front of them.

"Your waiter's name this evening is Donavan. He will be with you shortly. Please enjoy your evening." He bowed elegantly and stepped back from the table while waving at one of the bus boys to bring water to the table.

"So, Tony how have you been keeping?"

"Not so bad. You know, just another day, same old shit."

"Yeah, I know. So, how much did you and Jason discuss about this assignment? If I know you two, I would have to venture a guess that not much was discussed at all."

"Well, you ventured right." Tony answered, and that brought a smile to TNT's face. Tony liked the fact that TNT knew the situation between Jason and himself. That way he didn't have to keep his guard up around him or go into long explanations.

"Ok, let's get a drink ordered and get down to business then, shall we?"

Tony liked the sounds of that; because he had a lot of questions and wanted to get as many answered as possible. Small talk was exchanged while waiting for their drinks and food. After the waiter set their dinners down and left, TNT looked at Tony and got right to the point.

"So, I bet you're wondering why I wanted you on this so bad."

"As a matter of fact the question did cross my mind a few times."

"Well, I have reason to believe that there is more to this story than just those men getting killed."

"What do mean by that?"

"I have been privy to some information that makes me believe that this a conspiracy to draw attention to environmental issues in that area. The police are looking for a suspect from one of the environmental groups. Apparently the loggers that came onto the scene, witnessed one of them there. A woman, if you can believe that. I believe this is where the real story lies and you know how I feel about you as a reporter. Tony, find that suspect, and we'll have the scoop of a lifetime. Now anything you find out call me before you hand it over to Jason. This is a sensitive situation as it may involve a lot of important people."

"Where did this information come from? Is it reliable?"

"Sorry, I can't tell you the source but I can assure you that it is very reliable. Tony the important thing is to try and find this suspect. Offer her whatever you have to, to get an exclusive. Just be careful."

"What makes you think she's still even around there?"

"Again, I have been told that the police are pretty much positive that she is still in the area. If this conspiracy theory is correct, we could be sitting on a bomb here."

"Did your source tell you which environmental group might have been responsible for this?"

"No. Tony I don't trust anyone else with this. It's all yours, but like I said before, I want to know the progress before it goes to Jason"

"Not a problem there."

As they sat there finishing their dinners, Tony's mind had pretty much gone blank. All the questions he wanted to ask, just didn't seem all that important anymore. This was it, this was the story he had been waiting for. Finally, he felt like a reporter again. He would not fail on this.

CHAPTER 3

❖

It had been two weeks since the incident in the woods with the protesters and Frank had been keeping a very low profile. It had surprised him, that the police had not come knocking. He thought for sure that the protesters would have gone to them. Also, a lot of the other loggers felt that he had betrayed them some how, by letting these tree huggers, as they were called, get away so easy. He was especially avoiding George Ruber. He had heard that George was badmouthing him, calling him a coward. It wasn't that he was afraid of George, he just wanted to give everything a little time to cool off. There were a few people that took his side, but he never took much notice of that either. He was just the kind of guy that stood up for what he thought was right, whether anyone else agreed or not.

"A man ain't a man, unless he can stand up for what he feels is right no matter what other people think." His father had always told him. "It's real easy to follow the crowd, and damn hard to stand alone."

He had heard that George was becoming more aggressive toward the whole subject and was spending quite a bit of time in the city at meetings. No one seemed to know what kind of meetings these were, but every time George came back from one he was more aggravated. He was at one of those meetings tonight, so Frank took the opportunity to head down to the Ocean Port for a couple of beers and shoot a few games of pool. Frank knew that some people looked at him as being scared to confront George, and maybe in a way he was. Not so much as to what George would do to him, but rather what he might do to George. You can only call a man down for so long before he is going to fight back, and he was getting close to that point.

He finished his beer and said his goodnights. As he headed home he felt good. There was a warm glow flowing through him from the alcohol and he'd had a great visit with some of the guys he hadn't seen in a while. What he felt best about though, was that there had hardly been any mention at all about the evening involving the protesters or George.

It wasn't until he turned off the highway that he noticed the headlights following him. When he thought about it, it seemed as though they had been there ever since he left the bar. Maybe it was just someone heading in the same direction but his gut feeling was telling him otherwise. He decided to find out for sure. Ahead was a service station. Turning in he kept a close watch on the vehicle behind him. The headlights pulled over to the curb and went out. Frank could feel his cheeks start to turn red. A bit from the alcohol but mainly from the anger building inside. If that was George, then it was time to get this over with once and for all. Maybe it was a group of them tree huggers wanting to take revenge for their buddies. Well, bring it on, he was ready. As he headed into the building the thought of calling the police crossed his mind but he immediately dismissed it. He didn't have much faith in them after the way they hadn't done anything about the roadblock. No, he decided, he would take care of this himself.

The washrooms were located around back of the station and Frank walked around as if he was going to use them. Turning the corner, he cautiously took a look to see if anyone was getting out of the vehicle. There was no movement. He quickly made his way to the street on the other side of the station and started running. Working in the forest pretty much all his life, he made it around the block in no time at all. He had barely broken a sweat when he turned the corner and was behind the car. He could make out the form of a head behind the steering wheel. Frank stayed close to the shadows and watched for a few minutes to make sure no one else had stepped out and would return. Feeling comfortable that the driver was on his own, he decided to make his move. Stealthily he crouched low and made his way quickly to the rear of the car, where he dropped down to one knee and peered over the trunk. Nothing, the driver just sat there and moved his head a few times as if checking something on the front seat. Frank's mind was racing. Did he have a gun? Is that what he kept looking at? He decided that he would have to act quickly and make surprise his ally. He was feeling giddy with excitement. The adrenaline and alcohol mix was racing through him at an uncontrollable speed. He could feel his heart racing and the blood rushing through his veins. Taking a couple of deep breaths he got himself under control. That evening in the woods was nothing compared to this. Getting a visual plan in his head as to his next plan of action, he took another steadying deep breath and crawled around the car. Crawling on both knees, so that he wouldn't be noticed, he made his way to the driver's door. He fought back the urge to lift his head and look inside. Placing his hand on the door handle, he started to count to himself.

"One...two...thr..." he ripped the door open and grabbed the driver by the hair and shirt. With a vicious pull he threw the body out of the car onto the asphalt. He was shocked at how light this person was. Within seconds, he was on top of the driver with one hand around the throat and the other raised in a fist ready to smash it down onto the face of his enemy. Instead, his fist froze in mid air and his eyes widened. He was not looking into the hateful eyes of George, or the angry eyes of some unknown vengeful protester. No, these eyes he had looked into before. They were the soft eyes belonging to Sherri Maider.

Not realizing it, he still had a grip on her throat. Sherri had both hands trying in vain to pull his death grip from her throat. Her body twisted and jerked in an attempt to throw her attacker. As she continually tried to kick at him, she started to feel lightheaded. In desperation she raked her fingernails across Frank's cheek. Bringing him out of his shocked trance, he immediately swung off her so that she could get air. Sherri rolled over to her stomach and got to her knees, coughing and trying to pull air into her lungs.

"Jesus Christ!" Frank yelled. "Are you ok? I am so so sorry, I thought you were someone else."

"Are you crazy? You could have killed me." Sherri gasped, between breaths.

"I am really sorry. What the hell were doing following me anyways?" asked Frank, starting to feel a bit of the anger creeping back. Looking down on Sherri's small form, his anger suddenly turned to fear. He had come very close to disfiguring, if not killing her. The thought of it started to make his stomach feel queasy.

"I just wanted to thank you again for what you did at the roadblock that night, and see if I could buy you dinner."

"Well shit, you could have phoned."

"Hey, this was taking me a lot of nerve to do this. If you remember, we're not exactly on the same team here. I was just…just waiting for the right time to approach you, that's all."

"You ok to stand?" he gently asked.

"Yeah, I think so."

He placed a hand under her elbow and on her back, gently steadying her as she got to her feet. He could see the scrape on her forehead and blood coming from her nose.

"Are you sure you're ok? Listen, if I had known it was you, I would not have attacked you like that."

"I know. I shouldn't have been following you either."

"You're bleeding. I don't live very far from here, why don't you follow me over and we can clean that up."

"Well I don't know."

Frank smiled. "Come on, I'm not going to cut you up with one of my saws I promise."

Sherri couldn't help but laugh. She knew from the first time she looked into this man's eyes, that he had a gentle heart. Besides it would give her more time to talk to him about why she really wanted to see him.

"Ok, it probably is a good idea," Sherri said, rubbing her shoulder where she had landed on the road. Frank held the door for her until she got back behind the steering wheel, then climbing into the passenger seat, he moved the newspaper that laid on it. Sherri gave him a lift to his pickup truck.

As she stepped through the doorway into Frank's house, what she saw was nothing what she expected. There were no axes leaning against the wall, or any logging paraphernalia visible anywhere. Framed pictures of boxers hung on the wall and concert posters with ticket stubs hung on other walls. Models of Harley Davidson motorcycles and old cars stood on the stereo stand and bookcase. There were candles dotting the room and plants at every window. To Sherri, this man's house was tidier than hers. Frank came out of the kitchen with a cloth and some antiseptic.

"Come on over here to some light, so we can get a better look at that." He motioned for her to come over to the dining room table. "Now, this is probably going to sting a bit at first." He said, as he gently dabbed some antiseptic to the scrape on her forehead, that made her take in a sharp breath.

"It's nothing, just a small scrape. You won't even notice it in a few days."

"That's comforting to know." Sherri replied, trying to sound as sarcastic as she could. The truth was that she was enjoying being in the presence of this man and having him pay her so much attention.

After he was done, Frank picked everything up and headed back into the kitchen. "Can I get you anything to drink?"

"Well, that would be nice. What have you got?"

"Let see. I've got vodka, wine or beer. Any of those do anything for you?"

"Actually, I'm a rum lover myself but a cold beer sounds pretty enticing."

"A woman after my own heart. Two cold ones coming up."

Frank came out carrying the two beers and set them down on the living room coffee table. Taking this as a hint, Sherri walked into the living room and sat down on the couch. Frank picked the beers up and handed one to her.

"Cheers." He said, raising his bottle to toast with hers.

"Cheers."

"So, I realize that we were never really introduced. I'm Frank Cotis.

"And I'm Sherri Maider."

"So, how long have you been involved with this Nature's Select group?"

"About eight years now. How long have you been a logger?"

"Pretty much ever since I got out of school. Not much of anything else here to do to make a living. Logging has been keeping these families supported for generations now."

Sherri looked at him and wondered how far they should take this conversation. They were now getting into territory that they had totally different views on, and she was so enjoying his company. She quickly changed the topic to other areas. Sitting there they discussed where they had gone to school, families and even sports. Frank was delighted that Sherri was a sports fan and showed her all the boxing posters he had hanging in the living room. As they walked from poster to poster he told in detail the events of each night. Sherri listened intently, even though she wasn't much of a boxing fan, but because she could see and feel the passion that he had for the sport. After a few beers Sherri soon became quiet. She knew it was getting time to tell him why she really wanted to see him in the first place, and she also knew that it would probably be the end of an enjoyable evening.

"What's wrong? Did I say something wrong or has my babbling put you almost to sleep? You've become very quiet."

"Oh no, nothing like that. It's just that there was another reason why I wanted to see you."

Frank noticed that she was gripping the beer bottle in both hands and turning it constantly. Her grip was so tight, that the knuckles on her hands had turned white. He suggested that they move back to the couch.

"Well, if you squeeze that beer bottle much harder, I'm going to have to get the antiseptic out again."

Sherri sank back in the couch and stared down at the bottle in her hands.

"Well, I really don't know where to start. This whole thing is getting so out of control. When I first got into the Nature's Select, it was because it was something I was passionate about. Watching ancient forests disappear made me want to stand up and scream. Now there are people that don't even really care about what we're standing for. They just want to be around in case something should happen so that they can be involved. It's like they are hired guns that travel around and help cause disturbances. Not because they believe in anything. It's like they just like causing trouble. That night at the roadblock was the first time I have ever been so scared. When your friend hit Scott with that piece of wood, I knew for me things had changed."

She stopped and set the bottle down on the coffee table.

"Why didn't you guys go the police?"

"Well, a couple of nights later Nature's Select had a meeting, and I suggested just that. Some of Scott's friends, and these other people I was telling about, started talking seriously about having some kind of revenge. I told them violence wasn't going to work, it would only provoke more violence. I tried to make them understand that if they retaliated, it would kill any progress we had with public. Boy, I bet you're real sympathetic about that, eh." She said, smiling up at him. Frank returned the smile and raised his beer bottle. "Anyways, they basically told me that if I didn't like it, then I should maybe cut out and find some other cause. Shit, that's when I knew these people weren't in it for the same passionate ideals that I was. You don't just bounce around from one cause to another, on a whim. You get involved, because it's what you believe in your heart is right. They said that peaceful demonstrations weren't getting them anywhere and before one of them got seriously hurt, they had to strike back to show that they wouldn't be pushed around. Even though I know that what they are saying is so very wrong, I still can't help but feel as though I am betraying them. I have been a part of Nature's Select for so long. This whole thing is just so weird right now and I'm getting tired of it all."

Sherri had stopped talking and the room filled with silence. Frank sat back and stared at one of the posters on the wall, as if he was seeing it for the first time. He understood why she was involved with this so-called environmental group; he too had ideals he strongly believed in. Like the right for any man to make a living and support his family. He had watched as many good men, men much better than these tree huggers he was sure, lost homes and basically ended up on welfare because logging was all they knew. It was happening because people like her, were sticking their noses in and not even understanding the consequences of their actions. When it came to an old growth forest and a man's family, well the forest would lose in his books every time. Not that he didn't appreciate the majesty of it. Hell, he appreciated it more than these weekend warriors who thought of themselves as naturalists ever would. He worked around and amongst these magnificent monoliths every day. No, it would lose to provide a family a living. For every forest that got harvested, there were regulations that the area had to be replanted and a new forest started, and so the cycle went. He had always argued that it was much like the human cycle. We were all born to die one day and make room for the new.

"Do you really think they would do anything stupid?" Frank asked.

"Who knows, I never thought it would get this far. Just thought I should tell you, as you were there for us at the roadblock."

"I wasn't there for you. I just didn't want to see anyone get hurt, that's not why we were there. Maybe we should go to the police, at least put in a report so that it's on file."

They both sat in silence, for what seemed like a very long time. Finally, Frank got up and headed for the kitchen.

"Would you like another beer?"

"No thanks. It's getting late and I should head home. Thanks very much for everything and next time I promise to call ahead. Definitely, much safer."

Frank walked her out to her car and watched as she pulled out of the driveway. As he watched the car disappear around the corner, he wished he had met her under different circumstances. Why couldn't he have been a plumber and her a nurse. No conflict there. Shrugging his shoulders he headed back into the house. He went to the fridge and grabbed himself another beer, walked over to the television and turned it on. There was one of those new real life programs on. People had to stay confined in a submarine for so many months in order to win money. Stupid, he thought and his mind quickly drifted. How had things gotten so crazy? They were supposed to go and scare them off, instead George had to hit one of them. Now they were pissed off and planning a violent act in retaliation, and of all things he was falling for one of them. He tilted his head back and took a long drink from his beer. He laid his head back against the cushions of the couch and closed his eyes. He pictured Sherri with her black wavy hair and her big round dark eyes that made him melt. They reminded him of puppy eyes. She didn't have the body of a model but by no means was she overweight, just right he smiled to himself. It was her smile that really made him take a quick breath. When she smiled at him, he could almost see an aura glowing about her. Yeah this is going to be damn difficult, he thought to himself.

The ringing of the phone shattered the place Frank had taken himself, with such an impact, that when he jumped the remote control for the television went flying onto the floor. Picking the remote up, Frank hit the mute button.

"Hello." He said, sounding groggy.

"Yeah, it's me." Suddenly, his senses flashed alive. It was George. "I told you they would come back if we didn't teach them a lesson that night. Well, I just learnt that they plan on setting up another roadblock. This time they are going to get what they deserve. The rules have changed." Frank could hear the excitement building in George's voice.

"Listen, George, maybe you should just lay low for a bit. You don't want to draw too much attention from the police on this. Besides I've heard that maybe they are planning on a little revenge because you hit that guy with that chunk of wood."

"Good, now we've got even more of a reason to put a beating on these huggers."

"For Christ's sake, George, don't you think there's been enough violence?"

"Listen, we tried hanging back and letting the police handle things. We even tried your chicken shit way and where did it get us. Nowhere, that's where. It's time someone made these shit heads understand that we're not here for their amusement, and besides not all of us are afraid to stand up for what they believe in."

Frank felt the sting of the last statement, knowing that it was directed solely at him.

"Well, maybe some people believe there are a lot of different ways to stand up for something you believe in, without violence involved."

"Jesus Christ, you're starting to sound just like them now. What's the matter Frank, you starting to turn into a hugger too? There are people that are ready to make a stand, and do it without your cowardly ass."

Frank could feel the anger swelling and knew that he was about to lose control. He was gripping the telephone receiver so hard that his elbow was starting to ache.

"George, I'm going to pretend that you are just letting off some steam, because I'm getting real tired of your snide remarks and the way you're talking about me in public. I stand beside my fellow workers. I don't need a hot head like you telling me what I do or don't believe in. Especially someone who isn't thinking rationally. Shit man, we used to be friends. We used to work together, what the hell is happening to you? All I'm saying is sit back for a while and see what happens. These guys are all pissed off because you beat on one of theirs, just like we would have been had it happened to one of our guys."

"It wouldn't have happened if them assholes weren't there in the first place. I've been learning about how things work in their world. You can try to protect your buddies all you want but this time they are going to take a beating. Hope you had a nice visit with that hugger bitch. Personally, I think you're pussy struck." Even before it registered what George had said the receiver slammed down.

Frank stood frozen holding the phone to his ear. Slowly, he put it down getting angrier by the second. The son of a bitch had been spying on him. Damn this was not going good, someone was going to hurt, if not killed this time. He decided that after work tomorrow he would go see the police. He had to tell someone, this insanity had to end. He would personally deal with George the next time they met. Getting himself under control, he sat back and started to think of Sherri once more. He was not about to let a paranoid hotheaded jerk bring him down. He finished his beer and laid down on the couch. Hitting the mute button again on the television remote, he dozed off with the sounds of a game show as his lullaby.

Sherri pulled into her driveway and turned the ignition off. She sat there in silence listening to the traffic passing by on the freeway just a couple of blocks away. Had she done the right thing telling him? She couldn't shake the feeling that she had betrayed the group. After all they weren't the ones that threw the first blow. As she sat there in solitude, she knew that what these people were planning on doing was against what she believed in. All she was doing, once again, was making a stand. If they wanted her to go and make a stand for something else, she would just go ahead and do that. No more violence. She felt good now about telling Frank. As she got out of the car she suddenly wanted to be in the comfort and security of being with him. She grabbed the two bags of groceries she had bought at the supermarket on her way home. Awkwardly holding her grocery bags, she fumbled through her purse looking for her door key. With a smile coming across her face, she decided that she wanted to get to know this man better. That was to be the last thought she would have that night as the cloth doused with chloroform suddenly pressed against her nose and mouth.

CHAPTER 4

Paul was standing outside his apartment building with his suitcase and camera equipment when Tony pulled up. As Tony pushed the trunk button and watched Paul place his suitcase inside, his mind was still on his dinner meeting with TNT. The thought that this could have been planned by someone to make it look like the environmental group had done it, was a bit over whelming.

"Hey man, how you doing? Ready for a few days of fun and frolic?" Paul asked, as he placed his camera equipment on the back seat then settled into the front passenger seat.

"Always, you know me." Answered Tony. He was wondering if he should tell Paul about what had transpired with his meeting with TNT. He decided to wait until he had a chance to look around and check things out first.

"Man, I hope this is a good one. I gave up a few days with a sweet lady for this."

"Well, we're not going to find out sitting here." With that, Tony pulled the Firebird away from the curb and headed for the freeway turning north. It was a great drive to Newport. First they would get on highway one, which would take them through the city. It wound its way just on the outskirts of the city, then came alongside the coast. It followed the coastline until it connected to highway ninety-nine, that would take them directly to Newport. Tony had been to many cities before, but he always marveled at this city's night skyline. As he looked out at the scene, passing them by, he could see the lights of the cargo ships anchored in the inlet, waiting their turns to be loaded or unloaded before heading out to ports all over the world. Behind them, glowed the lights of the city. The vibrant colors of neon could be seen outlining some of the taller buildings, while the lights from traffic moved about beneath them. The bridge, which spanned the inlet, connecting downtown to the north shore seemed to hover over the ocean's blackness. It stood out front and center with its lights running along the full span on either side. Traffic seemed light this evening, which made Tony real happy. The drive up highway ninety-nine was made for the Firebird. It snaked its way along the coast rising and falling with the contour of the rugged mountain coastline. There had been all kinds of reports and specula-tion on how they should change the highway. Make it safer they said. Shit, it wasn't the highway that was unsafe; it was the idiots that didn't know how to drive it. Scared of the winding road, tourists would brake for every corner or cut into the on coming traffic lane as they tried to maneuver around it. When they came to a passing lane, they would immediately speed up instead of moving over to allow traffic to pass. This would infuriate other drivers who would then take chances that many a time ended up in an accident. Then there were those locals that seemed to have to drive it like it was the Auto-bahn. Idiots. No, he thought, don't change the highway, leave it for those who knew it and enjoyed it. If they wanted a safer highway then make a new one away from the coast. That's it, he decided, I'm going to do a series of articles on this.

He didn't have to worry about traffic tonight though, and they cruised along. Hugging the road, the Firebird effortlessly took charge of the curves.

"So, what's our agenda when we get there?" Paul asked.

"Well, we'll get booked into our rooms then head down to a bar and see if we can maybe talk to someone local. It will be a good place to find out what they know." Tony knew from experience, that a local bar could be the best source of information. It was amazing what just buying a couple of drinks could get him for information on stories.

"All right, I was hoping you were going to say something like that." Paul said with a smile.

"Thought you might like that."

As they came over a rise in the highway, they could see the lights of the pulp mill that was situated across the sound from Newport. It glowed like a city unto itself. There had been a town located there for the workers at one time. The town had long since been shut down and the workers now took a ferry across the sound, to get to work. They came around another bend in the highway and Newport suddenly spread out before them. The street and business lights shining brightly against the black night. They stayed on the highway until they could see the Travelers Eight Motel sign illuminating the sky. It was the newest motel in Newport, and at that moment, Tony liked the fact that Jason had always insisted on doing things top notch.

As Tony parked the car, Paul suggested that Tony go in and get them registered and he would grab the bags.

"You won't get no argument from me." Tony replied, and immediately headed for the lobby doors. Entering the lobby he stopped for a brief moment and took in the surroundings. The floors and reception counter were all done in a gray speckled granite and the wood trim was a beautiful red cedar. The walls were decorated with prints of old photos depicting earlier days in the history of Newport. Set into the far wall was a granite stone fireplace. It all came together to give the visitor a very warm and welcoming feeling. He saw the lady standing behind the counter, waiting on him and he made his way over to her.

"Good evening. How may I help you?" She asked, with a welcoming beam on her face.

"We've got reservations. Tony Parkins and Paul Pratt from the *Garibaldi Daily Newspaper.*"

"Ok, let's have a look." She said, as her fingers seemed to glide effortlessly over the computer's keyboard. "Oh yes, there you are. Will you be requiring rooms with a wet bar?"

"Yes, please." Paul piped up from the lobby doorway, as he pushed the baggage cart through. Tony looked up at Paul and saw the smile on his face. Hell yeah, why not, he thought. I always wanted Jason to buy me a few drinks.

"You heard the man, two rooms with wet bars." Tony confirmed.

"So you're reporters, eh? Are you here to cover those loggers being murdered?"

"Yes ma'am, we are." Tony answered. "Is there anything you could tell us about them?"

"Heck, not much more that you're going to read in our little local paper. I do know that there is a manhunt out for one of those huggers. Apparently she was seen at the murder sight."

"Did you say she?" Paul jumped in.

"Yes, the loggers that came across the killings saw her standing there with an axe in her hand."

Paul and Tony stood there looking at each other. It was apparent that they were feeling the same thing. This was going to be big.

They finished filling in the registration forms and got their keys. Thanking her for her help, they headed for the elevator. The receptionist told them she was happy to help and if she could be of any further assistance to just let her know.

"Jesus, Tony, what do make of that?" Paul asked, once they were in the elevator.

"I'm not sure, but what I am sure of, is that we have got our work cut out for us. This whole thing seems a little bizarre."

Their rooms were on the third floor across the hall from each other. They decided to settle in, get freshened up and then head downtown to a bar.

"Ok, meet you downstairs in say an hour?" Paul suggested. as he inserted the automatic key card into the slot.

"Sounds good to me." Tony replied. That would give him time to call Cats. He unpacked his bags and dialed her number. There was no answer so he left a message on her answering machine letting her know that he would try again in the morning.

"Well, Jason, time to buy the first one." He muttered. as he went to the small bar fridge. After unpacking his bags and setting up his laptop, he went out on the balcony and sat down looking out at the snow-capped mountains that stood guard over this small picturesque town. As he sat there sipping his drink, his mind sorted through what TNT had told him over dinner and what the lady downstairs had just told them. Could someone have set up this whole thing? Well, that was what he was here to find out. The repercussion that it would cause, seemed mind boggling to him, and yet he liked it. He tilted his glass back and finished the drink in one swallow. This was definitely looking like the story that would put him back into the scene. Getting up and heading back into his room, it was time to go to work.

When he got downstairs, Paul was already there chatting up the new receptionist that had come on shift. Both were laughing and it wasn't hard to see, by looking into the young ladies eyes, that Paul had her totally infatuated already. She didn't even look at Tony as he walked up and slapped Paul on the shoulder.

"Ready to go, or are you staying?"

"No, I'm coming. Was just visiting with Trudy. Trudy this is Tony my partner I was telling you about. It was a real pleasure to meet you. Maybe I'll see you again later or tomorrow?" Paul said, looking into her eyes and smiling.

Tony shook his head, as he watched the poor girl, unable to come up with an answer melt on the spot. A quick nod of her head was the best she could do.

"So, where are we heading?" Paul asked.

"Well, there's a pub downtown at the Ocean Port Hotel. It's one of the older bars in town and most of the locals hang out there. We should be able to make contact with someone, who would be willing to talk to us. We'll check it out anyway and if nothing comes of it we can always hit one of the other downtown bars.

The Ocean Port Hotel was the bar in the Newport downtown area. It had been one of the original bars, and over the years it had been given many a face lift. The walls had been painted in murals showing underwater scenes of coral, seals, fish and killer whales breaking the surface of the water. The shorelines showed the beautiful mountain landscape with bear and cougar roaming the land and eagles soaring in the sky. It truly was a sight to behold. An illuminated awning ran full length down two sides of the hotel, casting a light down on the sidewalk brightening up the entire scene.

"Man, I gotta shoot a few pictures of this in the morning." Paul exclaimed, as they walked up to the front of the building. As they walked in, a few people looked up but never gave them a second look. The floor was done in a hardwood, from an old warehouse and given an oil finish that made the natural colors and grain of the wood stand out. The walls had murals painted on them, with the same themes as those outside. A well stocked bar ran the full length of the room at one end. Under the front lip of the bar counter, ran a light that was hidden from view so that it gave off a halo glow. There were two glass garage type doors at one side of the room, that could be opened to the patio outside. Tony pointed to the bar where a couple of empty barstools stood and they made their way over to them. The place was busy, with waitresses precariously holding their trays with one hand above their heads as they maneuvered between the people standing about. He had always marveled at how they could do that and very seldom have an accident. They both settled up to the bar and ordered a drink from the bartender. She was a good looker, with a firm body and long blonde hair. Her smile was very welcoming and it made a person want to smile back.

"Bet she makes a killing in tips." Paul said, having to raise his voice to be heard over the music and crowd. Tony shook his head in agreement, as he looked around the room for someone he could possibly talk to. After years of doing this, he knew exactly what he was looking for. Best scenario, would be one or two guys, who weren't drunk, but had a glow on and were feeling good. The crowd tonight was quite young and he couldn't see anyone that he thought would be of any use. After all, he didn't want to waste his money buying drinks, if he wasn't going to get anything in return.

He returned his attention back to the bartender, who was enjoying a rare chance to stand back and take a breather. Paul was already chatting up a good looking lady standing beside him. He decided to try and see if the bartender might know someone he could talk to, after all they always seemed to know everything that was happening. Turning to see if he could get her attention, he noticed that she was talking to a man that seemed to be giving her some instructions. Tony figured he was either the owner, or the manager of the bar. This could be a good contact. The man was well built and had rings on almost every finger of both hands. His hair was jet black and slicked back tight to his scalp. After a couple of minutes, their meeting broke up with them laughing and the man started heading toward Tony.

"Excuse me." Tony called out, as he was passing by him.

"Yeah, can I help you?" the man stopped and looked at Tony. His black piercing eyes immediately caught Tony's attention. There was a definite air of confidence about him and his approach was very straight to the point.

"Hi, I'm Tony Parkins. I'm a reporter from the *Garibaldi Daily Newspaper*." Tony answered, with his hand held out. The man grabbed it and gave Tony a firm shake.

"And what can I do for you?"

"Well, we're here to do a story on those loggers that got murdered up in the Whallington Valley, and I was wondering if you would have some time to answer a few questions, or if maybe you knew someone who we might be able to help us."

He looked around the room, as if he was looking for someone in particular, then back at Tony.

"Yeah, sure. Just give me a few minutes and I'll be right back." With that he turned and headed back to the bartender. He said something to her and Tony noticed that he motioned towards him and Paul. The man then disappeared through a doorway leading out behind the bar. A few minutes later the bartender set a drink down in front of them.

"These are from Deric." She said with a smile.

"Is he the manager?" Tony asked.

"No, he's one of the owners." She answered, then turned immediately to fill the drink orders being barked at her.

"Man, this place is loaded with good looking ladies." Paul exclaimed, giving Tony a nudge on the arm.

"Yeah well, Romeo, just don't forget why we're here. Maybe you could see if any these dazzling damsels, know anything or anyone who might help us with this story."

"Not a problem there, it will be my pleasure. In fact I think I see a good place to start. See you later." He smiled, grabbed his drink and headed out into the crowd. Just as Tony had expected, Paul went straight to a table with three women sitting at it. Within minutes, Paul was seated at the table and had them totally engrossed in him. What a charmer, Tony thought to himself. He turned back facing the bar. The bartender was standing in front of him wiping down the bar top.

"Quite a ladies man." She said, nodding towards Paul.

"Yeah, he doesn't seem to have much trouble in that department."

"My names Trista." She introduced herself with an extended hand.

"Hi. Tony." He could feel the firmness of her grip from carrying loaded trays.

"So, I hear you guys are up here to do a story on them loggers. Shit, that was bad. The whole town went into shock over that one. Those guys were good men. Those damn tree huggers. If the police had shown some balls and arrested them in the first place when they wouldn't take their blockade down, none of this would probably have happened."

"What makes you think arresting them over the blockade would have stopped this from happening?"

"For a few reasons. One, they would have gotten the message that law would be upheld here. Another reason, is that maybe they would have been in jail rather than out loose to kill, not to mention, if the police had done there job, then those boys would not have gone out and trashed the huggers campsite."

"Do they know it was the tree huggers that did it for sure then?"

"Oh, they won't just come out and say it, but everyone knows it was them. Every logger that was killed was involved in the attack on the blockade. Excuse me." She turned and started filling more drink orders. Tony watched her as she grabbed glasses and beers, while the waitresses kept putting in their orders. As he watched her, he wondered how she could keep all those different drink orders straight, but in the end everyone had their orders and were on their way to satisfied patrons. He pulled out a small tape recorder, he always carried with him and made a note of the fact that the men that were killed, were the same men that were at the roadblock. He caught her eye and indicated that he would like another.

"Do you really believe it was them? I mean these environmentalists are usually very passive. They do roadblocks, sit ins, marches, that sort of thing. This was a brutal act of violence, it just doesn't seem like their style." Tony asked.

Now that he had her talking, he didn't want her to stop. This was a good source to get a feel as to how the locals were feeling about this. She set his drink down and stood back.

"Well, who the hell else would it be? The police are looking for one of them right now. According to the police, one of them women that were at the roadblock, was seen at the murder scene standing over one of the bodies with an axe. How much more proof do you think a person needs?"

He could hear in the rise of her voice that she was starting to get angry.

"Are any of the guys that came across the killings in here tonight? I sure would like to get their side of the story."

Trista scanned the crowd but shook her head no. He was about to ask her a few more questions when he noticed Deric standing at a hallway leading to the washrooms. Deric was motioning to him to follow. He grabbed his drink and followed him down a short hallway and through a door at the end of the hall. The room they entered looked as though it had once been a small restaurant or lounge. There were chairs and tables stacked up and several boxes sitting around. To one side was a table with chairs around it and Deric pulled one out and sat down.

"Ok, Mr. Parkins, what is it that I can do for you?" Deric asked, looking straight at Tony.

"Well, like I said before, we're here doing a story on those loggers that were murdered and I just wanted to ask you a few questions in regards to it."

"Ask away. Don't know how much help I'll be."

Tony reached in his pocket and produced the small tape recorder and set it on the table.

"Do you mind if I tape this interview? I have a terrible memory."

"No not at all."

"Did you know any of the men that got killed?"

"Yeah, they would come into the pub quite often. Good group of guys too, never had any trouble with them."

"Did they ever have any kind of run ins with any of the environ-mentalists?"

"Well, certainly. Never in a violent fashion though, if that's what you're getting at. There were always arguing sessions with a lot of yelling, but that's about as far as it would ever go."

"Did you know any of the people from the Nature's Select?"

"No, this place isn't quite their type of establishment. Most of them frequented The Brew, and I don't mind that a bit. Helps keep things a little calmer around here."

The Brew was another pub and inn down the street from the Ocean Port. They had their own brewery and had only recently been built. Tony made a mental note to stop by The Brew and see what information he could come up with. "After that night out at the roadblock, was there ever any talk as to what exactly went down out there?"

Deric sat there and looked at Tony as if he were searching for something in his face. He grabbed his drink and took a swallow.

"I think you would have top ask one of them that question."

"Well, from what I understand that might be a little hard seeing as how they were the ones that got killed. I heard that one of the environmentalists got hurt out there, the night the loggers went out and destroyed their campsite?"

"I heard something about that." Deric answered, looking as if he wanted to get this over with. Tony knew that he was holding something back, but decided to change the direction of questioning, he didn't want to lose him.

"Did these men have families?"

"Not all of them. If I'm not mistaken only two of them had families. We're having a fundraiser for the families next weekend. Maybe you can put that in your paper to help us out."

"You bet I can." Tony replied, knowing that it wasn't a request, but rather a demand if he wanted this interview to continue.

"From what I gather the consensus around town is that the environmentalists did this as an act of retaliation."

"Well, that is the feeling around here. Mind you who else would it be?

I mean, it's very unlikely that loggers would be going around killing other loggers. These guys have an incredible bond between them."

"Do you know of any loggers that might be willing to answer a few questions?"

"Not sure. Everyone is still pretty shook up over this. This is a pretty quiet little town; this sort of shit just doesn't happen around here. I guess that's another reason why they're looking at the huggers as being the ones who did this. Nothing like this has happened before until these people showed up and the town needs someone to blame. Then finding some of them lying there too, well it doesn't take a rocket scientist to figure that out."

Tony sat back in utter astonishment, this was the first he had heard about any of the protesters being found out there.

"Excuse me, are you telling me that they found other bodies out there besides the loggers? Why has no one else heard of this?"

"I don't know, but there is a rumor that more than just the loggers were found out there."

Tony needed to organize the information that just got dropped on him. This definitely put a new spin on the situation, and things just weren't making any sense to him. Surely they knew about this at the newspaper. This definitely was turning strange. Why had he not heard about this in any of the other news reports? Was this just a rumor?

"I know this may sound like a bit of a strange question, but did you know of any loggers that were friendly with the environmentalists?

The look Deric gave Tony at that moment, made him feel incredibly silly for even asking it. All Deric did was shake his head no and continue looking at him with that look. He wasn't even sure why he asked that question, but he knew that it was something he had to check out. From what TNT had told him and what he just got told, he wanted to make sure he had all the bases covered.

"Do you know if the cops have a lead as to the where abouts of that lady they are looking for?"

"No, not that I know of. I do know that if the police in this town solve this, it will be purely by accident."

"I take it you're not too impressed with the local law enforcement here? In fact it doesn't seem like anyone I've talked to is very impressed."

"Well, if they would have done their job in the first place none of this would have happened."

"You have no idea how many times I've heard that already."

"Well, it's true. It seems like something terrible has to happen before they will take any action. You get these people coming over here from other countries, nothing more than professional protesters as far as I'm concerned. They cause nothing but trouble, break civil laws and our authorities won't do a damn thing about it. Yet if one of us retaliates then we get grabbed and charged. So, to answer your question, no, me and a lot of other people in this town have no respect for these wanna be cops."

Well, thought Tony, I definitely have something to use to get people talking.

"Do you know who discovered the bodies?"

"From what I've heard, it was some of the guys that were working the same shift. Apparently they could hear the screams and saws and came running thinking that maybe a tree had fallen on one or more of the men. It does get pretty dangerous out there for these men. As for their exact names, I won't be giving them to you. Even if you did find out who they were, I wouldn't go and talk to them if that was your plan. I've seen men get shook up before, but these guys are strong and right now from what I've heard they're all getting counseling. After all, I'm not sure if I would have been able to keep it together, after coming across friends all cut to pieces, Jesus." Deric grabbed his glass and finished it in one gulp. Tony noticed the shake in his hand as lifted the glass.

"Listen I better get back to work." Deric quickly said, starting to stand up.

"No problem, just a couple more quick questions, if you don't mind?"

"No, I suppose not, shoot." Deric said, settling back down in the chair.

"Other than the environmentalists, were there any other people hanging around town that seemed interested in the logging and the protest that was going on?"

Deric sat for a moment giving the question serious thought. "Not that I can recall. The only people that I can remember asking any questions in regards to any of this, has been reporters."

"Are you sure, not even anyone commenting on it in passing?"

"Well hell, I guess someone might of, but do you have any idea how many people I talk to in a day?" Deric sounded a bit perturbed about the last question, so Tony figured he better end the interview here.

"If you do remember anything that might help me with my story, please get a hold of me. I'm staying at the Travelers Eight Motel, out on the highway. Thanks for taking the time to talk to me."

"No problem. Now, don't forget to mention the fundraiser next weekend for the families of those men."

"I won't. I will take care of that this evening."

As they got up to leave Tony asked, "One last question. Could you tell me the names of the men that got killed?"

"Sure, Billy Pacster, Bob Garrison, Willie Folero and Frank Cotis. There was one strange thing though, the body of a logger, no one had seen in a while, was found out there also. Don't have any idea what he was doing out there. George Ruber, was his name, I think. Probably the strangest thing was, that he didn't work with them anymore, but he was also one of the guys that tore the roadblock apart."

"Thanks again." Tony said, thinking how more and more bizarre this whole thing was getting.

"Not a problem." Deric replied and the two of them headed back out into the bar.

CHAPTER 5

As she opened her eyes, Sherri felt dazed and confused. The last thing she seemed to be able to remember was standing in front of her apartment. Her stomach felt nauseous and her mouth was extremely dry. She could hear voices in the background, but could not make out what they were saying. They sounded as if they were coming from a long hollow tube. Blinking her eyes, she tried to clear the blurry edges from her vision. Trying to raise her head, only caused a pain to shoot through it as if someone had hit her with a hammer. Wanting to grab her head in her hands, she tried to pull them up. At first, she couldn't comprehend why her hands wouldn't move, until she looked down at them and saw the straps restraining them. Her heart racing, she rolled her head to one side and could make out a table with people sitting around it, looking over what seemed to be maps. No one had noticed her wake up, so she lay there trying to clear her head and calm herself. The room appeared to be huge, much like a warehouse. As her vision and mind cleared, she realized that she was on a table much like those she saw in ambulances on television shows. The warehouse seemed to be empty, except for the table with the people sitting at it. Soon it all started to come back to her. Standing in front of her apartment, then that smell, and then the terror. She sat up with a start taking in a sharp breath that drew the attention of the people at the table.

"Well, our guest is awake." She recognized the voice, but couldn't remember where she had heard it before. Sitting there, still feeling a bit foggy, she tried to focus on the form heading toward her from the direction of the table. Soon the source of the voice came into view and the fear gripped at her once again. It was the man that had hit Scott at the roadblock. Wildly looking around at the rest of the group, as they approached her, the confusion even became more intense. Most were members of Nature's Select.

"So, how are you feeling? Sleep well?" George sarcastically asked.

"What's going on? What am I doing here?" Sherri asked, having to fight the words out from the dryness in her throat.

"Oh, we brought you here. We thought this would be the safest place for you."

"Safe, from what? I don't understand."

"Ok, you're right. This probably isn't the safest place for you. You'll find out all in good time why you're here. For right now, just relax and get yourself together."

The restraints were removed from her wrists and someone handed her a glass of water. She drank it down heartily, wanting to get rid of the dry taste in her mouth. As she gazed around at the people standing there, she noticed a couple of them that had been with her at the roadblock. When her eyes met theirs, all she got back was a steady cold stare. What was going on? What was going to happen to her? She handed the glass back and swung her legs over the edge of the table. As her feet hit the floor a pair of hands grabbed each arm to help steady her. They supported her and helped her to a chair at the table. She took a glance at the map spread out on the table and recognized it as geographical map of the Whallington Valley.

"So, you feeling any better?" George asked.

"I have felt better. So, you want to tell me what the hell is going on? If this is suppose to be a joke the humor ended a long time ago."

"Oh, this is far from being a joke. You see, you are going to become the greatest martyr the environmental cause has ever had."

"I don't understand what the hell you're talking about. In case you've missed it, kidnapping has been against the law for a very long time now."

"When this is all over, no one will know that anyone was kidnapped. Now we know that you went and saw Frank Cotis. Would you mind telling us what you were talking about?"

"I don't think that's any of your business." Sherri snapped. The blow came so fast and hard that she fell off the chair and couldn't hear anything other than the ringing in her ears. Her cheek was stinging with pain and the foggy sensation tried to make its way back into her head.

"We're not here to piss around. Now, what did you two talk about?" George screamed down at her.

Hands grabbed her and slammed her back into the chair. She rubbed her face where he had hit her and she could feel the blood on her hand even before she saw it. The look in his eyes as he concentrated on her, was like that of a crazed man. They were wide and vacant. A terror gripped at her stomach, almost bringing on panic. She looked pleadingly at the few people that had been with her at the roadblock. Why were they just standing there? As the next blow came, only darkness followed. The hands that had steadied her before now dragged her limp body across the floor and placed her back up on the table and her wrists placed back into the restraints.

"What the hell did you hit her so damn hard for?" one of the others protested.

"Because, I'm tired of playing stupid games. We are running out of time and we need to know what the hell she told him. Just make sure she's strapped down good. I'm going to call in and when I get back we'll find out anything we want and then some."

George turned and marched out of the warehouse. Those remaining, immediately went about the business of strapping her arms, legs and head to the table. A few minutes later George returned with a full glass of water. Standing over the still body of Sheri Maider,

George stared at the form lying before him. Sherri let out a gasp, as the cold water from the glass, splashed against her face. She instinctively tried to sit up, only to be met with resistance from the restraints.

"What are you doing? Have you totally lost your mind? Let me go, I don't know what it is you want. I promise, I won't tell anybody about this. Just please, don't hurt me." She pleaded.

Without a word, George walked over to where the others stood. Straining, she could hear them whispering, some seeming agitated, only to be met by a sharp response from George. Soon she could make out footsteps growing fainter, as they left. God, how she wished she could move her head and see what was going on. Suddenly, George was standing above her once again, and his look brought a scream to her throat.

"Oh, you can scream till your vocal cords are shot. It's not going to do you any good where you are. Hell, if you want I'll scream with you. Now you see, you had your chance to come clean, but you decided to take the rough road." As he talked, she could feel his hands running up the inside of her leg. Tears started rolling uncontrollably down her cheeks. This couldn't be happening. She stiffened every muscle as much as she could, bracing herself for the inevitable. His hands moved up over her breasts and she openly wept, pleading with him between sobs not to hurt her.

"So, you ready to tell me what I want to know?" George asked, his eyes scanning her body.

"Yes! I'll tell you anything, just please don't hurt me." Even as she said it, she felt ashamed at being lowered to groveling for her safety. If she was ever to get out of this, she swore to herself, that she would kill this man.

"All right, we're starting to get somewhere now." George said, feeling well in control. "Let's try again. What did you talk to Frank about?"

"Nothing. We just talked about what happened that night on the roadblock. That's all."

No sooner had she finished, when she could feel his hands undoing her pants and slowly pulling the zipper down.

"No, please." She begged, feeling total panic and helplessness.

"Well, you see I don't believe that is all you two talked about. Now, here is how we are going to play. Every time I think you are lying, I'm going to undo another piece of your clothing. You do understand, what could happen to a beautiful woman, laying helpless and naked on a table, and nobody even knows she's there. Now, would you like to try again?" he asked starting to undo the buttons on her blouse.

"What? I don't understand what it is you want me to say?"

"I want you to tell me what you talked to Frank about." He screamed in her face. He was so close to her that she could feel the warmth of his breath and the spittle that flew from his mouth. The foul smell from his breath, made her want to vomit. His hands were now fondling her nipples and she knew then, that no matter what she told him, he was going to violate her. The tears flowed hard, as her body shook from the crying. She tried to focus on something else, she just didn't want to be here. Franks' image flashed into her mind and she locked onto it. Sitting in his place, listening to his gentle voice, just feeling good being in his presence. She would get through this. She wasn't going to tell this monster anything; he could go to hell.

"Are you ready to talk to me yet?" he asked, grinning as he started pulling her pants down.

"You can go to hell!" She spat at him.

"I was hoping you were going to say that."

She could hear him undoing his pants and letting them fall to the floor. As she felt his hands caressing her thighs, she formed her hands into fists and could taste the blood from her lower lip, as she bit down hard on it. She was not going to let this slime hear her scream. George climbed up onto the table, maneuvering himself into position. His face had a wild animal look to it, as his eyes probed every inch of her body. She stiffened herself as hard as possible, feeling his manhood touch her, when suddenly his head jerked up from the sound of a door being opened.

"What the hell are you doing?" a voice screamed, echoing around the empty warehouse. She recognized it, but couldn't see who it was. "Get off her now!" Sherri could hear footsteps running toward them. The emotion of relief flooded over her and the tears started flowing again.

"I'm teaching this bitch a lesson," George yelled back," Besides, there's enough for both of us. After tomorrow night it won't matter anyway, might as well..." He didn't have time to finish, as Sherri saw two hands grab him and pull him off the table.

"We are not rapists, now get your damn clothes on and get the hell out of here. If they ever found out you tried shit like this, you would be joining her tomorrow night." The voice was dripping with contempt, as she could hear George putting his pants back on. "Now go get the others and we'll start packing up. It's time to get moving."

"You weak shit." Was all George said, as he turned and headed toward the door at the end of the building. Her tears were no longer from fear, but rather they were tears of happiness and relief. Soon the face that belonged to her savior, was standing over her and looking down into her eyes. At first she thought it was the water in her eyes that was playing tricks on her, but as she blinked the tears away, all she could do was stare in disbelief. Her savior was Scott Valta, the protester who George had hit with the board at the roadblock.

"Are you alright?" he asked. All she could manage was to shake her head.

"I'm going to undo these straps so you can get yourself dressed, and we'll take a look at your face. Looks like he did quite a number on you."

After undoing the straps, he gently helped her up from the table and onto her feet. She didn't realize how emotionally drained her body was, and almost collapsed, when Scott let go of her. Steadying her again, he held her while she got herself dressed.

"Scott, I don't know how to thank you."

"Don't!" he snapped.

"Please, tell me what's going on. I'm so confused and scared, nothing is making any sense here. That man hit you with a piece of wood and now you're saying you two work together. Scott, please tell me."

"You will find out soon enough, then you won't be so quick to thank me for anything. Now sit down and let me have a look your face. The others will be here soon, then we're out of here."

She couldn't help but notice that he would not look at her. He always acted as though he was busy with something.

"Scott, please, I have no idea what is happening tomorrow, so I can't say anything to anyone, please let me go."

For the first time since he helped her off the table he looked at her, and she could see the pain in his eyes.

"I can't. I'm so sorry Sherri." He immediately turned away from her again.

"Why, for Gods' sake? What harm can I possibly do when I don't know what the hell is going on?"

The pleads were falling on deaf ears and she had a bad feeling about tomorrow. All she could think about now, was how to get away. Running wouldn't work, she knew Scott would be able to run her down. Besides, she had no idea where the others were. Even while she was looking around, trying in desperation to find something, anything that might jump out and give her an idea as to how to get away, the huge overhead shop door at one end of the warehouse slowly started to open. The outside light slowly started to flood in, but was soon blocked by the shadow of a van pulling in. Behind them another door opened and Sherri turned to see George and two men that she had not seen before, heading in their direction. Instinctively she grabbed Scott's arm in fear. The van pulled up to them so that the side door was right in front of them. Someone on the inside slid the door open.

"Get in." George snarled and gave Sherri a push in the back. Scott spun and stood directly in front of George before he could shove her again. Both men stood there like two gunfighters, waiting for the other to blink. George finally snickered and climbed into the front passenger seat shaking his head. Scott grabbed Sherri's arm and helped her into the van. There were two other people in the van, the man who had opened the door, and the driver, a woman with red hair and a scar that ran across her forehead.

"So, that's the one, huh?" the red head asked. "Well, it's a real pleasure to meet you. How does it feel to become a legend?"

"Shut up and drive the van." Scott snapped at her, pulling the van door closed. The red head turned forward in her seat and started to pull the van out of the warehouse. The side windows of the van had been blackened out, so all Sherri could see was through the front windshield. No one was talking, they all seemed to be wrapped up in their own thoughts. George had turned in his seat, so that he seemed to be constantly staring at her, which made her skin crawl. Scott sat across from her on the floor, but did not look up at her. He kept his gaze straight out the front windshield as if expecting to see something he had been waiting for. The other men sat to the front of the van, so that they to had a view out the front windshield. Having George's eyes on her, made her feel as if she had been violated. She just wanted to climb into a hole and hide. The thought of what had almost happened, back in the warehouse, was making her feel nauseous. She could still feel his hands and eyes on her naked body. She felt dirty.

She looked over at Scott and asked, "Where are we going? What did she mean by becoming a legend?"

Scott turned his head and his eyes met hers. As they looked at each other for a few seconds, he turned his attention once again to view out the windshield without answering.

"Well now, how about if I come back there and we get comfy and I'll tell you all about it? Doesn't seem like Scott wants to talk to you, but you know I'll always talk to you." George said. The red head laughed, looking at Sherri in the rear view mirror.

"Leave it alone." Scott was glaring at George. Sherri could see the redness of his ears and the veins in his neck starting to rise. George just laughed and shook his head again.

"Pathetic." George murmured, as he turned to the face the windshield. Sherri noticed that the red head looked over at George and gave him a smile and wink. Sherri tried hard to see out the windshield, trying to get her bearings. The best that she could determine, was that they were on highway one, but couldn't make out which direction they were headed. As if seeing what she was trying to do, one of the men slid over and positioned himself so that her view was blocked. With a sigh, she sank back against the van wall and felt very cold and alone. One minute she was having a wonderful evening and the next she's in this confusing, scary, unbelievable situation. No one to tell her what was going on. She had to know. Not knowing was becoming worse than what was happening. Scott seemed to be her best bet, if only she could get him away from the others, she felt he might talk to her. George and him obviously had no love for each other, and maybe she could somehow use that to her advantage. She had to come up with some type of plan, that would pit the two of them against each other. As she sat there trying to conceive a plan, she noticed the wooden toolbox at the back of the van for the first time. It looked a lot like the ones she always saw in the back of logger's pickups. The ones they kept their axes and chainsaws locked in.

"What's in the toolbox?" she asked.

"Your destiny." The red head replied, staring back at her. The scar across her forehead creased and gave her eyes the look of something not human. Sherri quickly brought her attention back to the box.

"So, when are you going to break it to our little princess what is in store for her. Maybe she would like to come up front here, or I would

be more than happy to go back there and be her fortune teller."
George taunted, directing the words at Scott. The tone in his voice
made Sherri shrink back hard against the wall and she flashed Scott a
pleading look.

He wasn't looking at her, but the response he gave, made her even
more apprehensive. She couldn't comprehend what was transpiring.
She had to know.

"You say anything to her before the allotted time and I personally
guarantee you go with her." Scott's voice oozed with venom, daring
George to say anything. Everybody's head snapped to look at her as
the frantic pitch of her voice startled them.

"Please, will somebody tell me what's going on? I need to know,
please!"

All eyes returned to Scott, in anticipation, to see if he was going to
say anything. She could tell by the way he hung his head and turned
to meet her eyes, that he didn't want to answer her. As his eyes met
hers, she silently mouthed, please. He lifted his head slowly and
stared at the toolbox before returning his gaze to her.

"Please, Scott. I don't understand. I need to know."

"Sometimes it's best not to know everything."

"I'm scared and confused. You're all acting so strange. Please,
please tell me what's happening."

The intensity of his eyes as he locked onto hers, made her freeze.
"You are about to give the ultimate sacrifice for the cause."

"What sacrifice? I support the cause, you know that. I support it
more than most. What are you talking about?"

His voice was almost inaudible when he gave the answer. She
wasn't sure if she heard it right the first time and demanded that he
repeat it.

"Your life."

She felt like some one had hit her in the back of the head. The
space inside the van suddenly became very claustrophobic and she
couldn't seem to draw enough air into her lungs. Her stomach was

becoming nauseous and she felt like vomiting again. She looked around the van and everything seemed to be spinning. Terror and panic were starting to overwhelm her. Suddenly, she sprang for the back door of the van grabbing frantically for the door handle. Trying in desperation to open it, her only thought was that just on the other side of that door, this nightmare would end. If only she could get the door open. Why wouldn't it open? She didn't even feel the hands that grabbed her at first; she was so focused on getting to the outside. Suddenly, her movements were being restricted and the panic came in a massive rush. She started to jerk her body, violently trying to loosen herself from the hands that were holding her back from reaching sanity. Every muscle and fiber in her seemed to be stretched to their limit in an effort to break free. The hands forced her to her knees and bent her over the toolbox. Out of desperation she brought her leg up as hard as she could manage. The sensation of it hitting something and the scream of agony seemed to bring her senses back. The grip that had held her slacked off and with acrobatic quickness, Sherri flipped onto her back and drove both her legs straight out at her captor. Her feet made solid contact with the man standing over her. The quickness of her attack took her assailants by surprise. The man was driven back and as he lost his balance, he fell hard against the back of the driver's seat. The red head had been watching in the mirror, but was not prepared for the suddenness of the blow to the back of the seat. It jarred her forward sending the van screeching side ways across the highway. Bodies were tossed across the van and slammed into the wall. Sherri jumped up and lunged for the side door handle. The van swerved violently in the opposite direction as the red head fought to keep it under control. This threw Sherri against the side door giving her control of the door handle. Quickly, she flipped the handle up and pushed the door back. The air came rushing in and she could see the pavement passing by in a blur. Voices were yelling behind her and she could feel a hand brush at her back trying to grab her. As she leapt for the open doorway, the van suddenly swerved once more causing her to loose her balance, falling backwards into the van. Her hand snapped out and grabbed the doorframe as she managed to keep herself positioned at the open door. As the van slowly seemed to come under control, she sprang toward the freedom that awaited her. The suddenness and force of the jerk that pulled her back into the van, was so hard that it knocked the wind out of her. In an instant, she was laying on her back and George was staring into her face.

"Now, this is a familiar position for us, isn't it? You aren't going nowhere bitch."

Without thinking, Sherri slashed at his face with her fingernails. Even as she heard his gasp of pain, she brought her knee up into his stomach. She was about to roll out from his grasp, when other hands grabbed her. George turned to look at her and she saw the damage that her nails had inflicted. For the first time since this nightmare had started, a smile came across her face. There was blood coming from the side of his face and eyelid. Sherri braced herself for the blow that was coming, as George held one hand over his eye and with the other reached for something under the passenger seat.

"Don't even think about that shit." Scott barked, as George held the tire iron in his hand. "Start paying attention everyone and get your heads out of your asses. Get a cloth ready, we'll put her down till we get to the valley."

Scott looked down at her and she could have sworn his head moved side to side, ever so subtly, giving her the no sign. He kept his eyes locked on hers and she seemed to be drawn to his stare. That was the last thing she saw, as the soaked cloth was once more placed over her mouth and nose.

CHAPTER 6

Frank truly loved what he did for a living. Even as a young boy growing up in the mountains, he had always enjoyed being out in the woods. It was his turn this morning to drive around and pick the other guys up for work. They would take turns driving the company crew cab home on the weekends and then picking everyone up for work. There were usually five men that would travel together in this group. Allan Pacster, Bob Garrison, Willie Folero, George Ruber and himself. Frank wasn't sure what ever happened to George, as there were only four of them at this point. There were rumors that George had gone to work for someone down in the city. Frank had a hard time believing that, as George had a love for the woods, as strong as any man did. Another rumor had it, that all these trips he had been taking into the city were for retraining, but no one seemed to know what the retraining was for. None of the men ever brought George up in conversation, as they understood the tension between George and Frank.

His first stop brought him to Allan Pacster's place. Allan was a young father of four and had a beautiful wife. They lived in an old log house, that had been renovated several times over the years to accommodate his growing family. It had been his parent's house, where he and his siblings had been raised. Now it was handed down to him and he took great pride in the fact that it was now his to hand down to one of his children. His wife ran a small flower shop in town and between the two of them, they seemed to be happy with the lives they had forged for themselves. As Allan came out of the house, his wife followed out to the doorway and gave Frank a wave and smile.

"So, how was the weekend?" Allan asked as he threw his lunch box on the seat between them and closed the door.

"Aw, not bad." Frank answered. He thought that maybe he should tell Allan about the conversation he had with Sherri, but decided not to. There was already too much emotion over this and there was no sense in getting everyone worked up again.

"How was yours?" Frank asked.

"Busy as hell. Between constantly working on the house, now Sheila has decided that she would like to have a couple of green houses, so that she can grow some of her own flowers to sell. You would think, she would be busy enough. Oh well, that's my lady." He laughed and waved goodbye to her as they pulled out of the driveway and headed down the road.

Next they pulled into Bob Garrison's yard. He was a young man and had just recently met a beautiful lady. He definitely didn't have trouble in that department though. Bob was in his early thirties with blonde hair, blue eyes and a smile that seemed to draw women to him. His body was lean and muscular, as he had been a hard worker all his life. They pulled in and gave the horn a couple of quick blasts. Bob was never known for his punctuality. There had been mornings, when the horn was his wake up call. None of the guys minded though, as Bob was just a great guy to have on a crew. This morning he was heading out the door, even as the last blow from the horn was sounding. As he walked up to the truck he had his trademark smile on his face.

"Morning guys. How the hell are ya?" Bob greeted them.

"Just finer than frogs hair." Allan answered.

"Did you catch any of the football games over the weekend?" Frank asked, knowing Bob was an avid football fan.

"Not all of them. I was playing in a golf tournament all weekend. Now that was a blast."

Soon Allan and Bob were discussing the finer points of a chip shot, while Frank drove on, smiling to himself. As the truck approached Willie Falero's driveway, Frank could see Willie standing out by the road waiting. Willie was single, after going through a nasty divorce about two years ago. He was a quiet man, but still seemed to have a good time whenever he went out. Everyone enjoyed being around him. He lived upstairs from a small shop, where he repaired small engines on the side. Willie enjoyed wrenching on things and always had some kind of mechanical project on the go. When the truck stopped, Willie hopped in the back seat with Bob and soon the men were discussing every thing from what they had heard on the news that weekend, to what was on the agenda for the day. It was a ritual that played itself out every morning, and no one seemed to get tired of it. The day was beautiful, with the sun shining and no threat of rain. Of course, that meant being out in the woods and everyone knew, the bugs would be out in full force. Every man had his supply of bug repellent, and would make sure that they were ready for the onslaught.

As they headed up the winding logging road, taking them deep into the interior of the Whallington Valley, Frank looked around at the scenery and a comforting feeling seemed to engulf him. He was truly where he loved to be. Maybe he would see if Sherri would like to come out here with him on a weekend and they could spend a day by one of the many streams that flowed through here. If nothing else, they shared the love of nature. He had been thinking a lot about her lately and had finally decided to see if maybe she would be interested in spending sometime, trying to start a relationship with him. As they pulled into the work site, the guys were teasing Bob hard about one of his drunken antics at a recent golf tournament. The truck was filled with laughter and everyone inside it had a feeling that today would be a good day.

They grabbed their equipment and headed up into the forest. It was agreed that they would meet at a clearing by a small stream, where there was a nice pool, for lunch. All four men loved working in the forest, and respected it greatly. As Frank headed off away from the others, he filled his lungs with the freshness and aromas that surrounded him. He could never get enough of it and always looked forward to being out here. While most people in town waited for the week to end and the weekend to start, Frank wanted the weekend to end and the week to start. He just couldn't imagine why anyone would want to sit in a room behind a desk all day. To him, it just seemed like such a waste of life. His dad had taught him to love nature and he wanted to do that one day for his own children.

He reached the area where he was to begin falling trees. He would carefully select only those that would be of any use, or that would be a hazard to anyone of the crew that would be coming in behind him to collect the logs. Putting on the safety leggings, that would protect him from the chainsaw, in case of a kick back, his mind was on Sherri. He kept seeing her eyes and smile and knew that he wanted to be with her. Soon he was suited up with goggles, hardhat and ear protectors. He pulled on the cord and the chainsaw fired to life. Soon he was busy with the task at hand and everything else was put aside for now.

The van slowly pulled up beside the crew cab and parked. Sherri was awake by now and getting helped out of the van. While she had been under, a bandana had been tied around her mouth, to prevent her from screaming. George and the other men were lifting the wooden toolbox out of the back of the van. They pulled out two chainsaws and each man grabbed either an axe or small hatchet. Her eyes were watering from shear fright, as her mind imagined these instruments being used on her. The red head had a firm hold of her with one hand and held a small hatchet in the other. Scott stood on the other side of the toolbox, strapping a hunting knife to his leg. When he was done he looked up at Sherri. This time, she definitely noticed the no sign being made by his head. What was he trying to tell her, why was this happening? She didn't want to die, nor could she understand why these people wanted her dead.

"Won't be long now and you will get to join your logger sweetheart." The red head whispered into Sherri's ear. "Oh, I'll make sure you die right beside your boyfriend. He is pretty damn cute. What a shame he has to die, and just think everyone will think he killed you. After all, he was just protecting himself from you fanatic environmentalists."

Sherri tried to scream but to no avail. Working with all her might she tried to escape the grip that the red head had on her, but had to stop as the red head placed the hatchet against her throat.

"What the hell is going on over there?" Scott demanded.

"Nothing. Our little princess here thought maybe she was going to go somewhere."

The red head shoved Sherri over to where the men were standing. With tears streaming down her face, she tried desperately, pleading with these people, but the bandana restricted her from saying anything. Her stomach was in a knot and she felt as though she was going to urinate at any moment.

"Ok, we all know why we are here. If there is anyone here not committed to this, or is feeling uncomfortable about it, then stand down now. Once we head into there, there is no turning back." Scott emphasized, as he pointed the axe he was holding in the direction the loggers had gone.

"For Christ's sake, can we just get on with it and quit with the moral searching. It's a little late for that, don't you think? Besides, you know we wouldn't be able to let anyone leave here alive." George pushed his way past Frank.

"Alright, let's go. We'll follow George, as he knows this area best. When we get there remember, split up and surround them, we don't want any witnesses."

Sherri shook her head fiercely from side to side. This was not happening, this was not happening, she kept repeating to herself. The red head pushed her in the direction the others were going and soon the forest swallowed them up.

Frank looked down at his watch and noticed that it was almost lunchtime. He set his saw down beside the axe he had leaning against a tree, picked up his lunch box and headed for the spot where they had agreed to meet. When he got there, Willie and Bob were already there and not long after, Allan popped out of the trees and into the small clearing. It was a great spot and the stream had created a pool where a log had fallen into the water creating a small dam. Over time the rushing water washed away an area and now green moss carpeted the edge and ferns grew from the rotting wood. The men found a log or stump to sit on and started having their lunch. The conversation was light and hearty, with their laughter echoing back at them from the trees. At one point Bob thought he had heard something, but when they all listened it was quiet. Soon, he was being ribbed about being scared and asked if he wanted to go home. Each man offered to hold his hand, to make sure he got back to his area safely. All they got in response, was a stiff middle finger being shown to them, which was met with a roar of laughter.

As the group got closer, they could hear the laughter of the loggers. Sherri could make out Frank's voice and laughter. Her heart screamed for him to help and to warn him of the danger. They stopped and Scott motioned to the men to split up and go in opposite directions. As one of the men turned to leave, he stepped on a twig and the laughter from the loggers stopped. Everyone stood motionless, holding their breath. The red head had the hatchet pressed so hard against Sherri's throat, that the axe felt as though it was cutting Sherri's skin. Soon the laughter started again, as one of the loggers was getting teased by the others about being scared. Sherri looked at George to see if hearing his old friends' voices would bring him to his senses. The look in his eye told her that he was beyond caring. Soon everyone had left except for her, the red head and Scott. They stood there in silence, for what seemed forever.

Frank was packing his lunch box away, when the sound of chainsaws broke the tranquility and a body came flying past him stumbling to the ground. The other men jumped up yelling in confusion. Frank stood frozen, as he recognized the body laying before him, as Sherri. Her mouth was tied with a piece of cloth and her eyes were wide open, looking as if they were going to pop out of her head. Frank heard Allen's scream, and spun in the direction from which it came, only to watch in horror as the chainsaw chewed its way through Allan's skull. From the corner of his eye, Frank caught the glimpse of an axe coming toward him. Instinctively, he drew back just as the blade grazed his chin. Diving for the ground, he rolled and came face to face with a body that used to have the head of Willie Folero on it. Blood seemed to be pouring out every where. He jumped to his feet and screamed as he saw the red head raising her hatchet above Sherri's stomach. Even before he could react, one of the attackers that he recognized as Scott, from the roadblock, drove an axe into the back of the red head and her body lurched forward. The hatchet she had been holding, went flying into the air and landed at Frank's feet. Quickly, he bent over to grab it and felt the swish of air as an axe came by where his throat used to be. He heard another horrifying scream and looked up to see Bob driving an axe into the forehead of one of the assailants. As he twisted to see what was happening to Sherri, he saw Scott, cutting the rope that bound her wrists. Frank yelled a warning, at Scott, as he saw a man wielding a chainsaw come running behind him. Frank stared in confusion and disbelief, as he recognized George as the man with the chainsaw. Bob's scream for help, broke his seemingly trance, he had fallen into at the sight if George. There were two men after Bob and he could see the blood coming from where Bob's right arm used to be. Charging over, Frank brought the hatchet down hard, burying it in the head of one of the attackers. The other man turned with the chainsaw, waving it at Frank. Before he could get close, Bob threw himself against the man sending them both tumbling to the ground. Bob howled in pain, as he came down on his severed limb. Frank snatched up the axe from the ground and hacked at Bob's attacker. Blood sprayed every where and covered Frank. Quickly glancing down at Bob, he saw his eyes wide open but empty. In the scuffle, Bob had rolled onto the chainsaw and it ripped its way through his midsection and protruded from his chest. Frank spun when he felt the hands grab him. He raised his fist to strike out when his eyes met Sherri's. The terrified look that she had, was like nothing he had ever seen before. Before anything could be said, a gurgling sound was heard as the chainsaw worked its way into Scott's heart. Screaming, Sherri grabbed her head and dropped to her knees. Frank, still standing covered with blood and holding the axe, turned to face George. Everything seemed to stop for a moment, as both men stood and stared. Frank could barely recognize the man he now faced. He looked like total evil and seemed to be enjoying this. Anger, like none he had ever experienced before, rushed over him. All Frank could think of, was that he had to kill this man and do it quickly.

Suddenly, George revved the chainsaw and swung it upwards charging toward Frank. Quickly raising the axe, Frank managed to block the chainsaw just in time. The sudden force though, knocked the axe from his hands. George swung the saw again and it tore through Frank's shirt and ripped a gash open in his chest. Frank stumbled back, clenching at his chest, where the saw had opened him up. He could see that it drove George even crazier. George was smiling, to the point of almost laughing, as he came at Frank with the saw again. Frank saw the chain coming down, and rolled quickly to one side. He could feel the teeth of the spinning chain grab at his shirt. When the saw hit the ground, it struck a rock and the chain flew apart. Grabbing at the axe laying on the ground, Frank swung it wildly, hitting George on the inside of the knee. George dropped immediately grabbing at his leg. The blade of the axe hadn't hit, but the force of the blow had shattered his kneecap. By now Frank was starting to feel weak, from the loss of blood. Picking himself up, George hobbled over and jumped onto an ever weakening Frank. Grabbing Frank by the throat, George squeezed, making it impossible for Frank to take in a breath. Frank tried in desperation to claw at George, but soon there was no strength left in him. Frank heard, what sounded like a bat hitting a softball, as George released his grip and rolled off Frank. George was grabbing at the back of his head and moaning in pain. Frank looked up and saw Sherri standing with an axe, hanging by her side. Dropping the axe, Sherri leaned over and tried to help Frank up.

Her voice came to him as if she were whispering, and the vision of her was becoming blurry and then clear again. She had one of his arms around her neck and was trying to get him on his feet, pleading with him to stand up. Everything seemed to be happening in slow motion. As he looked up at Sherri, he saw the tears streaming down her face, he saw her lips moving but could not hear the words. There was nothing but silence now and the realization that his life was over, flowed over him. He reached out and grabbed Sherri's hand and with tremendous effort tried to mouth the word, "Run". A second later life left him.

George's moan and movement made Sherri jump. She had been kneeling beside Frank, with her one hand over the ugly gash in his chest and the other hand gently stroking his forehead, as if to comfort him. When she saw George, trying to get to his feet, a sudden rage took control of her. She grabbed the axe that was lying on the ground and walked over to where George was starting to stand. Later, she would not even be able to recall the events that happened at that moment. Seeing him favoring his one knee, she hit it again with axe, sending George rolling on the ground writhing in pain. Walking up to him, she looked down at his face and brought the axe above her head. As she started to bring it down on his head, over and over again, she kept screaming, "Why?"

When she no longer had the strength to swing the axe, she stood there and stared at the carnage that lay around the ground. Parts of bodies were laying everywhere in pools of blood. It was as if the forest floor had started to bleed. Suddenly, her body started shaking violently and she didn't know when but she had urinated.

"Holy Shit!"

The scream made her snap her head to the side, to see where it came from. Standing frozen staring at the sight that lay before him, was a man in clothing much like Frank and the others had worn. He brought his eyes up to hers. She saw the horrific look on his face, as he stared at her standing there. Lying in front of her, was a body whose head was nothing more than a puddle of mush and blood dripped from the axe she still held in her hand.

"My God, what have you done?" She could hear other voices now and men crashing through the bush heading towards them.

"Get over here quick! She's killed them all!"

As the words slowly registered in her mind, "She's killed them all", her eyes moved down to the mashed form laying at her feet and the axe in her hand. The sickening scene grabbed hold of her mind. Dropping the axe, she started running, screaming "No!" There was no thought of why or where she was going, just that she had to run. The branches from the trees scraped at her face and arms, but she kept charging on, trying to put as much distance as she could between her and the madness. The vision of Frank's mutilated body, seemed to follow her. Then the sight of George's head, lying at her feet, with bone and blood mixed in a mush, drove her to scream out. She wasn't sure how long she had been running, or even in which direction she had gone, but when her lungs finally screamed for air, she couldn't continue anymore and dropped to her knees crying uncontrollably. Getting control of herself, she sat against a tree in total exhaustion. They can't really believe that she was responsible for what happened there. God why did this happen? The events that had happened over the last day seemed so unreal, that her mind struggled to maintain a focus on what was real and what wasn't. As she looked at the blood and bits of skull splattered on her clothing, she suddenly vomited violently.

Evening was starting to approach and she knew that she either had to get out of the woods, or at least find some place to settle in for the night. She had taken survival courses and spent lots of time camping and hiking, so she was confident on what to do to survive the night. Looking at the sky, she figured which direction would lead her back to the road, but wasn't sure as to how far that would be. She had no idea how far she had run. Striking out in the direction that she now considered the way out, she tried to figure out what the best course of action would be, to let the authorities know what had happened. She decided that she would go to the local police station when she got to town and explain everything to them. They would sort this nightmare out. After a couple hours of walking through the woods, she knew that she would have to spend the night, so she started looking for a good spot to bed down. Her training told her to find some place on higher ground, so that if it rained she wouldn't wake up in a pool of water. Also, she was fortunate to be in a cedar forest. It was easy to find a tree, where she was able to lay under its huge branches, using the fallen needles for a soft bed. Breaking off some of the lower branches, she covered herself with them to protect her from the cold of the night. They weren't the most comfortable blanket, but they definitely did the trick. It wasn't long before she fell fast asleep. She wasn't sure what it was that had woken her, maybe a chattering squirrel or perhaps a deer passing by, but something made her sit up with a start. She sat still for the a few minutes, intently listening. After a while, she felt secure in the fact that there was nobody out there. No one had followed her and was watching her. The light of dawn was starting to invade the blackness and the fresh smell from the forest floor gave her a sense of well being. Sherri stood up and brushed as much of the needles off as she could. She then took a branch and scraped the dried on particles from her clothing. The thought of it and the flashback started her crying again. Grabbing her shoulders and squeezing as hard as she could, she slowly got herself back under control. Heading out again for the road, she was surprised at how far she had run. A few times, she stopped to check the sun, wondering if perhaps she was heading deeper into the woods. Not sure how long she had been hiking, but estimating perhaps a couple of hours, she broke through onto an old logging road. It was overgrown with grass and small shrubs, but it gave her spirits a lift. Noticing that to the right, the road seemed to climb further upward, she decided to turn left and head down. Hopefully reaching the valley floor.

Eventually, she came across the main logging road and felt better about her chances of making it to town. Picking up her pace, she turned and headed down the road. At first when she heard the vehicle approaching, her instinct was to try and flag it down for a ride. Deciding otherwise, she dashed into the bush and hid until it had passed. She was certain that every logger around, would have heard the news by now and there was no telling what would happen if they found her out here by herself. The truck passed by and Sherri was glad that she had hid. As it passed by her hiding spot, she counted three men sitting in it and they didn't look as if they would have been willing to listen to her plead her case. After the truck was well out of sight, she came out and started back down the road. Surprisingly, it wasn't far before she came to the intersection, that she recognized as the one where they had turned with the van. Was it possible that the van could still be there? And if so would there be police around? She decided to take the chance, after all, if the police were there, she could explain it all to them. She started up the road staying close to the edge, in case she had to make a quick dash into the woods to hide. As she came around the bend in the road, Sherri saw the van parked along side the loggers crew cab pickup. The wooden toolbox was gone and yellow police tape was wrapped around both vehicles. Sherri sat in the bushes along side the road for quite a while, making sure that no one else was around. When she felt it was safe, she ran over and tore the tape from the van and climbed in. Her body started to shake at the memories that lingered inside the vans space, but once more she grabbed hold of herself and fought it off. Reaching under the dash, she retrieved the keys. George had insisted, that the keys be left behind incase something happened, that way they would always have a way of getting out of there.

The instant the engine came to life, she shifted to drive and sprayed gravel from the spinning tires as she raced away from there. The radio was on and seemed like nothing more than background noise. It helped her keep her mind occupied, so that she wouldn't keep reliving the past twenty-four hours. When the news came on, she turned the volume up. Sure enough, the headline was about the killings.

"Authorities are still bewildered, about what exactly happened to four loggers found murdered, in the Whallington Valley. Information is still a bit sketchy at this moment, but we do know that they are looking for a female, believed to be one of the killers. She is believed to be dangerous and should not be approached. Witnesses at the scene, say they saw her head off into the woods and she hasn't been seen since. Police describe her as standing approximately five feet six inches tall and weighs about one hundred and twenty pounds. She has dirty blonde hair and was last seen wearing a green t-shirt and blue jeans. Again we stress, do not approach this person, as she is very dangerous. If you see her, notify the local police department immediately."

Sherri reached over and turned the radio off. My god, they really believe I killed those people, she thought in disbelief. Why had they not mentioned the other bodies there and only the loggers? As she drove off the logging road and turned onto the highway, she decided to find someplace to stop and try to figure out what to do. As she came into Newport, she noticed a service station on the side of the highway. There wasn't anybody around, so she pulled the van around to the side of the building where it would be out of sight.

Carefully, she rolled the window down and looked around to see if anyone was paying any attention to her. After a few minutes, she climbed out of the van and quickly made her way into the ladies washroom, locking the door behind her. Leaning on the sink, she lowered her head and let out an exhausting sigh. Everything was going to be ok, she told herself. Once they heard what really happened, they would have to let her go. Turning the water on, she started washing her hands. When she looked up in the mirror, a shocked gasp escaped her. Her hair was matted and her face covered with dirt and dried blood. She was not sure if it was George's blood, or her own, from the branches scraping against her when she fled the scene. Quickly she scrubbed her face and stuck her head under the tap washing her hair as best she could. She removed her t-shirt and washed it in the sink scrubbing it with the hand soap that had been provided by the station. After ringing the t-shirt out she slipped it back on and did the same with her jeans. The wet clothes felt uncomfortable, but she felt better after being able to clean up a little. Realizing that she hadn't eaten for sometime, she started feeling hungry, but decided that she would just have to wait till she got home. Slowly, she opened the door and peered out. Seeing no one, she stepped out and was about to walk to the van, when she saw the police car pull up on the other side of the van. Her heart felt as though it was about to jump out of her chest, and the almost familiar feeling now of panic, started to grab at her. They couldn't see her as they were on the other side of the van, so she quickly stepped around the corner of the building.

"Yeah, this is the van alright." She heard the one officer say. "Check with the attendant and see if he saw anything. I'm going to check around."

"Do you think it was her that drove it down? It had to be, eh? Hard to believe someone can snap like that, and for what, a bunch of trees. Good thing we got that phone call about her."

Confused, she wasn't sure what she was hearing. What phone call, and what did they mean snap like that? She wanted to run out and demand to know what was going on, but something inside her told her to stay out of sight. Something was very wrong here, and until she had a better idea of what that was, she decided to try and stay hidden for as long as she could. Lifting her head up from behind the air compressor, which she was hiding behind, she saw the one officer talking on his radio. He had his back to her, so she decided to take the chance and make her way over behind some parked cars. She knew that if she stayed in one spot too long, they would definitely find her. Walking quickly, she made her way across the open space between her and the cars. With her heart pounding in her chest, she immediately dropped behind one of the cars and held her breath. No footsteps were heard running toward her, and no voices alerting anyone that they had spotted her. Sherri cautiously stood up and peered through the back window of the car, watching as the other officer made his way back to the van.

"The attendant said he noticed her pull in, but didn't pay any attention to what she did or where she went. Man, she sure did a number on those poor bastards. How in the hell, was she able to get all four of them like that?"

"Now there's a million dollar question. Radio dispatch informed me that they found a letter at her place, and plans as to how she planned on ridding the world of all those who were harming it. We are definitely dealing with a nut case here. Let's hope we catch this bitch before she goes crazy on someone else."

She watched as the officers climbed back into their car. Her heart was pounding and her breath seemed to be coming in short gasps. She was living in a nightmare and there didn't seem to be anyway of waking up from it. She was being framed, but by who and why? Never before had she felt so alone. Who could she turn to for help? She had friends in The Nature's Select, but then she wasn't sure whom to trust there. She had always thought of them as family, but that had all changed now. No, she would have to try and find a way to get to the bottom of this on her own. But where to start?

⚜

CHAPTER 7

"Ok, I told him exactly what you wanted me to, but I still don't know why you wanted him to know about the others." Deric asked into the phone. He had made the call as soon as he was back in his office, just as he was instructed.

"Well, you just let us worry about the whys and you take care of the dos. Now keep an eye on him and let us know how close he starts to get." The voice on the other end ordered. Deric had never met the man behind the voice, but the generous cheques he had been receiving from him, had made this relationship a very profitable one, so he never asked too many questions. He just knew it was in his best interest not to.

"Yeah, no problem. I'll get back to you as soon as I know anything." Deric replied, then hung up the receiver.

Tony found Paul still sitting at the table with three ladies. He took a mental note of what everyone was drinking and walked over to the bar. Trista took his order and brought the drinks over to him. He paid and carried the drinks back to the table.

"Ladies, this here is my partner in crime. Tony meet Aline, Chantal and Valerie." The three women looked up smiling and said hi. Tony set the drinks down and pulled up a chair between Chantal and Valerie.

"So, how'd things go?" Paul asked.

"Good, and you?" Tony raised his eyebrows, looking over the top of his glass as he took a sip.

"Well, you will probably be interested to know that Valerie works for the logging company that the victims worked for."

Tony turned and smiled at her. Returning the smile, she extended her hand. "A pleasure to meet you. Paul has been telling us a lot about you."

"All good I hope."

She had short black hair and beautiful green eyes. When she smiled, it seemed to make her eyes sparkle. As Tony took a quick glance, he noticed that she seemed to be in excellent physical condition. He figured she must either work out at a gym, or played some sort of sport.

"I hear you're writing an article on what happened to Frank and the boys." Valerie said, her face showing the pain as she looked down at the table.

"Yes, we just got in tonight, so we really haven't had time to do much yet."

"Well, if there's anything I can do to help please do not hesitate to get in touch with me."

Tony knew that he would definitely be doing that. He would be able to get a lot of background material on the men. That would give him a direction to get started on, plus he was finding this lady very attractive.

"Thanks very much, if it isn't a bother, I will take you up on that offer." He said smiling and looking deep into those enticing eyes. Taking a card from her purse, she wrote her home number on the back and handed it to him, telling him to call anytime. He put the card in his wallet and the conversation took on more of a social tone. They stayed until the bar closed, said goodnight to the ladies, and headed back to the Travelers Eight Motel. They agreed to meet early in the restaurant downstairs, and both headed for their rooms. When Tony opened the door, he noticed the red light flashing on his phone letting him know that there was a message waiting for him. He took his coat off and walked over to the desk to retrieve the message.

"Hey you, how's it going? Got your message. Give me a call when you get in. Don't worry about the time. Knowing you two, it will probably be after the bar closes." It was Cats, and Tony immediately smiled at the sound of her voice. He also had a twinge of guilt, as he had made a date to get together with Valerie on a social level. They had hit off immediately, and there was something about Valerie that he just couldn't explain. It just felt comfortable being around her. He picked up the phone and dialed Cats number.

He knew that he had woken her up, by the groggy sound of her voice.

"What's the matter? You getting old and needing to go to bed early these days?"

As soon as she heard his voice, her tone picked up immediately. "How are you guys doing up there? Get settled in ok?"

"Oh yea. We went down to one of the local pubs and found out some very interesting information. Were you aware that they found some of the protesters' bodies lying out at the scene?"

"Are you shitting me? This is the first I've heard of it."

"No. Do you think maybe you could see what you could dig up there? Something is very wrong here. I can't for the life of me understand why this was not reported in the news when it broke. Talking to the locals, there hasn't been any mention of it. It's like they don't know anything about it."

"No kidding it's a little strange. How did you find out about it?"

"Talked to a guy here that owns the bar we were at, and he filled me in. Now, he may not know what he's talking about, but I have to find out for sure. It's just not making any sense to me at all."

"What did TNT have to say for himself at your dinner meeting?" Cats asked.

"Well, he seems to think that this was all a big conspiracy to draw attention to environmental issues in the area. He claims that he has a source, and they say it involves some very powerful people. He didn't really elaborate. He did tell me that the police are looking for a female suspect that was seen at the killings. He also wants me to report to him any progress I make before taking it to Jason. That should push Jason over the edge, when he finds that out."

"Yeah, I heard about the suspect, it's been on the news. He can't be serious about a conspiracy. This is one strange story." Cats' voice sounded a bit sarcastic to Tony.

"You're telling me. He told me his source is very reliable, but wouldn't tell me who it was. Anyway, I'm going to get some shuteye. I've got a lot to do tomorrow and we plan on getting an early start. If you can try to find anything out about the other bodies that were suppose to have been found out there, it sure would help me out here."

"Yeah, not a problem. You take care of yourself."

"You know I will. I'll call you tomorrow, and don't worry, I'm a big boy. Besides I've got Paul to watch me."

"Oh hell, I forgot. Now I'm really worried." They both laughed and said their goodnights.

Something kept eating at Tony, but he couldn't put his finger on it. Sleep didn't come easy that night, as he kept waking up running everything through his mind. Why did none of the news services have anything about the other bodies? Why was Deric the only one that had mentioned it? Was he bullshitting him? Surely the bartender knew, or even Valerie. After all, it was some of the men who work for the same company that came upon the scene. There would have been talk amongst themselves. He had to talk to someone who had been out there. He decided to get a hold of Valerie in the morning and see if he could get a name of one of the loggers who found the bodies.

When he got downstairs to the restaurant, Paul was already sitting at a table with a coffee in front of him and a copy of that day's edition of the Garibaldi. They said their good mornings, and Tony ordered a coffee while Paul went back to reading an article he seemed to be engrossed in.

"Anything of interest in there this morning?" Tony asked. He was interested to see if there was anything else from the news wire about the killings.

"Can you believe this? They're going to increase the taxes on liquor and tobacco again. Jesus Christ, a person can hardly afford to go out now as it is. I just can't figure out why anything that is fun, these jerks have to mess with. I'm telling you, they are going to price it so bad, until no one can afford it and then what are they going to do to replace all that tax income?"

Tony couldn't help but laugh. All over the world dramatic events were shaping the world, and the only thing that interested Paul, was the fact that the price of his favorite drink was about to go up. Paul didn't even smoke, but just the fact of another tax increase sent him ranting. They sat there and discussed what they would do that day. When Tony mentioned about the other bodies that were suppose to have been found at the murder scene, he could see the excitement jump into Paul's eyes. Tony decided to go down to the local police station to get an official statement and maybe see what kind of reaction he would get by asking about the other bodies. Paul was going to go downtown to take some pictures, so that they could do a small piece on the town itself. As they were walking out, Tony suddenly remembered that he had promised to put something in the paper about the fundraiser for the logger's families, and headed to a pay phone to call the newspaper.

He dropped Paul off downtown and they agreed to meet at a small sidewalk café in an hour. Tony pulled away and headed for the police station. As he drove, he looked around at the beauty of the town and surrounding scenery. All this violence seemed so out of place in such a beautiful tranquil setting. He parked his car in front of the building that housed both the police and fire department. Stepping inside the station, he entered a small room, with a door and a glass partition. There was a buzzer on the wall beside the glass partition, with a small sign instructing everyone to press the button for assistance. Tony walked up and pushed the buzzer. After about a minute, a lady appeared at the window and asked how she could help. Tony explained why he was there and she told him to wait for a minute while she got someone who would be able to help him. Standing there, he looked around the room and saw a camera peering down at him from one corner. On one wall were posters of missing children and wanted criminals. On the other wall were pamphlets and bro-chures on everything from how to protect your valuables to report-ing a drunk driver. Soon an officer came to the window looking as if Tony had just interrupted something important and emanated noth-ing but attitude. Just great, Tony thought, this guy's going to be a great help.

"What can I do for you sir?" the officer asked.

Once again, Tony explained who he was and why he was there. The officer didn't seem too interested in what he had to say until Tony asked, "I have heard rumor that there were more bodies discov-ered than just the loggers, I was just wondering if anyone could clar-ify that?"

The officer seemed to stand suspended in time for a few seconds, just staring at Tony. He then instructed Tony to hold on and he would get someone that was familiar with the case. Tony saw that he had hit a chord. My God, he thought, if this is true, something big is definitely being hidden here. But why? Who would benefit from hid-ing something like this? It wasn't long before the officer returned escorted with another man in a suit.

The man in the suit was introduced to Tony as Detective Darrin Daikon. The detective opened the door leading into the main station area and asked Tony to follow him. He was lead down a hallway past the holding cells in the back. They soon left the brightly lit area visi-ble to the public and made their way down a dully lit hallway, to a small foyer with three small offices off to the side. On one side was a room with lockers, that Tony figured was the change room for the officers. The detective asked Tony to be seated at a bench, next to the door of the locker room, and then walked into one of the offices. As Tony sat there, he could hear voices coming from the locker room. Officers were mingling around inside and suddenly Tony's full attention was drawn to the conversation being carried on.

"...is supposed to be the woman that we're looking for in those loggers' deaths. Can you imagine, first stealing the van from the crime scene, then just driving it into town and then disappearing?"

"Well, she still has to be around here, cause there is no way she got through the roadblocks, and we have every means covered. It's only a matter of time before we nail her."

Tony slid as close to the locker room door as the bench allowed, so that he would be able to hear better. His attention was so focused on the conversation, that he hadn't noticed Detective Daikon come up behind him.

"Would you follow me please?" Detective Daikor motioned for him to follow. Tony jumped at the sound of his voice. He got up and followed the detective into one of the small offices. As soon as Tony entered the room, he knew exactly where he was. This was one of the interrogation rooms. A metal table stood in the center of the room, with a folding chair on either side and one up against the wall. On one wall was a two-way mirror, so that other people involved in a case could watch and listen in on the questioning.

"Please, have a seat." Daikon pointed at the nearest chair. "So how can I help you Mr. Parkins?"

"Well, I have a few questions I'd like to ask for my story." Tony pulled out a small tape recorder he always carried with him. "Do you mind if I record this?"

"Sorry, but I would rather you didn't."

"It's just so that I don't forget anything or misquote you."

"I can arrange for a note pad and pen for you to take notes, if you would like." Daikon sat staring at the tape recorder, to make sure it wasn't being turned on. Tony found this a bit unusual, but agreed. He picked up the recorder and went to put it back in his pocket. Tony cleared his throat and at the same time pushed the record button. Instead of putting it in his pocket, he laid it on his lap. He wasn't sure how well it would work from there, but he wanted every thing on tape. He reached in his other pocket and pulled out a small note pad and pen.

"We always come prepared, just in case. So, how is the investigation going? I understand you are looking for a suspect." Tony asked, wanting to get the interview started.

"Yes, there was a suspect witnessed at the scene, the day of the murders. We are quite confident that we will have her in custody shortly."

"Do you really think that one lady could be responsible for the death of those men, or do you think there were others?"

"Officially, we cannot comment on that at this time, as the investigation is still in its early stages." Daikon was staring hard at Tony now and almost leaning across the table. "You put that pen down for a minute and I might be willing to tell you what I think unofficially." He whispered in a low steady tone.

Tony's heart felt like it was going to jump into his throat. Was this the break he was waiting for? Quickly, he took a glance down at the tape recorder, then laid the pen down.

"If I hear or read about anything I am about to tell you, before I say it's ok, you'll never get out of whatever prison, I choose for you. Is that clear?"

The intensity in Daikon's look at that moment, told Tony that the man was dead serious. They looked at each other for a few seconds and Tony calmly replied, "I understand."

Daikon got up and walked out of the room. Bewildered, Tony sat there looking around the room. His eyes settled on the two-way mirror and wondered if anyone was on the other side. When Daikon came back into the room, he was carrying a piece of paper that he laid down in front of Tony. Tony picked the paper up and read it. The words on it made his hands start to shake. Embossed on the top of the sheet was the local seal for the police department and Newport's town seal, along with the words, Media Release. It was pretty much what all the other news reports had been saying about the murders. It was the words written on the bottom of the page, that made Tony's heart race.

"There were other bodies. Can't talk here." The words seemed to jump off the page at him. He was still staring at the words, when Daikon's voice brought his attention from the paper.

"Mr. Parkins? Mr. Parkins, are you all right?" Daikon was looking at him, trying to get Tony not to show, any clue, that there was anything on the paper other than the official press release.

"I hope that will answer all your questions. That is the press release we are issuing at this time and if there are any new developments in the case, we will be issuing a new statement." Daikon said, as he started to rise his chair.

"Um, yes, this is fine. Thank you." Tony smiled, his mind reeling.

"Good then. If there is anything else I can do for you, please do not hesitate to contact me. Here is my card, just give me a call anytime." He handed a business card to Tony, and on the back he had his home number written down. With a quick glance at Tony, he turned and opened the door. Tony walked out in a daze. He was trying to put everything into perspective. He shook Daikon's hand and thanked him again for his help. As he walked through the station, he felt lightheaded. He wanted to break into a run and get out of there. It felt as though everyone was watching him. He could feel the beads of sweat forming on his forehead. Just as he was reaching for the door, he heard is name called. The voice was right behind him. The urge to run was almost uncontrolable, but he knew he wouldn't get far. Tony stopped and turned around. Standing behind him, was the officer that had met him when he first arrived.

"Hope we were able to help you Mr. Parkins." The officer said as he reached for the doorknob to open it. The change in his attitude was like night and day, from their meeting earlier.

"Yes, thank you. I pretty much got everything I need."

Tony smiled and started through the door, the officer was holding open for him. As he brushed past the officer, his knees went weak at the words the officer whispered to him.

"I was there. Please, let people know the truth."

Tony stood motionless, unable to move as the door closed behind him. He stood in the small entry room trying to compose himself. Everything had changed, dramatically, in the last few minutes. This was almost too strange to be true. He felt like he was living in the twilight zone. He needed time to sort this all out, but right now he had to find Paul and give Cats a call. He was definitely going to need help. Tony walked out of the station into the sunlight and fresh air.

He found Paul pretty much where he had expected; shooting photos of the Ocean Port Hotel. He pulled up and parked. Paul waved at him and kept taking photos.

"We need to have a drink." Tony said as he walked past Paul giving him a slap on the back.

"Yeah, sure. What's up?"

"I'll explain inside. You are not going to believe this."

Paul could see in Tony's face and hear in his voice that something big was up. He immediately replaced the lens cover on his camera and was fighting to get it into the carry case while he was hurrying up the steps, leading into the pub. They found a table in the corner by a window and sat down. After the waitress dropped off their order, Tony reached into his pocket and pulled out the tape recorder and press release. He slid the press release over to Paul and hit the play switch on the tape recorder. The recording was barely audible, as the most important part had been spoken in almost a whisper.

Tony looked up, as Paul took in a deep breath, after reading what was written on the bottom of the release. As Paul finished reading, he looked up at Tony. Tony noticed that Paul's face had gone white.

"Is this for real?" Paul asked in disbelief.

"Yeah, I'm pretty much positive this is the real deal. That's not all, I over heard two officers talking and they believe that the woman their looking for, is still in the area. If we could find her, shit man do you have any idea what it could mean?"

"No kidding. Where do we start?"

"Well, I'm going to give Cats a call, when we get back to the motel. I've asked her to check a few things out for me. Then, I'm going to get a hold of Valerie, to see if I can somehow get in touch with one of the loggers that came across the scene."

They quickly finished their drinks and headed back to the motel. Tony noticed the red light on his phone, was flashing once again. He went over and retrieved his messages. The first one was from Cats, which he was expecting, the second message was from Valerie, suggesting that she pick him up for their date, as she knew her way around town better, the last message came as quite a surprise. It was from Detective Daikon. He decided to call Cats first, to fill her in on what he had learned.

"So, how are things going?" Cats asked when she heard his voice.

"Not bad. Things just keep getting weirder here. Just confirmed that there were more bodies found at the sight. Why they haven't been reported on, that I don't know. But I sure as hell am going to find out. Were you able to come up with anything?"

"No nothing new here. Pretty much just the same old stuff that has been on the wire."

"You all right?" asked Tony. She hadn't reacted quite the way he thought she would of, at such astonishing news.

"Yes, I'm fine. Just getting a little concerned for you. Please, be careful, this is getting all so strange."

"I'll be careful. I promise." Tony reassured her.

They talked for a while longer. After he hung up, he made arrangements with Valerie to be picked up later, and then he called Daikon. All he got was his answering machine, so he left a message asking if they could get together somewhere, tomorrow morning. He had a shower and walked out to the balcony, it had been an incredible day. As he stood there, he noticed a homeless lady standing amongst the cars in the parking lot, looking lost and scared. Her hair was in disarray and her clothes were torn and dirty. He watched her for a while longer, walking between cars, her head constantly darting this way and that as if watching for something. Tony turned and walked back into the room, feeling sorry for the poor lady. He was buttoning up his shirt when he froze solid. That was her. That was the face in the newspaper. He ran back out on the balcony and looked frantically around. He couldn't see her. Running from the room, he ran down the hall to the stairs. As he headed down the stairs, he was skipping them two and three at a time. Bursting through the door, he found himself standing in the parking lot, with his shirt half-done up and no shoes on his feet. He turned around one way, then the other, hoping to get a glimpse of her. He walked over toward the back of the motel, to the kitchen entrance, where the garbage bins were. Just as he was passing the last row of cars, he heard a shuffling sound behind a delivery van. His heart started racing and he could feel his blood pounding at his temples. Slowly, he walked around the back of the van. As he turned to the back, she came out with such a force, that it sent him stumbling backwards. As he fell, he shot his foot out and tripped her up as she tried to dash past him. He could hear the wind come out of her, as she hit the asphalt. Tony ran over and wrapped his arms around her, trying to prevent her from escaping. He was amazed at how hard she could fight. She was twisting and kicking in an attempt to free herself.

"Stop fighting. I'm not going to hurt you. I don't believe you are the one that killed those people." This seemed to take a little fight out of her.

"Let me go then." She spat back at him.

"No, I won't let you go; and if you continue to fight like this, we're going to draw attention, and the next thing you know the police will be showing up." That did it, she calmed down and nodded her head in agreement. Tony did not release his grip though, for fear that she might make a run for it.

"Listen, we can't stay out here. I've got a room upstairs where we can go. You'll be safe there." She looked at his face for the first time. He was taken aback by the fear he saw in her eyes. Her eyes had black rings around them and large puffy bags. "I promise you, I am not here to hurt you, or turn you in. I'm from the *Garibaldi Daily Newspaper* and I'm here to find out what really happened out there."

Tony helped her up and led her toward the rear entrance of the motel. Just as they were about to go inside, she stopped and looked up at him. Tears were streaming down her cheeks and her body had started to shake. "Thank you." She said. Tony wrapped his arm around her shoulder to steady her and led her upstairs.

CHAPTER 8

⚘

Tony helped her to sit down on the bed, then got her a drink of water. He stood in the center of the room, staring at her in disbelief. She was so small and frail. How could anyone think she had killed anyone, especially those burly loggers? She took a long drink, then handed the glass back.

"Thank you." She said, not meeting his gaze.

"You're welcome. My name's, Tony Parkins. Is there anything else I can get you? Are you hungry?"

She lifted her eyes to him and he could see the answer. She must not have eaten in a while now he thought.

"Ok, I'm going to order room service. Try to relax. You're safe here. Nobody knows you're here, so you'll be ok. Is there anything in particular you would like?" She shook her head no. Tony turned to go to the phone and order.

"Sherri Maider."

He turned and looked at her questioningly.

"My name, it's Sherri Maider." Tony looked at her and smiled.

"It's a pleasure, Sherri."

After he placed the order, he suggested that she might like to have a bath or shower to clean up. She jumped at the chance to lay in a tub and soak. After she closed the door and he could hear the water running, he called Paul's room.

"Ok, you are not, in your wildest dreams, going to believe this." Tony exclaimed.

"Hell, the way this whole thing has been going, I would believe just about anything right now."

"She's in my room."

"Christ, that was fast. I thought you weren't suppose to see her until tonight."

"What?" Tony couldn't figure out what Paul was talking about right away, then it hit him. "No, not Valerie, Christ. I'm not seeing her until later. The one they're looking for. Remember the woman that was in the newspaper? The one the police are looking for? She's in my room, having a bath."

"Bullshit! You've been into the Crown Royal a little heavy, or what? You are shitting me, right?"

"No. She's right here. I saw her in the parking lot, hiding between vehicles. Listen, I'm going to get her fed, then I'll let her rest while I'm out with Valerie. Give me about an hour, then come over. I want her to know that someone is close by that she can trust. She is really freaked out. You know, I don't believe she had anything to do with those killings."

"Yeah, not a problem. Tell me something. Do you think this can possibly get any stranger?"

Tony stood there for a moment with the receiver to his ear, then calmly said, "Without a doubt."

Sherri still hadn't come out of the bathroom when the room service arrived. Tony was a little concerned, so he walked over and knocked on the bathroom door.

"Food is here." He said as he pressed his ear against the bathroom door.

"I'll be right there." Tony could hear the splashing of water as she climbed out. After a few minutes, the door opened and she came out with a bath towel wrapped around her. Her hair was wet hanging down on the front of her chest.

"Sorry, but my clothes were so dirty, I just couldn't bring myself to put them back on again. It's been a while, since I've been able to clean up and relax. I would really like to thank you for helping me." She said looking at him, then her eyes moved to the plate of food on the table and Tony could see her eyes widen.

"Listen, don't worry about it. Why don't you sit down and have something to eat and I'll get one of my shirts for you to wear." He hadn't even finished, when Sherri was already heading for the table. While she ravenously started to eat, he went into the closet and pulled out a button down shirt. He laid it on the bed and told her that when she was finished, she could put it on while they got her clothes cleaned. There was a public Laundromat across the street, so he picked her clothes up and said he would be right back. Tony went over to Paul's room and asked him, if he would take them across the street and wash them. When Paul saw the bundle of clothes, he gave Tony a "you've got to be kidding me" look. Tony explained that he didn't want to leave Sherri alone for too long. Reluctantly, Paul took the bundle and made sure that Tony understood, that he was going to owe him big time, for this one.

When Tony got back to his room, he found her sitting at the end of the bed, in his shirt, watching television. He couldn't help but be taken by the way his shirt hung off her lean, hard body. Quickly, he turned his attention to the television. It was an old mystery, he remembered seeing as a teenager.

"Now that's an old classic." He said. Sherri just looked up and nodded. "Listen I gave your clothes to my partner." Her head snapped up and he saw the fear in them. "It's ok. He's on our side. I have a meeting tonight, so he's going to be around if you need anything. His room is right across the hall. Are you ok with that?"

"Guess I don't have much choice. Do you have to go to this meeting?"

"Yes, I do." He walked over and sat down beside her on the bed. "Sherri listen, I do not believe you did what they are saying, and we're going to do everything we can to prove that." She laid her head on his shoulder and he could see the tears once again begin to flow. Putting his arm around her, he could feel her body throbbing from the sobs.

"Will you be up to possibly talking about this tomorrow?" He felt heartless for asking, but he knew that time was not on their side.

"I think so." They sat there for what seemed like hours. When the knock came, they both jumped. Tony got up and motioned for her to go into the bathroom.

"Who is it?" he asked, looking through the security hole.

"Wing's Laundry. Who do think?" Tony unlocked the door and let Paul in. He had the clothes in his hand all folded, and his eyes were scanning the room, then back at Tony. He shrugged his shoulders and raised his one hand in a questioning manner. Tony motioned toward the bathroom, then told him to put the clothes down on the bed.

"It's all right Sherri, you can come out. It's Paul with your clothes all washed."

"Could you hand them to me please." Tony picked the bundle up off the bed and walked over to the bathroom door. Sherri was standing just inside the doorway, looking frightened. She searched his face questioningly.

"I promise you, it's all right. He's a friend." She took the clothes and closed the door. Tony turned and went over to the bar fridge and offered Paul a drink.

"She's really shook up. You'll have to be very careful about what and how you talk to her. Valerie is coming to pick me up in about two hours, so I would like you to stick around and just keep an eye on her to make sure she's ok."

"Oh sure, first laundry, now babysitting. I get stuck in a motel room all night, while you go out and have fun with a beautiful lady." Paul joked.

"No need to thank me."

The bathroom door opened and Sherri hesitantly made her way out. She gave Paul a quick glance then walked over to where Tony was standing. Placing a reassuring hand on her shoulder, he motioned toward Paul.

"Sherri this is Paul. Paul meet Sherri."

Paul stepped forward smiling with his hand extended. "Please to meet you." Sherri shook his hand and nodded.

"Paul is going to be here in case you need anything while I'm gone. Sherri he is a friend and you can trust him."

"Not to mention I'm a great listener, or if you prefer I can talk your ear off." Paul humored, trying to lighten the moment. He did notice a softening to her eyes. "I'm right across the hall if you need anything, but Tony was saying that you could probably use some rest, so I'll leave you to settle in and I'll check on you later."

"Thank you." She said, now smiling openly.

"So, any idea when you might be back?" Paul asked Tony.

"Not really sure, but shouldn't be too late. Well, I better get ready. Sherri make yourself at home, and Paul I'll get in touch with you in the morning."

Sherri's request caught them both by surprise. "Would it be all right if I stayed over in Paul's room tonight? I'm just not sure if I want to be alone tonight." She had felt so alone these past few days, that having these men around made her feel good. Paul smiled and told her it wasn't a problem. They left and Tony climbed into the shower.

He was standing outside the motel when Valerie pulled up. As he leaned to climb into the car, he had to take a quick breath, he was not prepared for how beautiful she looked. Her green eyes and warm smile left him standing there staring.

"So, are you getting in the car or is something wrong?"

"No, I'm definitely getting in." he said climbing into the car but his eyes remained on her.

"What?"

"Nothing. It's just that you are incredibly beautiful."

Valerie let out a chuckle and shook her head. "Is that a line that usually works for you?"

"Only when I'm around a beautiful lady."

"Well, thank you. So, what would you like to do tonight?"

"I don't know. After all it's your town."

"Well, why don't we go have a couple of drinks first, then figure it out from there."

"Sounds good to me."

Valerie turned out onto the highway and took a quick glance over at Tony, only to find him staring at her and she smiled. After driving a short distance out of town, they pulled into a small neighbor hood pub called the Cedar Tree. As they walked into the pub, Tony couldn't take his eyes off of Valerie. He was absolutely mesmerized. She was wearing a tight white top that hugged the contours of her breasts and back. It was just short enough that it left a thin exposed area of flesh showing her hard flat stomach. A long white wrap around clung to her hips and when she moved it flowed about her. They got a table out on the deck and ordered drinks.

"So, how's the investigating going?"

He suddenly had no interest in talking about work, but the question brought him back to why he was there.

"Not bad. Some very interesting turns of events have arisen."

"Oh, like what?"

He wasn't sure if he should tell her or not, but something told him that she could be trusted, besides he needed her help, so she would eventually find out anyway. Tony looked around to make sure no one was eavesdropping on their conversation.

"Well, just for starters, did you know that they found other bodies at the scene besides those of the loggers?" Her eyes shot wide open.

"Other bodies? What do you mean other bodies?"

"I'll know more tomorrow, but I'm pretty sure that some of the attackers were found dead at the scene also."

"There was no mention of that in the news." She said skeptically.

"I know, that's what's so puzzling about this whole thing. Do you think any of the loggers that came upon the scene would be willing to talk to me?"

"I'm not sure. When I think about it, the men that were on that crew have not been seen or heard of much. It was very dramatic on them and it's like they just disappeared into their own worlds. Oh, you see them around town every now and then, but not out socially anymore, or talking to anyone. It's like they don't want to have anything to do with anyone. Some have even moved."

Tony could see the pain in her eyes. He wanted desperately to comfort her. "I guess you knew these men and their families pretty well."

"Yes, they had worked for the company for a while. I became friends with their families and now it's like I never knew them at all. Her eyes started to swell up with tears. Tony reached over and laid his hand on hers and gently squeezed.

"Valerie, I sure could use your help getting to the bottom of this."

"How can I help? I really don't know much at all about what happened out there."

"Maybe not, but you do have access to company files, and that in itself could prove to be a great help. You see, I have reason to believe that there may be some kind of cover up happening here, with the logging industry, environmental activists or the government."

"You're not serious. Why would anyone want to cover this up? What could they possibly gain by it? That is just too unbelievable."

"Valerie, the answers to those questions right now I don't know, but I sure intend to find out. If I am wrong at least we might be able to figure out who did do this and why. It might help a lot of people put closer to it." She was looking hard into his eyes. He was still holding her hand gently rubbing his thumb across the softness of it.

"Ok, what can I do to help?" she asked with a look of conviction coming over her face. Tony smiled at her and gave her hand a firm squeeze.

"Did any of the men that came back from that day say anything in regards to the killings?"

"Well, the men never came back to work for a couple days after that. The police took them away for questioning that day and then they seemed to change."

"What do you mean?"

"Like I was saying before, they seemed to keep to themselves."

"Could you possibly try and see if you could get one of them to talk to me? You can assure them that no one will know. Their names will never be mentioned."

"I will try but no guarantees."

"Fair enough." Tony said and then took the conversation in a different direction. They spent a good part of the evening sitting there talking about each other. Tony found himself becoming more and more attracted to this beautiful lady sitting across the table from him. They decided to go and have dinner at a fish and chip restaurant called the Wigan Pier. Valerie said that it had been written up in quite a few articles as being one of the best in the area. As they were leaving, Tony excused himself and said he had to report in to the office. He really wanted to call Cats and tell her about finding Sherri and see if she could check into Sherri's background for him.

"So, what's the latest?" she asked cheerfully. The guilt was almost too much for him to handle, for he knew how hurt she was going to be when he finally told her about meeting Valerie. That would have to wait for another time though.

"Not bad at all, we found the lady everyone has been looking for."

"What do you mean you found her?"

"Now I know this is going to sound a little unbelievable. Hell, I still find it hard to believe, but she was hiding out in the parking lot at the motel. Paul's keeping an eye on her now. Can you do a background check on her for me? Find out where she's from and how involved she was with that group Nature's Select. Her name is Sherri Maider."

"Yeah, I can do that. So, she's at the room right now?"

"It just seemed like the safest place for her. Oh, can you do me one more thing and tell TNT that we have found her. He wanted to be kept up to date on how things are going." He could see Valerie standing outside waiting. "Listen, I've got to go, but I'll give you a call again tomorrow evening."

"Ok, not a problem. Say hi to Paul for me."

"Consider it done. Talk to you tomorrow." He hung the receiver up and headed straight out to Valerie. As he approached, she turned and smiled at him. He thought his heart was going to explode, she looked so radiant.

"What are you smiling at?" she asked him. He hadn't even realized that he was.

"Just a happy man, I guess."

They had an enjoyable time over dinner, talking about their pasts and laughing about experiences that had happened to them. There was a pause in the conversation when Valerie suddenly looked up at him.

"Thank you. I haven't been able to just go out and have an evening of feeling good for a while. I can't believe some of the things we talked about, but I feel so comfortable around you."

Tony reached out for her hand, but this time she extended it to him.

"I know exactly what you're saying. After my marriage fell apart, I tried to keep to myself. I thought that if I didn't let anyone get close, then I couldn't get hurt. With you though, it's different. I want you to get close." His heart skipped a beat, he didn't want to seem like he was coming on too strong and scare her off. This time she squeezed his hand and smiled letting him know that it was ok. After dinner, he decided that maybe he should get back to the motel. As they left the restaurant and walked out to the car, he asked if she would drop him off at the motel. She stopped walking and glanced up at his face.

"Well, I was wondering," she was looking down and then back at him with a very nervous expression. It happened so fast that Tony almost jumped back. Valerie had leaned over and kissed him. She pulled back and looked into his eyes. Reaching around her waist, Tony pulled her close to him and they stood there sharing a passionate kiss. As he felt her lips touch his, the desire in him for her grew. He could feel her tongue gently separating his lips. Tony wrapped his other arm around her and slid his hand down to rub her firm ass and pull her closer so she could feel him. A soft moan escaped her throat.

"Let's go." He said, smiling at her as they separated. Valerie smiled back at him, not so much with her mouth, he thought, but with those hypnotizing eyes. They drove to Valerie's place, which was located in a very quiet suburb, high on a plateau overlooking Newport. The house was built from solid red brick and had two huge maple trees standing guard out front. The driveway went up from the street, then disappeared into a double car garage.

As they entered the house, Tony found himself standing in a large entryway with a staircase leading upstairs and one leading down. Valerie stepped in front of him, as he was looking around, and brought her lips up to his. They stood there for awhile, passionately exploring each other with their hands and tongues. After a long while they hesitantly pulled apart and held each other in a rocking hug.

"Are you feeling what I'm feeling." Valerie whispered in his ear.

"I am sure that I am." He replied squeezing her a little tighter.

"How is this possible? We just met. This is incredible."

Tony pulled back, looked in her eyes and smiled at the beauty he was beholding. She was right he thought, this can't be happening. He had told himself he wouldn't allow himself to let go again. The pain of betrayal had almost destroyed him once and he didn't want to go through it again. This was different. He could feel it. This just felt so good and so right. A sudden burst of joy came over him and he let out a laugh, then brought her close and kissed her again.

They went upstairs and Valerie got them both a drink. Tony suddenly thought about phoning Paul to make sure every thing was all right, but as they sat down on the sofa and Valerie curled up next to him, his mind emptied of everything but her.

Tony soon found his hands exploring her body. As they moved over her breasts, she took in a quick breath, then pressed herself closer to him. He gently kissed the curve of her neck and moved his hand down to her thighs. He felt her body move to his touch and she positioned herself to feel how hard he was. Standing up she grabbed him by the hand and led him down the hallway to her bedroom. The room was large by most standards and there was a king size bed against the one wall. As they reached the bed she sat him down on the edge and stood directly in front of him, slowly removing her clothing as his eyes scanned up and down her body. As her clothing hit the floor, Tony reached around and placed his hands on her soft buttocks. He pulled her in close gently kissing her navel, slowly he moved down, kissing her as he went. She placed her hands on his shoulders and pushed him back onto the bed. As he laid there looking up at her, she gazed directly into his eyes, smiling as she started to remove his clothing. He could feel her warm breath, as she bent over to remove his pants and shorts.

Pressing her hands against the inside of his thighs, he responded by opening them for her. When she took him in her mouth, a shot of excitement went through him like nothing he had felt before. The fire swelled inside him to the point that he felt like he was going to explode. Then as if on cue, Valerie slowly brought herself up, kissing him till their lips met. She pressed herself to him and he could feel the firmness of her nipples against his chest. As they moved on the bed, his hands moved down between her legs until he could feel her wetness. They rolled over so he was on top and she opened her legs invitingly. Slowly, he entered her and they both purred with the passion that consumed them. They made love until both laid back, gig-gling from exhaustion.

Tony was shaking and laughing at the same time. "I have never experienced anything like that before."

Valerie laughed and gave him an understanding kiss. They both laid there, enjoying the moment they had just shared, then drifted off into a peaceful sleep.

CHAPTER 9

✿

Paul couldn't help but notice how restless a sleep this lady was having, laying there before him. He had been wondering what was holding Tony up, but then figured he was a big boy and could take of himself. There was no way he could have known about the two men, silently entering Tony's room, for they were professionally trained and were there to retrieve the girl.

He got up and went over to the small bar fridge to mix himself another drink. They had sat up for awhile talking before she laid her head back and fell asleep. When he opened the fridge he noticed that he had drank all the gin. He thought about phoning downstairs and seeing if he could order more, but then decided to go over to Tony's room and grab a couple of bottles out of his fridge. He checked on Sherri one last time and then quietly left the room. A door could be heard closing somewhere as he entered the hallway, but other than that there was no sign of anyone. Paul walked across the hallway and slipped the key into the slot and entered the room. Even before his hand could find the light switch, the blow came down fast and hard on the back of his head. He felt a sharp shot of pain, then blackness. They rolled him over and shone the flashlight in his face.

"Shit, this isn't him." One of the men said disappointedly. "And where is the girl? I'm positive this is the room number they gave us."

"So, what do we do now. You know if we leave him, the cops are going to get involved."

"Well, not much we can do. Trash the room a bit, see if you can find anything of value in his suitcases and we'll make it look like a burglary." The man bent down and checked Paul's pulse. "He'll live, but sure is going to wake up with one hell of a headache."

The two men went about their business, like two well oiled machines. They grabbed Tony's laptop computer and a few other things that would be worth something at a pawnshop, even though these items would end up in a trash bin some where in another town. When they came across Tony's briefcase, they checked the papers inside and saw his name on them, confirming they had the right room. After a brief discussion, they decided to get a room and wait it out till the time was right to make their move. After all, no one had seen them, so nobody knew what they looked like. They left the room and made their way out the back fire escape.

Tony headed into the lobby of the motel, saying hi to the desk clerk, who was checking in two men in suits. One of the men turned and gave him an acknowledging nod. Tony couldn't help but feel like the man was staring at him as he past by. He opened the door to his room and turned on the light. At first, his mind didn't register at what he was seeing. The room was turned upside down and Paul laid face down on the floor. He ran over and knelt down beside Paul, immediately checking his pulse. Thank God, he thought to himself. Then he noticed a small patch of blood on the back of Paul's head. Suddenly, he wondered where Sherri was, and feared for her safety. As he tried to pick Paul up from the floor, he could feel him starting to stir. After a few minutes he managed to get him up off the floor and onto the sofa. Tony went and got him a glass of water and a couple of aspirin from his overnight bag.

"Are you all right? What the hell happened?" Tony asked, handing Paul the aspirin.

"Shit, I wish I knew. The last thing I remember is walking over here across the hall. Man it feels like a truck hit me."

"Where's Sherri?"

"She's sleeping on the sofa in my room. What the hell hit me?"

"It looks like you came across someone burglarizing my room." Tony scanned the room, then noticed that the laptop was missing. He let out a short burst of profanity, then started to go through everything to see what else was missing. After making a short inventory list of the missing items, he asked Paul for his room key so he could check up on Sherri. Before he left, he checked Paul's wound, then went across the hall. He entered the room and saw Sherri still laying on the sofa sleeping, unaware of the events happening around her. She looked so peaceful, compared to the woman he had fought with in the parking lot, just a few hours earlier. He left her sleeping and went back to make sure Paul was doing ok. He was standing by the window holding a damp cloth to the back of his head.

"Man, you are lucky. You could have been killed." Tony headed over to the fridge and mixed himself a drink.

"Yeah, I suppose I am. Could you mix me one to? I sure could use it."

Tony mixed Paul a gin and tonic, then called the police and asked for Detective Daikon.

"Daikon here, can I help?"

"Daikon, it's Tony Parkins. My room got burglarized and my partner got attacked."

"Is he all right? I'll call for the paramedics to come check him out."

"No, he's fine, just a bit of a headache."

"Well, he should still get checked, in case of a concussion. Ok, don't touch or move anything, I'll be right over."

"Ok, not a problem." Tony replied then hung the receiver up in its cradle. He walked back over and checked on Paul once again.

"Detective Daikon thinks you should get that head of yours checked out, in case of a concussion."

"Aw hell, I'll be all right. Isn't the first and won't be the last time, I'll take a smack on the head." Paul finished his drink and handed the empty glass to Tony, asking him if he would mind mixing him another. After he gave Paul another drink, Tony said he was going to go over and check on Sherri again. Just as he was about to leave, the phone on the nightstand rang.

"So, what's going on up there?" it was Jason and Tony resented the intrusion. "I haven't heard anything from you, except the odd rumor. I would really like to know that our money is being spent wisely." Jason finished with a sarcastic tone.

"It's going good. This is going to be one hell of a front pager. Until I get all the details, there is no sense in printing anything on this. I can guarantee you though, we will blow everyone else out of the water. Oh, Jason don't sweat it too much. After all, it isn't your money that's being spent." Tony enjoyed the mental picture he was having of Jason steaming on the other end.

"Look, I don't give a shit if anything goes to print, but I want to see something in here by the end of tomorrow. At least a draft, to get us caught up on what you've found and where the story is heading. If there's nothing on my desk by the end of tomorrow, you are off the assignment. Is that clear?"

"It was nice talking to you too." Tony said. He could hear Jason screaming on the other end as he hung up. He wasn't going to take no threats from that shit. He turned and saw Paul looking at him and shaking his head.

"Let me guess. Your best buddy, Mr. Jason Burke."

"Yeah, you guessed right. Could you go check on Sherri, I'm going to give Cats a call."

"Not a problem." As Paul headed out of the room, Tony sat down and stared out the window at the snow-capped mountains, not looking forward to making this call. He knew he had to tell Cats that he had met someone that made him feel alive again, but he also knew the pain it was going to cause her. How do you tell someone that cares for you, something like that, without making them feel as if they weren't able to touch you that way? When in fact it was quite the opposite, but in a different way. He decided that this would have to be done in person and decided to wait until he got back to the city. He picked the receiver up and dialed the number. After a few rings she picked the phone up. It wasn't the tone in her voice that made him hesitate, it was the click, as if another phone had been picked up or a tape recorder had just been turned on.

"Hello? Hello is anybody there?" Cats called into the phone.

"Hi, it's me. So how are things?" Tony concentrated to see if there were any unusual noises from the other end.

"I'm fine, how about you guys? Jason is all pissed off because you haven't checked in."

"Yeah, I know. Just got a phone call from him. Not much I can do right now anyways, had my room broken into and they stole my laptop. The police are on their way over to check things out."

"My God, are you all right?"

"Oh yeah, I'm fine. Paul walked in on whoever it was and took a blow to the back of the head, but with that hard head he'll be fine."

"Oh no! Did he get a look at either one of them?"

The question made Tony hesitate. That was odd that she asked "either one of them", as if she knew there were more than one. He shrugged it off, after all how could she possibly know?

"No, it was dark and he got hit from behind. He just left to go and check on our guest."

"She's staying in Paul's room? I thought she was in yours?"

"I had to go out for awhile, so we felt it was better that she stayed near someone. Did you manage to find much out about her and her involvement with Nature's Select?"

"Yeah, I emailed it to you but I guess that isn't going to do you any good right now. Nothing exciting. She grew up in the prairies on a farm. Her family sold the farm and moved into the big city in her late high school years. She's been with Nature's Select for eight years now. She is apparently one of the protest organizers and is on hand to deal with media. I did find out that she was at the blockade the night the loggers attacked them."

"Good work Cats. Listen, when I get back we have to get together. There's something I need to talk to you about." He could feel the lump forming in his throat.

"Sure, not a problem, always a pleasure to get together with you. Tony, you guys be careful. There are some real assholes out there." He heard the sharp gasp.

"Are you ok?"

"Yeah. I, uh, just pricked my finger."

"Ok. Well, I better get going the police are going to be here soon."

"Take care of yourself. I'll call you next time." If he wasn't mistaken, she had put emphasis on the last part.

"That sounds fine with me." As she hung up the receiver Tony knew he heard the second click. Their conversation had been listened in on, but by who? He hung the phone up and pulled another small bottle form the fridge. He slowly picked the receiver up again, but made sure that the button in the cradle remained pressed down. He then set the bottle on the button and dismantled the voice end of the receiver looking for a bugging device. There was nothing there, so he put it back together and did a search of the room but found nothing. Paul and Sherri walked in as he was bent over checking behind the television.

"What are you doing?" Paul asked, as they watched him slide the television back into place.

Tony waved at them to follow him out to the balcony. "I think this phone line may be tapped. From now on, we do all phone calls from your room."

"Ok, this is starting to get a bit freaky. Why would anyone want to tap our phone line? What would we know or have that would make someone bug us?" Paul asked.

Immediately, they both looked at Sherri. It suddenly occurred to Tony that maybe that's what the person or persons that broke into his room were looking for. But how did they know she was there. The only people he had told were Cats and Valerie. He did not like the implications.

"So, how are you feeling." He asked Sherri, even though he could see she was doing much better, but still looked shaken.

"Not bad. The rest did me good. Do you really think someone already knows where I am?"

"I'm not sure, to be honest with you. Listen the police are on their way over, so I think it's best that you stay over at Paul's room for now." She shook her head in agreement and Paul escorted her back to his room. Tony sat down at the table and proceeded to write everything down that had happened since he got to Newport. He was hoping that by doing that, he would be able to figure out how he could have led them to her.

After she hung up the phone the man listening on the extension smiled at her.

"Nice job Cats."

"You go to hell and my name's Cathy! Only my friends call me Cats and you're no damn friend of mine."

"Oh, I can see how you treat your friends. I'm not sure I would want to be a friend of yours." He said mockingly.

"Fuck you!" she yelled at him, as she stormed out of the room. She hated these people and what they were making her do. Her insides were in pain for the betrayal that she was putting on Tony, but these men were from the government, and if she didn't do as they said, they were going to go after her parents. Her parents had owned a small business and like everyone, had done what they could to avoid paying the high taxes forced on them. These animals had dug back into their records and had found most of it and what they didn't find, she was sure they made up. Her parents were now retired and weren't aware of what was happening. When she got the visit from the first government agent, she had it explained to her that if she didn't co-operate, they would go after her parents for tax evasion. He told her that they would go at them so hard that they would probably receive a jail term. She couldn't allow that to happen, no matter what the cost. She just had to get a message to Tony to warn him, but she was under constant surveillance.

As Paul was unlocking his door, a man walked past carrying a bucket of ice. He seemed to be paying particular attention to Sherri. Passing by he smiled and greeted them. They both acknowledged him and went inside, locking the door immediately.

Tony kept looking over his notes, and kept wondering if the intruder in his room was a burglar or had he been looking for Sherri. At the same time he was becoming more and more confused. How did anyone know that she was there with him? He just couldn't imagine Cats telling anyone and Valerie didn't know until tonight. But he did hear that clicking sound on the phone. Someone was definitely paying them some attention, but who?

A knock at the door gave him a start. After placing the papers in the drawer of the nightstand, he walked over to the door.

"Who is it?"

"Detective Daikon." He recognized the voice and opened the door. As Daikon and a uniformed officer entered the room, Tony noticed one of the men, he had seen downstairs earlier, walk past and take a quick glimpse inside his room. Tony watched him as he turned the corner down the hall never looking back.

"So, have you determined how much has been taken?" Daikon asked, looking around the room, as the uniformed officer was removing equipment to begin dusting for fingerprints.

"As far as I can tell, it was my laptop, briefcase and some money that was in my briefcase." This suddenly seemed so redundant to him, as the thought of this not being just another burglary kept haunting his mind.

"Well, if you could put together a list and description of the missing goods, we will check around at the pawn shops to see if any of it has turned up. To be quite honest though, very seldom do we ever recover items like this. Most of the time they fence them for quick cash to buy drugs."

Tony thought of telling Daikon about Sherri, but he knew that until he figured out who was keeping tabs on him, he would have to suspect everyone. The officer was diligently moving about the room dusting and taking pictures. Soon there was another knock on the door, and when Tony opened it, the manager of the motel was standing there. She was a very well dressed lady and greeted him with a smile.

"Mr. Parkins?"

"Yes." Replied Tony, impressed by her calmness, considering there were police in her establishment investigating a burglary in one of her rooms.

"Hello, my name is Nancy McField. I am the manager, and I cannot tell you how sorry I am to hear about your room being broken into. This is the first time in our history of operation, that anything like this has happened." She was trying desperately to look past Tony to see what was happening in the room, when she spotted Daikon.

"Darrin, how are you?"

"Hi Nance. I'm doing good, how about you?" Daikon walked over to the door to greet her.

"Obviously, could be better. Do you mind if I come in to check the room out? Motel policy, I have to make sure the room wasn't damaged too badly. Plus, I have to do an inventory of the motel's property in case they took any of it."

"No, not at all. Just be careful not to touch anything." By this time Tony had walked back into the room, leaving the two of them standing at the door visiting. The two of them continued their chat as

Nancy did her inspection of the room. It was soon over and she left, after telling Tony that his stay would be complimentary. He thanked her and walked her to the door.

The uniformed officer was putting his equipment away, when Daikon walked over and quietly whispered something in his ear. The officer acknowledged with a nod, picked up his bag and left the room closing the door behind him. As soon as the door was closed, Daikon turned to Tony and asked him to sit down.

"So, do you have any idea who might have broken in here?" he asked, as he continued to scan the room as if looking for something he might have missed.

The question took Tony by surprise. "No, I haven't got a clue. How in the hell would I know who broke in here?" he replied defensively.

"Had to ask. You see I've got this feeling that this was not your everyday break in."

Tony's senses went on immediate alert. "And what would make you come to that conclusion?"

"Well, for starters, the way the room was broken into. Who ever did this was very much a professional. As I entered the room, I didn't notice a single sign of forced entry. Not a scratch. Now we're talking a keyless lock system here. This type of break in artist doesn't bother with people staying in motels. They target the big money customers, the ones that stay at the big hotels with the valet parking. These boys would even be museum heist type clients. The other thing that is bothering me, is that the room looks too organized for your every-day burglar."

"What do you mean too organized? They turned everything upside down."

"Exactly, it's too neat. The normal burglar is in a rush. His heart is racing he just wants to get in and get out. He doesn't have time to take every drawer out and tip it upside down. He will reach in and just throw everything out trying to find your stash of valuables.

Whoever did this, was not worried about time or even getting caught."

They both sat in silence for awhile, gazing around the room. Tony fought the urge to tell Daikon about Sherri and about the phone call with someone listening in. Finally Daikon turned to Tony.

"You asked me about other bodies at the scene. There were, all associated with Nature's Select, except for one. He was a local logger from here, George Ruber."

"Why hasn't any of this been made public knowledge?" Tony asked, his insides doing flips at this news.

"We were pulled off the investigation."

"By who?"

"Before we could even get started investigating the crime scene, these guys from the secret service show up and tell us that it has become a matter of national security and that they would be taking over. When we got back to the station there was a guy there waiting for us. We were taken into a room and told that if we mention anything of what we saw out there, we would find ourselves up on federal charges. He also said that mentioning any of this, could jeopardize the lives of many people including our own. He said he was unable to go into any further detail, but that under no circumstances were we to talk to anyone about this. If we did, the consequences would be dire for us. All of us have had to live with this, and from what I can figure nothing is being done about it. This national security thing is bullshit and so is the hunt for the woman that was spotted out there. There is no way one woman could have caused all that carnage. It doesn't take a rocket scientist to figure that out. They just need someone for the public to focus on, so it looks like they are doing something."

"What about the loggers that came across the scene. Would any of them talk to me?"

"I'm not sure. Probably not, I would imagine they were warned even worse than we were. They have families they have to worry about. Something stinks really bad about this whole thing and I would love to find out what it is. I did not become a cop to turn my back on something like this."

They discussed in detail what Daikon had seen at the crime scene. How the bodies had been found and what types of murder weapons had been used. Both agreed to set up a rendezvous time to meet again. At the end of the street from the motel was a fast food restaurant with picnic tables out by the road. If a meeting were to take place, a stone would be placed at the base of one of the legs.

Daikon left and Tony headed for the shower. When he got out and dressed, he headed over to Paul's room. They decided to order some food in and to start getting some answers from Sherri.

CHAPTER 10

T hey had finished their meals and were sitting around Paul's room talking. Tony decided to slowly work his way up to the events of the murders, rather than jumping in with both barrels firing. After all, it wasn't everyday a woman saw the type of human butchering that this lady had seen. How she handled it, emotionally, was something he could not even comprehend. He was afraid that she might not be able to cope with it, if he came on too strong. She had agreed to have the tape recorder going during their discussions.

"So, tell me about Nature's Select. What is their main mandate and how do they operate?

"Well, they were set up to help protect the environment from over development. More and more animals are losing their habitat and species are on the brink of becoming extinct. Someone must be responsible for protecting them, otherwise the greedy corporations would just walk in and damn the cost or consequences. They don't seem to understand that once these animals become extinct, there is no bringing them back. They're gone forever." It was easy to see the passion that she felt for this. Her eyes seemed on fire with it.

"So, exactly how does Nature's Select go about protecting these animals and stopping corporations from moving in?"

"We try to educate the public as to what is going on, lobby our government officials and try to hit these corporations where it hurts the most. In the wallet. If we can get people to boycott their products, they have to start listening. If that doesn't work, we organize public protests, so that the media gets involved and carries our message to more people."

"So, even if people depend on these resources to pay their bills, feed their families and send their children through school, you still believe they are doing a bad thing?" He could see her face starting to turn red and he knew he was getting to her. If he could keep her going on this path, he was sure he would learn more about Nature's Select than he had ever hoped to.

"It's not that we have a problem with people making a living and supporting their families, but when what they are doing is hurting our environment, then someone has to take a stand." She suddenly went silent, as the memory of the night at Frank's place raced through her mind and the things he had said on the subject.

Tony could tell that this was a well-rehearsed reply that she had probably used on many a reporter. This is not what he wanted. He wanted her honest opinions and after all, he figured he deserved it. He leaned over and turned the tape recorder off. Paul gave him a questioning look and raised his hands slightly. Tony sat back in his chair and stared at Sherri for a few minutes, which made her very uncomfortable.

"What?" she asked looking right back at him. "I'm answering your questions. What else do you want?"

"I want the truth. I want your own personal opinion on things, not rehearsed propaganda that you're so used to feeding the media, that I'm not even sure if you hear what you're saying. There is not much I can do to help you, if you're not going to be totally up front with me. The time of defending the cause is over. You are now in a fight for your own survival right now, and your best bet is the two of us, in this room, with you right now." Tony looked straight in her eyes and could see the tears starting to form. "Are you ok to begin again? This time what do you say we just get to the point and get this over with?"

She shook her head yes and Paul handed her a box of tissue. They spent the rest of the day going over the events that lead up to the meeting in the parking lot. Several times they had to take breaks for Sherri to recompose herself. Paul objected a few times, saying that they should start again tomorrow and give her a rest, but Tony pushed on persisting that time was of the essence. Sherri also said that she just wanted to get it over with. She relived the night at the blockade, the night she was abducted, the van ride to the logging area and then the killings. Here she stopped quite often, as the gruesome visions of the blood and the horrific screams pierced her now controlled state. As she recounted the events, she would try to concentrate on the evening she had spent with Frank and how he had made her feel so good inside. She could not hold on to it though, as the memory would be shattered by the sight of him lying on the ground with his chest ripped open.

Tony returned to certain parts, asking questions to make sure that nothing was being missed. Sherri then told them how she managed to get to town by taking the van. She told them about the conversation she had heard between the two police officers at the service station and how she was convinced that she was being framed, but didn't know why. Tony believed that himself. They finally took a break for dinner and Tony gave Valerie a call. He desperately wanted to talk to one of the loggers that had been out there that day.

"Hey you. Miss me?" he said, upon hearing her voice.

"Haven't been able to think about anything else." She purred. His heart was pounding with desire at her voice.

"Would it be possible to get a list of the names of the men that came across the killings?" He felt bad asking her, as he knew the sadness it brought her.

"I can get that for you, but I don't know what good it will do you. Like I said before these guys don't talk to anyone."

"Well, I would like to at least try."

"Ok. Am I going to see you again tonight?"

"There is nothing that could keep me away."

Valerie let out a giggle and said she would have the information for him when he got there. They set a time and Tony hung up the phone. He then asked Sherri if she could draw them a map on how to get to where the killings took place. He wanted to go out there and have a look around. As he was getting a pen and paper for her, he decided that he would see if Detective Daikon would take them out there. It would be an excellent time to discuss what each had learned and possibly tell him about Sherri.

He asked Paul if he wanted to come with him downtown. He wanted to go see Deric again at the Ocean Port. There were a couple of other questions he wanted to ask him. Paul declined saying he would stick around to keep Sherri company, and that he thought he would probably head out that evening. Tony liked the idea of having one of them around, especially after the day they had just put her through. He opened the door to leave and noticed one of the men from the previous night walking towards the elevators at the end of the hall. It seemed to him that every time he opened a door, one of them was there. He was beginning to question whether it was just coincidence. He made a mental note to give Daikon a call, to see if maybe he had a couple of men keeping an eye on them.

As the Firebird jumped to life, Tony turned the tunes up and pulled out onto the street. He loved being in this car. It was his world that no one else could penetrate, unless he wished it. He was running everything through his mind, as he maneuvered through traffic. As he turned off the main road and headed into the downtown district, he caught the glimpse of a dark blue sedan turning with him. He wasn't sure if he was just being paranoid, but hadn't that same car pulled out of the parking lot behind him. It might just be coincidence that they were both headed for downtown. He decided to find out for sure. Driving around town, he pretended to look at storefronts and even stopped at a convenience store. The sedan seemed to disappear but as soon as he returned to traffic the sedan showed up a couple of car lengths behind him. Tony drove out of the downtown area and headed for the highway. He figured his best bet to lose whoever was behind him, would be out on the winding highway. As soon as the Firebird pulled out into highway traffic, Tony pressed the accelerator down hard. He felt the ever so slight hesitation as the tires spun, then was pressed back in his seat as they grabbed the asphalt. The smile on his face came instantly. He loved the way the car hugged the road and responded to his every request. Soon, he was darting in and out of traffic, keeping an eye on his rear view mirror. The sedan had also picked the pace up, but wasn't as maneuverable through traffic as the Firebird. Soon Tony could see that it was falling farther behind and the driver was starting to take more chances. He was now on open highway and there was no sign of the sedan behind him. As he came up on a side road, he turned the steering wheel and hit the brakes, sending the car into a sideways skid, immediately he shifted down then hit the gas shooting the car straight onto the side road. When he was a short distance down the road he stopped and put the car in reverse, watching for the sedan. Within seconds it raced by and he pressed down on the gas pedal, backing out of the road and headed back to town.

Racing back to town he decided to scrap the idea of going to the Ocean Port. He was now certain that someone was spying on him and the only thing he had that anyone would want, was Sherri. He pulled into a service station and called Valerie. It was imperative that he get Sherri somewhere safe.

"Well, hi there. You missing me that much?" she teased.

"I'm always missing you. Valerie, I have a favor to ask of you."

"Sure if I can. What is it?"

Feeling safe about being on a pay phone, he went into detail about how his room had gotten broken in to and then the car following him. He explained how he needed to get Sherri somewhere safe and asked her if she would mind hiding Sherri at her place.

"Christ, this is getting pretty bizarre. Who would be doing this? Yeah, of course she can stay at my place. Does this mean we're not going to see each other tonight?"

"Oh, we'll be seeing each other tonight. Just not for the reason that we were both thinking of." He laughed.

"And what reason were you thinking of?"

This is crazy, he thought. I've just been followed by God knows who, Sherri's life could be in danger and all I can think of is laying in bed next to this beautiful woman.

"I'll tell you tonight. I would still like to get those names, if you don't mind." He had to get his mind on something else.

"Not a problem. I will bring it home with me. So when do you think you'll be by?"

"It's going to have to be after dark, so that we can sneak Sherri out of there. I was hoping you could help us with that to."

"You don't want much, do you? What is it you need me to do?"

He explained the plan he had come up with on his drive back into town. She was to park her car in the car park at the motel, as close to the lobby doors as she could get, and leave the keys in the ashtray. Then she would go into the lobby and ring Paul's room to let them know that she was there. She would then take the elevator up to their floor and walk past the room. If no one was in the hallway, as she passed the door she would raise her hand as if she was brushing her cheek. He would be watching for her through the security glass in the door. At that time he would come out and join her in the hallway. They would leave using the elevator, as it was close to the room where the two men were staying. He was hoping that if they were watching him, they would try to follow them. After a few minutes Paul and Sherri would leave using the staircase, get into Valerie's car and meet them at her place. They would follow Paul and Sherri for a bit just to make sure they weren't being followed. If they were, Tony was prepared to run interference. Once he was sure that they weren't being followed, he would drive around for a bit longer making sure that they themselves weren't being followed.

Even as he explained it to Valerie he wasn't sure if it would work, but he had to try something. Just sitting in the motel room made him feel too much like a sitting duck. After he was done giving her the instructions, he asked her to repeat them to him. Once he was satisfied that she understood what had to be done, he headed for the restaurant to leave Daikon the signal that he wanted to meet. As he stepped out of the phone booth, he saw the sedan passing by on the road. Recognizing the driver as one of the men from the motel, he quickly slipped around the corner of the phone booth so as not to be seen. It didn't appear as if the driver even looked his way, but to be on the safe side, Tony remained there another half an hour before leaving. He drove to the restaurant, ordered a burger and went out to the picnic table and sat down. To his surprise there was already a stone placed the way they had agreed to signal a meeting. If a meeting were to take place, the stone would be placed inside the leg under the table; otherwise it would be placed outside the table between the legs. As he sat there eating his burger, he continually glanced around to see if anyone was watching him. He was beginning to feel as if he was constantly being watched. This, he was pretty positive, was just paranoia, but then you can never be too careful, he thought. Especially when you didn't know who was watching you. Tony acted as if he had accidentally dropped a napkin and bent over to pick it up. As he did so he moved the stone out between the legs.

Parking the Firebird, Tony noticed the sedan parked at the far end of the lot. When he got up to the room he went over his plan with Paul and Sherri. He noticed that Sherri began to get nervous and the scared look returned to her eyes.

"Don't you worry, we're going to help you." Tony said sitting down beside her and laying a reassuring hand on her shoulder. He then looked up at Paul. "Keep an eye out for anyone in the hall.

When we leave I'm hoping they are going to follow us thinking I'm with Sherri. Just watch to se if they take the bait and follow us out."

"And if they don't?" Paul asked.

"Well, we will wait outside for a few minutes. If I don't see them coming out, I'll have to play it by ear."

"That's it!" Sherri suddenly blurted out. "You'll play it by ear? In case you haven't noticed, people are dead for Christ's sake, I am being hunted by someone and your plan is to play it by ear!" She stood up and started pacing around the room. Paul looked over at Tony and shrugged his shoulders.

"Well, unless you have a better plan, yes we will have to play it by ear, if my plan doesn't work. Now, if you do have a better idea by chance, please feel free to share it with us, otherwise try to calm down and work with us on this." He knew the fear she must be fighting to keep under control. The trauma of what she had been through would probably haunt her for the rest of her life, and there weren't too many men that would have been able to handle it as well as she had, up to this point. He needed her to stay calm though, because they would have to all be alert and avoid panic if something should go wrong.

Sherri stopped pacing and looked at Paul then at Tony. "I'm sorry, it's just that not everyday I have someone frame me and then try to kill me. I really, truly do appreciate all you've done. It had gotten to the point where I thought I was all alone and didn't know where or who to turn to."

"It's ok. I really do understand, but we all have to stay calm and keep our heads." Tony calmly explained to her.

The rest of the day was spent in Paul's room, waiting for Valerie's phone call. They went over the plan a few more times making sure there were no misunderstanding, on what everyone had to do. Every now and then, Tony would walk over to his room to see if either of the men were in the hall. Only on one occasion, did he see one of the men walking down the hall towards him. When he came back from his last trip, it hit him, that if they were listening in on his phone line, maybe he could send them on a wild goose chase, and that would give him more space to put his plan into action. The three of them worked out a story and Tony went back to his room to make the call.

He dialed Cat's number and waited for her to answer. When she answered, he noticed how fatigued her voice sounded. She was not her usual upbeat self. He also heard the second click again. Ok, you bastards he thought, it's time to play.

"Hey Cats it's me. How are you doing?"

"Not bad. How about you?"

"Hanging in. Needless to say things are a bit crazy up here right now. Listen, I just wanted to tell you that we're going to make a move with that lady they're looking for."

"Tony you don't have to tell…" she didn't finish as Tony cut her off.

"It's ok, I know. I just wanted to tell someone, so that if anything should happen, someone else will know where she is, and they can help to get the story out."

"Don't talk like that. Nothing is going to happen."

"Cats, it's ok really. Anyway, we're going to move tonight. There's a hotel downtown called the Brew Inn. I'm taking her there tonight and Paul's going to stick around here. As soon as we have her safe, I'll give Paul a ring and he can phone you."

"Tony, I can't anymore, they're listen…" the line went dead. Tony sat there for a while realizing that she knew they were listening and hadn't warned him. H e knew Cats, and was now worried that they had gotten to her. What had they threatened her with, to keep her quiet? She tried to finally warn him and they shut her down. A fear ripped through him that they might have killed her. He suddenly became ill and had to rush to the bathroom and vomit. He wanted desperately to call her back but felt that as long as he kept communicating with her, they wouldn't hurt her. She was being useful to them at this point. She was their contact to him and he swore to make them pay for that.

Cats was lying back on the sofa where the man with the headset had thrown her.

"You stupid bitch, do that again and not only are your parents going away for a long time, but they may never see their pretty daughter again. Do you understand, you stupid bitch? That was so stupid!" He was screaming at her and slapping her with every other word. Her tears flowed uncontrollably as she tried to cover up from the blows. This was a nightmare. One that she desperately wanted to wake up from.

Tony opened the door slightly and listened. Within a few minutes he heard a door open and close. Peering cautiously down the hall he watched as one of the men entered the elevator. Quickly, he ran across the hall and into Paul's room.

"Well, do you think they bought it?" Paul asked.

"I'm pretty sure. I didn't have time to go through our whole plan. Cats tried to warn me that they were listening and the line went dead. I think they're controlling her somehow."

"Damn, I hope she's ok." Paul said, his voice strained with worry.

"Me to." was all Tony could say. They set about finding clothes that would come close to fitting Sherri. What didn't fit, they folded and tucked until she didn't look at all like her former self. Tony went next door and grabbed his suitcases. As he entered the hallway, he heard a door open, looking down the hallway, his eyes met those of the other man. They both stood looking at each other for an awkward moment. Tony had a sudden urge to run down the hall and confront him, but instead he continued over to Paul's room. As Paul opened the door, Tony glanced over and watched as the second man entered the elevator. Tony hoped he was off to join his partner waiting somewhere downstairs.

Valerie pulled up and parked as close as she could to the lobby doors. After placing the keys in the ashtray, she headed for the lobby to make a phone call up to Paul's room. As she crossed the parking lot, she didn't notice the blue sedan with the two occupants, sitting in the dark corner of the lot under a burnt out light. The two men took no notice of her entering the lobby, as their focus was on watching for Tony and the big pay bonus that would be accompanying him. The driver was especially anxious, as it was his job to kill the man, that had made him look bad by loosing him. The only way to save face now, would be to dispose of the jerk.

Valerie walked into the lobby and headed over to the bank of in-house phones. She picked up the receiver and dialed Paul's room.

CHAPTER 11

❀

The sound of the ringing phone made the three of them jump. Tony went over and picked up the receiver.

"Ok, I'm here." Valerie whispered into the phone.

"Good. Are there any men standing around the lobby?"

"No, just me and the lady behind the check-in counter."

"Ok, good. I'm pretty sure that both men left, but we'll stick to our original plan. As you go past our room, just give me the all clear signal and I'll come out and join you."

"This is so exciting. I feel like a spy or something." Tony could detect the excitement in her voice, and prayed that he wasn't getting her involved in something that could eventually harm her. His thoughts went to Cats, and the nausea returned to his stomach. He had to make this happen, as he was anxious to make the meeting with Daikon.

"Well, just be careful. We still don't know who these guys are, or what their intentions are." Tony cautioned her. As he hung up the phone, deep down he knew exactly what their intentions were.

"All right guys, we're good to go. Are you sure you have everything down, as to what you have to do and where you're going?"

"Not to worry." Paul answered. "We will be ok. You just make sure you guys make it safe."

Hearing the elevator doors open, Tony peered out the security hole in the door and waited for Valerie to pass by. As she walked past the door, she brought her hand up to cheek. Tony took a deep breath, opened the door and whispered to himself, "This is it."

He didn't even stop to look back, but stepped out and fell in beside Valerie. They made their way to the elevator without speaking a word to each other. Once inside the elevator, he let out a huge sigh that was cut short by the kiss Valerie placed on his lips. His heart took a jump and calm came over him. As the elevator doors opened, Tony could feel his heart starting to race again. Would the men be standing outside waiting for them? Would this plan work? Was he about to get his friends killed with this stupid idea? Before panic gripped him totally, Valerie gave his hand a squeeze, as if she could sense the conflict rising in him. They exited the elevator and headed for the lobby doors.

"Mr. Parkins?" a cheery voice called out to him. He looked over and saw the manager, Nancy McField. "You have a message. It just came in." She had a folded piece of paper in her extended hand. He smiled, walked over and took it, thanking her and walked out the door.

The evening air felt comforting as they exited the lobby. There was a slight breeze blowing, feeling warm as it brushed against their faces. Tony stayed in front of Valerie, hoping that the men sitting in the sedan would not be able to notice, that it was not Sherri. As they approached the Firebird, Tony wanted to look over to see if the men were watching them. He certainly didn't have to. He knew that they were, he could feel their eyes boring hard at them. When they got to the car, he stood with his back facing them and opened the passenger door for Valerie. Walking around the back of the car to the driver's side, he climbed in taking a quick glance over to the sedan.

"Did you see them?" Valerie asked.

"No, but they're there and believe me they are watching us." He answered, keeping his eyes focused on the rearview mirror. As the

Firebird started up, Tony took a deep breath and said, "Here goes." Valerie slid her hand over and gave his leg a rub and smiled at him. When his eyes met her hers, he told himself that he would make this work, for everyone. His mind thought of Cats and wondered what was happening to her. He shook his head trying to clear it of any thoughts other than what was happening right then. He also did it to hold the feeling of guilt back. Tony slid the gearshift into reverse and backed out of the parking lot.

"Lets do it." Valerie said in a confident tone.

Pulling out onto the street, Tony looked in the mirror and saw the headlights of the sedan come on. He was glad to see that his plan seemed to be working. It made him feel better about Paul and Sherri.

Starting the sedan up, seemed to energize the two men with anticipation, like two bloodhounds chasing their prey.

"I still think one of us should have stayed behind. What if that wasn't her? I didn't get a good look, and besides we should take care of that other guy." The driver said as he concentrated on the Firebird in front of him.

"We can always get him later." Replied the passenger. "Right now, let's just make sure we don't mess this up again. I'll take care of the bitch and you can have your payback with that little prick driving."

This made the driver forget any doubt, as he was anxious to get his hands on Tony. They now pulled out onto the highway, staying a couple cars back.

Paul watched as the sedan followed Tony and Valerie out of the parking lot. Immediately, Sherri and him left the room and headed downstairs to Valerie's car. As they climbed into the car, he noticed how tense Sherri had become. Her head darted around, constantly checking for anything that might appear as a threat. He reached over and gave her a reassuring squeeze on her shoulder.

"It's going to be all right." He smiled.

"I pray it is. I feel that because of me you people may have put yourselves in danger."

"Well, we are all in this together, so let's not dwell on what could be, but on what we have to do to make this work." He found the keys and they left the motel's parking lot.

Tony darted in and out of traffic, keeping an eye on the sedan, making sure that it was behind them. He wanted to get them as far away from Valerie's place as possible and with Valerie knowing the area, he hoped that would be an advantage when it came time to lose them.

They drove around the downtown area, always trying to stay where there were a lot of people. Tony figured these guys wouldn't try anything, as long as there were witnesses around. Eventually, they were driving through a residential area that wound its way up the side of a steep hill. Knowing the maneuverability of the Firebird, he thought this would be a good place to lose the sedan He pressed down on the gas pedal and started to pull away. With Valerie giving him directions, he was happy to see that the sedan was falling further behind. He was feeling good about the way things were going and knew that once they lost them and got to Valerie's place, they would be safe.

"Ok, just up ahead turn right. There is a small side road that nobody uses, except the locals that know it's there. It will take us back down to the highway."

"Sounds good to me."

"All right, turn here." She said, as they came upon the small inter-section.

Tony turned the wheel sharp and they shot around the corner and down the narrow road. Suddenly, like a wall jumping out of nowhere, the headlights shone on a concrete barricade placed across the road, with construction warning signs on it. Wheels screamed as Tony slammed on the brakes, something he did not want to do, as the glare from the brake lights shone into the night, like a beacon. With the nose of the Firebird inches from the barricade, they both stared in disbelief. The construction sign informed the public of their tax dollars working for them, doing an upgrade on the road. Tony was about to back out when the glare from headlights shone into the Firebird, lighting them up like a spotlight.

"Shit, they must have seen the brake lights." Tony yelled.

"What are we going to do?" Valerie's voice sounded shaky.

The two men sat in the sedan looking at the cornered prey. "This is going to be like shooting sitting ducks," the passenger exclaimed. Tony saw the headlights make a slight rocking motion and knew the men were getting out of the car.

"We have to run!" he exclaimed, as he reached for the door handle. He saw that Valerie wasn't moving. "Now!" he yelled, snapping her out of her trance she seemed to be in. They both jumped from the car and ran around behind the barricade. Tony heard the first bullet hit the barricade, sending concrete dust flying into the beam of light from the cars. He grabbed Valerie's hand and half ran and half stumbled down the road. Running was difficult as the road had been dug up and the dirt was loose with rocks protruding everywhere. He couldn't hear the sound of the guns being fired and figured they must have silencers. What he did hear and notice was the bullets snapping into the trees and ground around them. Suddenly Valerie gave his arm a hard jerk sideways and he followed her.

"There's a trail somewhere here, that hikers use." She said, between breaths. They ran down the side of the road, being partially covered by the overhanging branches. In the dark, Tony didn't know how they were going to be able to find it. A bullet shattered a twig above his head and the debris stung his face. He wasn't sure if it was his imagination, or if the men were catching up to them, but he thought he could hear footsteps getting closer. The fear and panic that rose inside him became an inward battle of control. Another bullet struck the ground, between their feet, just as they dashed into what seemed like solid forest.

"Here!" was all Valerie said, as she steered them onto the trail. It was narrow, making them run in a single line. Tony focused on Valerie's back as they frantically made their way down the trail. In the background, they could hear the confused voices of the men, trying to find where they had disappeared. Tony knew that it was just a matter of time before they found the trail, he just hoped that it would give them time to get away. Soon he couldn't hear anything, except their heavy breathing and the sound of their footsteps crashing over the twigs and leaves that laid on the trail's floor. Soon they came to a cross section in the trail and Valerie came to a stop. There were signs at the intersection, indicating where each individual trail led and gave the name of each trail. Valerie indicated to trail that headed to the left and started off down it. They were moving at a brisk walk now, feeling safer with more distance being added between them and their pursuers. Tony noticed that the further they headed down the trail, he could hear the sounds of the town getting louder. They hadn't talked since being on the trail, in fear of letting their pursuers know where they were. The sound of their footsteps on the ground, seemed like it was resonating off the wall of trees that loomed around them. Breaking out of the narrow dark trail and onto a paved stretch of road, Tony threw his arms up and did a small dance. It felt like breaking free from some unseen cacoon.

"Where are we?" He asked, his voice sounding raspy from all the heavy breathing.

"This road leads to town or back up the hill to a new subdivision. Christ! Can you believe that shit? They tried to kill us!" She was sounding hysterical and angry at the same time.

"Valerie, when we get back to town, we'll leave your place. They don't know who you are and I don't want to put you in any more danger. If anything happened to you, I would never forgive myself. Ever."

They stood in the night air staring at each other when she wrapped her arms around his neck and kissed him deeply. They held each other's hand and started walking down the road heading for town.

"You aren't going anywhere. I've waited all my life for you. I have put up with men that told me they loved me, but were never there for me when I needed them. So, if you think for one moment that you are just going to up and take off, forget it. I'm in this with you and together we will get through it."

This time it was Tony who stopped them and grabbed her. Never before had he ever felt like this, and she was right, they would get through this together.

"Ok, then let's get going. We've got a lot to do yet." They headed down the road with a quicker pace, feeling as if they just had a shot of energy injected into them.

The two men got to the intersection in the trail and stood there, knowing that once again they had lost their prey. "Damn it! This can't be happening again." The driver shouted. He was taller of the two and had a distinctive scar above his right eyebrow, where a fishing hook had snagged him. His six year old nephew hadn't paid attention to where he was casting and hooked him instead of the fish.

"Well, there's no sense in standing out here. Let's get back to the car and get the hell out of here, before someone comes along." The other man said, slapping his companion on the arm and heading back up the trail. He was shorter and more muscular. His thick neck seemed to disappear as it met his broad shoulders and chest. His face had pock marks from a bad case of acne as a young man.

"What are we going to say when we report in? You know how pissed off they were when we didn't find her before anyone else." The taller one asked.

"Going to have to tell them the truth. You know what would happen if they ever found out otherwise. We will get these walking dead." Walking dead was a term they had come up with for any target that was to be terminated. They returned to the sedan, but not until they stopped and took their frustration out on Tony's Firebird, by firing several shots into it. The shorter man grabbed the cell phone, took a deep breath and dialed the number they were given to report to. As the phone rang, he wished that just this one time, no one would answer. At the sound of the receiver being picked up, his heart gave a skip. "Shit" he thought to himself.

"Yes, what have you got for me?" answered the deep familiar voice on the other end.

"We lost them again. They headed into the woods and we lost their trail." He braced himself for the lashing he was about to receive, instead there was only silence. If it wasn't for the sound of breathing coming from the phone, it would have been as if no one was there at all.

"We're heading back to town now. I'm sure we will pick them up again and this time they will not get away. I guarantee it." He quickly continued before the voice had a chance to say anything. After what seemed an eternity, the reply came. Not what he had been expecting at all, but rather calm and almost forgiving, but he knew better. These people expected results and he had witnessed what happened to those that failed to produce results.

"I want you to go town and go to the Ocean Port Hotel. Ask for a man by the name of Deric. He'll be expecting you. I am going to recruit you some local help, as it seems that you two are incapable of handling this yourselves." The last statement stung as it was meant to. He had always taken pride in his ability to carry out any assignment and resented the fact that his professionalism was now being questioned.

"What ever you say." He knew better than to question any order given, as over the years he had seen what happened to agents that did. Most of them just seemed to disappear, or would meet with an unfortunate accident.

"Good. I'll be expecting good news by tomorrow night. No more mistakes, or excuses. Do you understand?" the tone was now unmistakably threatening.

"I understand." The phone went dead.

"Well, what's up? How pissed was he?" his partner asked.

"Let's just say, we're not his favorite anymore. He's getting some local bumpkins to help us with this."

"Shit, they had better not get in my way, or they may end up like our targets are going to."

The short man looked over at the man with the scar and wondered how long it would be before he would disappear. He had a temper and an attitude to go with it. It seemed that it would only be a matter of time, before he would cross the group and they would have him removed.

The night air suddenly seemed to take on a chill, and he gave a shudder. "Come on and get in the car. We have work to do and we better get it done. They aren't going to stand for many more mistakes." They both climbed into the sedan and headed for town to meet their local help.

Paul found Valerie's place without any trouble. They got everything inside and were now sitting around waiting. He was trying hard not to get too concerned, but Tony and Valerie were now about an hour late from when they should have been arriving. Sherri was sitting in the living room, staring out the window. He walked over and closed the curtains.

"Don't want anyone noticing strangers in the house and calling the police." He said answering her questioning look.

"Oh, that's all right. I was just thinking about that day out in the forest and keep asking why."

He went over and sat down beside her. "I can not imagine what witnessing something like that would be like. You are a very strong person, Sherri. Many men would have folded under the strain of it."

"I'm not that strong. Sometimes I think, I just haven't had time to snap yet and it's sitting there inside me waiting to come out. I admit that there have been moments, when I felt incredibly close to doing so."

"Say, are you hungry?" I'm going to see what she has in the fridge. We haven't eaten anything since this morning and besides, it will help pass some time."

Sherri gave him a weary affirmative nod. "Do you think they're all right?" the question came on a shaky voice, as if she were about to cry.

"As you have probably noticed, Tony is a very resilient soul. If anyone can do this, he can. I'm sure they're fine, just probably taking him a bit longer than he had planned to lose those men." He hoped his voice didn't give away any of his fear. Quickly he headed for the kitchen, ending any further discussion about Valerie and Tony. The kitchen was fairly large, with cupboards circling the perimeter in a horseshoe shape. Off to one side stood a small table with two wooden chairs pulled up to it. The appliances were all a brilliant white, that seemed to lighten up the room. At the far end was a glass curio cabinet, that held what appeared to be antique china. Probably handed down from generation to generation, Paul thought. He made his way over to the fridge.

As he started chopping up some vegetables, he heard the sound of running water coming from the bathroom. A sigh escaped him, as he felt a relief for Sherri. Soon, she would submerse herself in a warm bath and be taken away for even a brief moment of time. He admired this small lady and the courage she showed. He just hoped she would be able to hold up until this was over. His mind then wandered off, hoping Tony and Valerie were ok.

A car approached down the road and they slipped in behind bushes, until it had passed. Stepping back out onto the road, Tony grabbed Valerie once again and gave her a kiss.

"What was that for?"

"Just because. You are an incredible lady and I feel so lucky to have you here with me."

"Well mister, when you finally get me out of this mess, I have plans for you, so that you can show me just how lucky you feel." She giggled and started back down the road.

Tony felt his heart fill with desire for her and yet he was also feeling stung, because it was him that had gotten them in this mess, as she had put it. He just hoped that he would be able to get her and everyone else out of it. Soon they came upon an intersection with a service station and convenience store on the corner.

"Stay here." Valerie said. "I'm going across the road to call a cab."

"Are you crazy? Someone might see you." Tony had a grip on her arm not wanting to let her go.

"And so what if they do? Nobody knows about me. Let alone that I'm here with you. I'll call the cab and when he arrives, I'll tell him our car broke down. You start walking that way and I'll have him pick you up."

"You don't think he's going to wonder what I'm doing walking, instead of being here with you?"

Valerie laughed and gave him a heart melting smile. "You know men. We had an argument, because you were suppose to have the car fixed. You decided you were going to walk home. Stubborn." She laughed again and this time, Tony had to chuckle and shake his head. A very incredible lady he thought to himself. He gave her a kiss and told her to be careful. After assuring him that she would be fine, they separated and Tony headed off in the direction that she had indicated. It didn't seem to him that he had gone very far, when the cab pulled up beside him. He sat in the back seat, staring out the window, praying that Paul and Sherri were ok. He couldn't imagine why they wouldn't be, unless there were more than just those two men. He shook that thought off and turned to make up for forgetting to get the car fixed.

CHAPTER 12

❀

Deric hung up the phone and smiled. He could not believe his fortune, the amount of money he had just been offered, would set him up for quite awhile. All he had to do was find that journalist, his photographer and that lady everyone was looking for, then dispose of them. He knew most of the street people in town. He found them to be opportunists and they were always willing to work for cheap. If anyone could find this journalist and his little group, they would. The thought had crossed his mind to ask for more money, because he figured these people must be very important, for what the group was willing to pay to have them removed. He also knew, that he also could be permanently removed. No, take what you're offered he thought and picked up the phone.

Tony and Val got out of the cab and went into the house. Paul and Sherri met them at the top of stairs.

"Where the hell have you been? Where's the Firebird?" Paul demanded, sounding very relieved.

"We ran into a bit of a problem." Tony replied, looking at Valerie and raising an eyebrow. "The Firebird is at the mercy of those two thugs right now and I'm not liking that one bit." He turned to Valerie and asked her if she had anything strong to drink in the house.

"As a matter of fact, I have a bottle of Crown Royal with your name on it." She winked and headed off.

Tony looked at Sherri, "How are you doing?"

"Much better now that I know you guys are all right." She replied smiling.

Valerie brought Tony his drink and they sat around the living room as he told the story of what had happened. Every now and then, Valerie would cut in and correct or add a point that she felt was crucial to the story. Tony seemed to welcome the intrusions, knowing that it was an experience that they had shared and made it through, together. As the story ended, he sat back reaching into his pocket to see if he had remembered to grab the keys from the Firebird. He pulled out a piece of crumpled paper, it was the message he had gotten just before leaving the motel. Carefully he unfolded it and read the message.

Forget the meeting place. Call me as soon as you can. Have some very interesting information. Detetive Daikon.

Tony got up to use the phone. Valerie directed him down stairs to her office. He tried Daikon at home, but got no answer. Then he tried him at the station and got through.

"Where are you at? I've been trying to find you all night." Daikon asked with a twinge of irritation in his voice.

"I've been, kinda busy. I was going to explain it all to you when we met. What's up?"

"I've been doing some background checking on the men that were found dead with the loggers. Two of them worked for a company called, Enviro Magna. This company does freelance environmental studies and then submits reports on how to solve different types of problems."

"Ok, now this isn't all that intriguing. Obviously, they felt the loggers were an environmental problem."

"Exactly, but here is the interesting part. The company is owned by a limited holding company, that also finances the logging industries main lobbying board. So, why would people who wok for a company, that is funded by a company that supports logging, be out there killing loggers? And why was George, a local logger, out there with them?"

Tony knew the answer to the last question, as Sherri had filled him in. However the rest was very interesting. "Very good question. Listen, we have to talk. There is something you need to know. How is your day tomorrow?" He had decided to tell Daikon about Sherri and the men that had tried to kill them.

"It can be very open if it has to be."

"All right, I'll meet you at the restaurant for breakfast around eight."

Daikon agreed and hung the phone up. Tony sat there for a while mulling over in his head, the information he had just received. He needed to get more information on this holding company and decided to get a hold of the one man that would be able to pull enough strings to get that info. He would call TNT in the morning, after his meeting with Daikon. Besides that, he wanted TNT to make sure Cats was safe. If anyone had the connections and influence to do it, Terrence Neil Tibbet could do it.

Valerie appeared at the door. As he looked at her, he realized how scruffy the two of them looked, after charging through the woods. Reaching down, she grabbed his hand and pulled him up out of the chair.

"I think a shower is in order, don't you?" she said, as she started to lead him up the stairs.

"Most definitely, but I will be needing someone to scrub my back."

"Oh, I'm sure we will be able to arrange that."

Tony woke up the next morning, feeling refreshed. After a shower and night of love making, who wouldn't have slept well? He got out of bed and got dressed. He had to make it to the breakfast meeting with Daikon and then phone TNT. It was time to get some help. This whole thing was getting way out of control on him and he didn't want to get anyone killed.

As he headed down the hall to the kitchen, the smell of fresh brewed coffee greeted him. Sitting at the table watching a small television that was placed on it, was Sherri, looking tired and fatigued. She looked up at him and gave him a weak smile.

"Morning. How did you sleep?" he asked, already knowing the answer.

"Have had better." Her voice seemed incredibly frail.

Tony poured himself a coffee and sat down at the table with her. For a long time they both sat and stared at the television. Not really seeing what was showing on it. It was something to numb the mind.

"You know, I killed one of the men there." Sherri suddenly said cold, staring straight ahead at the screen. Tony shot a look over at her, not quite sure if he had heard her right. She turned from the television and her eyes were red from the pain that was devouring her soul. The tears flowed endless and the redness confirmed that they had been flowing most of the night.

Tony got up and went over to her. Placing his arm around her shoulder, he hugged her comfortingly. At the same time she buried her face in his chest and wept, as though she were a lost child. He gently hung on and rocked her back and forth reassuring her that everything was going to be all right and at the same time telling her that it was ok to let it out. Between sobs, Sherri told him of the recurring nightmares of the scene in the forest that day. How she could hear the screams and the saws ripping into the men. She told him of how she had grabbed an axe in a moment of rage and continually smashed it into George's skull. She hadn't been able to remember that until last night. It came back to her in a dream and she had been sick for most of the night. They sat there for some time, Tony holding her and Sherri letting out the pain and anger that was being held inside. He didn't want to leave her, but knew he had to make the meeting with Daikon. Giving her a firm squeeze he said he would be right back. He woke Valerie up and explained to her that he had to go out and would she keep Sherri company. Valerie gave him a passionate kiss, said she would and told him to be careful.

Tony left with Valerie's car, feeling fairly secure in the fact that they wouldn't know it, therefore he should be able to move about without being noticed. When he pulled into the parking lot of the restaurant, he did a quick scan of it to make sure that the blue sedan wasn't parked anywhere. Inside, he saw Daikon sitting at a table beside the window. This made Tony nervous, as he would rather have a table in the center of the room where no one could see him from outside. He parked as close to the door as possible and went inside. As he approached the table, he noticed that Daikon had an irritable look on his face and was looking at him clenching his jaw. Something wasn't right and suddenly he wanted to run out of there. Keeping himself calm, he made his way to the table and sat down. Daikon sat there staring at him and not a word was said until the waitress had left with Tony's order.

"You want to tell me what the hell is going on? Your Firebird got towed into the compound, all shot up. Want to explain that to me, and while you're at it, if there is anything else you feel I might be interested in, please feel free to enlighten me. I was under the goddamn impression that we were both working together to solve this fucking thing. I gave you information that could bury me and you sneak around behind my back." Daikon's face had taken on a reddish hue and his voice had gone up in volume. The anger was impossible not to notice.

"If you'll calm down and give me a minute I would love to explain it to you. The bastards shot my Firebird up? Shit, shit, shit! Is it real bad? Will I be able to fix it?" He could see Daikon was starting to get even angrier with him, for not talking to him about what he knew, but right now he was more concerned about the car.

"Yeah, they shot up your car and if you don't start being straight with me, I'll personally make sure that it ends up in a crushing yard somewhere. Now you tell me who they are and what exactly is going on. I've been busting my ass trying to find answers and sharing them with you, and you are apparently heading off in your own direction and leaving me out. I've got a multiple murder to investigate, without my bosses finding out, and now people are shooting up cars in town and I don't know anything about it."

Tony could see the redness getting brighter in Daikon's face, so he decided he better jump in quick. As they sat there, Tony explained to Daikon how he had come across Sherri in the parking lot of the motel. He told Daikon, what he had found out to that point, from talking to Sherri. He had decided on the way over, that he would keep the fact that Sherri had killed one of them, to himself. He continued telling Daikon about the two men who suddenly appeared at the motel, watching and following him, and of his plan to move Sherri to a safe place. Finally he covered the events of the previous night and how they had been shot at running for their lives.

"Why didn't you tell me this before? Somebody could have gotten killed."

"Ok, now think about this. There is a brutal murder and then you find out that there were more murders at the scene, but they were not reported. Who do you think has the capabilities to cover that up? You guys, the police, that's who." Even before Daikon could retaliate Tony continued. "Suddenly, there are two men tailing me. I didn't know if they were your men, or someone else. Now, after all that, I sure as hell wasn't ready to just throw my trust to just anyone."

"So why are you trusting me now?" Daikon asked appearing much calmer.

"Because, I need help keeping my friends safe and you are my best bet. I hope I'm not wrong."

"Well, at this point I am your best bet. Is the girl safe? I will need to talk to her soon."

"Yes, she's safe. Now what have you got for me?"

"I, like you, have not been able to figure out what or who, is behind holding back on the fact that these other people were killed out there. I decided to find out who they were. I got hold of the files made by the original officers who arrived at the scene and started doing some digging on my own. One of the first things that peeked my interest, was the fact that their files were not kept in the usual place. I ended up finding them in the evidence locker. The only way I found that out, was to get one of my fellow officers, that had made the report, drunk and then coerced it out of him."

Daikon took a quick glance around the room to see if anyone was paying attention to them. He continued. "As I started to check the backgrounds out on these men, the one thing that kept coming up on everyone of them, was this Enviro Magna name. The only one that didn't seem to have any connection, was the woman that was also found dead out there. After taking fingerprints, I would have to say she drove the van to the site. Other than that, she is a complete mystery. I can't find anything on her."

"Maybe she was a girlfriend to one of the men? I thought you said only two of the men worked for this company." Tony cut in.

"That's right, I did. At that time, I hadn't been able to look into the other men's background. Now after saying that, there were only two of them that worked directly for this Enviro Magna, all the others were involved with a subsidiary company of some kind. Everyone of them."

"Ok now, can we check the holding company that owns this Enviro Magna and the loggers lobbying board in detail? Who are the major shareholders, just for a start? There has to be some kind of connection here that we're missing."

"I am already on that." Daikon said.

"Good. Next is it possible for us to go out to the crime scene and have a look around?"

"I can't see a problem with that. Now, when will I be able to talk to this lady?"

"Let me check with her. She is in pretty rough shape emotionally right now. I don't want to push her too hard."

"Ok." Daikon sighed. "But it's going to have to happen soon. I need all the help I can get right now. My ass is definitely on the line, if anyone finds out I'm working on this, I could get suspended."

"I'll see what I can do. So, when can we go out to the scene?"

"I'll call you tomorrow. Where can I reach you?"

Tony hesitated. "I think it would be best if I contact you."

"I thought you said you trusted me." Daikon snapped.

"I do. It's just that I have other people to consider, and I don't want to be making decisions for them. If they don't have a problem with you calling us, then I'll give you the number." Tony hoped this would appease him for now. "What would be a good time to call you?"

"Give me until noon." Daikon said, staring at Tony, not sure if he had just been given the brush off. As the two of them got up to leave, Daikon quietly said, "You are not wrong. You can trust me."

Deric couldn't help but laugh as he saw the two men enter the room. They reminded him so much of Laurel and Hardy. He watched as the men approached the bartender, then they were directed over to him. Soon the taller one, Laurel, he mused, was headed in his direction with Hardy, the short muscular one, following hot on his heels. Deric was sitting at one of the high bar tables and as they approached, he couldn't help himself, but chuckled again. This should be fun, watching the short one climb up on one of these high chairs, he thought.

"Are you Deric?" the taller one asked, when they reached the table.

"That would be me. And you two are?"

"We have a mutual friend who asked us to look you up. He said you would be expecting us and would be able to help us with a problem we're having."

Deric wanted to burst out with laughter. These were the men that were sent to take care of the reporter and his friends. You gotta be shittin me, he thought, but he knew that these men had probably hunted and killed more people, than most hunters had killed game, during hunting season.

Deric grabbed the drink he had sitting on the table and motioned for the men to follow him. They went behind the bar and down a hallway, to Deric's office.

"Want anything to drink?" he asked them.

"No thanks." The shorter one replied. "Have you got anything on where the hell the reporter and that woman are?"

"Not yet, but it shouldn't be long. This town isn't that big and I've got eyes out there looking."

"Just so you know, when you do find them no one is to do anything, just get in touch with us, and we'll take it from there."

"My instructions were to find and eliminate them." Deric said, wanting to get the money, he had been offered, if he killed them.

The taller man stood up from his chair and leaned across the desk, staring Deric in the eyes. "We don't give a shit. You find them, you tell us where they are and we will do the rest. Are you understanding me?" Deric could feel the man's breath on his face, he was leaning so close to him.

"The only thing I am understanding right now, is that you just told me to ignore an order from the group and I'm sure they would want to hear about it." Deric could see the second of hesitation in the man's eyes. Then what seemed quicker than a blink of the eye, the man whipped a gun out and held it to Deric's forehead.

"That would be a very stupid thing to do on your part." The man's voice had a definite growl to it.

"So would killing me, as you would probably never find these people. From what I've gathered, you don't seem capable of being able to keep track of your mark, once you do locate them." Deric's eyes never left the big man's eyes. He could see that he was seriously contemplating killing him, but he also knew that that wouldn't happen. Not now at least, maybe after the reporter was found.

"Ok, that's enough of this shit." The shorter man cut in. We've got a job to do and if we don't get it done none of us will have to worry about what the smart thing to do would have been. As far as I'm concerned, the smart thing to do is to find the reporter and that girl and do our jobs."

Inside, Deric felt relief pour over him as the man withdrew the gun and placed it back in its holster strapped under his jacket.

"Well gentlemen, are you sure you wouldn't like a drink? It might be a bit of a wait." Deric asked, remaining calm and collected, almost to the point of taunting. "So, what do I call you guys? You know my name, but you haven't given me yours."

"And it's going to stay that way." The big man snarled.

"Fine, suit yourself. Guess you won't mind if I just call you Laurel and Hardy then." If this were at any other time, he was sure he would be dead by now. Under these circumstances though, he knew he was protected. At the end of this, he was sure that he would have to kill the one with the scar.

"When this is over asshole, I'll come calling."

The ringing of the phone, broke the tension and all three men drew their attention to it. The two men shot a look at Deric, telling him to pick it up. Deric let it ring one more time, just to irritate them a bit more.

"Deric here."

"I just saw your man talking with that cop, Daikon." It was Kurt, one of the eyes he had employed to help find Tony.

"Where were they?" Deric asked with a sense of urgency in his voice.

"They were at the Foghorn Restaurant, out on the highway."

"Are they still there?"

"I'm not sure."

"Well get your ass back there and find out." Deric ordered.

"All right. I'll call you right back." The phone went dead and Deric smiled at the two men standing in front of him. They were like two kids, waiting to hear some exciting news. He thought about lying to them, but knew that would only get him in trouble.

"Well, we've spotted him. He's been talking to the cops."

"Where is he?" It was the shorter one now who seemed ance.

"The reporter was seen at a restaurant, out on the highway. We will find out in a minute if he's still there."

Suddenly, the three of them seemed to come together, focusing on the same goal. They could sense that the hunt was soon to end.

As Tony got back to Valerie's place, he went downstairs to call TNT. Valerie followed him down and asked how things had gone with his meeting. He went over his meeting with Daikon and told her about them shooting up the Firebird.

"Now that must hurt, I know how much that car meant to you." She said giving him a kiss.

"That's all right, they are going to get theirs. Listen, I have to make one more phone call, then let's try to have a relaxing night. I know I sure could use it and I imagine everyone else could to."

"I love the way you think." She said kissing him again. "Make your phone call, I'll be upstairs." She headed out and he dialed TNT's number.

CHAPTER 13

"Tony, how are you?" TNT asked sounding concerned.

"Hanging in there."

"Where are you? I've been hearing rumors that you have been having some trouble down there."

"Yeah, we've got a situation on our hands all right. That's why I'm calling you. Cats called me and I think she may be in trouble. Can you check on her and make sure she's safe?" Tony asked, almost pleading.

"Sure not a problem. Cats called me and said that you have found the lady everyone is looking for. That's great news. Where are you? I sure would like to meet her and hear her side of the story."

"We're still in Newport. I know this probably isn't going to sound very good to you, but right now, I can't give out our location. I was wondering though, if you have ever heard of a company called Enviro Magna?"

"Yeah, that's some kind of environmental consulting firm, if I'm not mistaken."

"It seems that some of the people killed out here, worked for or were involved with them somehow. So, I was wondering if you could get as much information on them as possible. Also, do you think you can get the name of the holding company that they're operating under, along with a list of companies that also operate under them?"

"I think I can handle that. Damn this is exciting. I haven't been given an investigative assignment in years." TNT laughed. Tony had always enjoyed listening to TNT's laugh. It seemed to come from the bottom of his stomach and slowly rolled out.

"Listen, I am really concerned about Cats though. Can you check on her, just as soon as possible?"

"Just as soon as we are done here." TNT reassured him.

"Thanks. I think this story is going to be bigger than any of us could have imagined. I am beginning to think that there may be some evidence here of your conspiracy theory."

"Well, if there is anything I can do, just let me know. You know I will do what I can."

"I know and thanks again. I will call you in a couple of days to see what you've found out."

They talked for a few minutes longer. TNT told him how furious Jason was because he hadn't been checking in like he was suppose to and how he felt Tony should be fired. This news made Tony smile. Making Jason mad, always seemed to give him pleasure. Besides, when he did write this story, Jason would be kissing his ass, not trying to can it. When his call to TNT was over, he made his way upstairs to the rest of the group. As he looked upon everyone's faces, he could see the toll this was taking on them. Paul's face seemed to be showing lines that hadn't been there before and he wasn't his usual lighthearted self. Sherri was looking the worse, and with good reason, he thought. Her eyes looked black, from the bags that had formed under them, from her lack of sleep. Her hair hung down unattended, sticking out in all directions. Valerie was holding up well, but then he had just drug her into this madness. He felt good that he had called TNT. It was the only way he knew of, to try and make sure Cats would be ok.

Deric rushed over and answered the ringing phone. The news was not what he wanted to hear. When Kurt had gone back to the Foghorn, the reporter was gone. After talking it over with the two men in his office, they decided to keep an eye on the detective that Kurt had seen Tony talking to. They figured that all in good time, the two of them would get together again. Minutes after the phone call from Kurt, the phone rang again, but this time it was the familiar deep voice of their contact with the group.

"So, tell me what you've learned so far? Have the other two contacted you yet?"

"Yes, they're here." Deric answered, looking over at the Laurel and Hardy duo.

"Well, talk to me, what have you found out?"

Deric swallowed and proceeded to explain about how they had spotted the reporter, talking to the police and their plan to keep an eye on the detective until the reporter contacted him again.

"I guess I should be thankful that you have some kind of plan. I want this taken care of quickly and quietly. Do you understand?"

"Perfectly." Deric answered, cold and to the point.

"All right and as for the cop he has to been talking to, you'll have to take care of him to. We have no idea how much he knows by now."

"Wait a minute, you're talking about killing a cop. Do you realize how much heat that is going to bring down here?" Deric could feel his stomach turning into a tight knot. Looking over at the two men sitting in front of him, they looked like two hounds waiting to be sent out after the hare. Their eyes shone with interest on the conversation they were listening to.

"I don't really give a rat's ass what you think. What I think, is that you don't have much choice at this point. Now give me one of the other two to talk to." Deric numbly handed the phone over to the taller man and sat back looking out his window. He was getting a bad feeling about this, but knew that he was in too deep and would have to go the distance on this.

"Ok, let's get started. I'll take the first watch on this cop. Can you get that guy you were talking to in here. We will need him to point out which cop it is we have to watch." The taller man said anxiously.

The excitement showed in his face and the scar above his eye seemed to turn a dark crimson color. Deric said he would have Kurt there in an hour. They decided to meet back in his office in one hour and would work out a schedule for keeping surveillance on the detective.

As TNT hung up the phone, he sat and stared at nothing in particular. This was supposed to have been so easy, without all these complications. He was confident that it would work itself out, after all, he still had his ace in the hole. Tony's trust. He had a slight twinge of guilt for using Tony the way he was and that at the end of it all, Tony would have to be killed. But then, something's in life would have to be sacrificed to maintain the power and balance, that him and the others in the group yielded. The first thing he had to do was to get Cats, and show Tony that he was working with him. He picked up the phone and dialed Cats number.

"Hi Cats, how are you doing?" he asked in a fatherly tone.

"TNT." He could hear the relief in her voice at hearing someone familiar. He could only imagine the strain that this must be putting on her. He hoped that when it was all over, she could be spared.

"I'm fine, so glad you called." She looked over at the man listening in, with all the hatred she could muster and got a smile and a wink in return.

"I just got a call from Tony and he was concerned about you. Are you sure you're all right?"

She wanted so badly to tell him that no she wasn't all right. There were two men in her home, watching and listening to everything she said and did.

"Well, I'm coming over to pick you up and we're going out for dinner." TNT continued. The man listening in was shaking his head no and the smile had been replaced with a cold stare.

"That's very kind of you, but it's ok. I think I'm just going to stay home and relax this evening."

"Nonsense, I'm not taking no for an answer. Laurie and I will be by there in about an hour. It will be good for you to get out. See you then." Before she could object, the phone went dead. She looked over at the man sitting there and was surprised to see how relaxed he was looking at her, with a very indifferent expression on his face.

"You lucky girl, looks like you're going out for dinner. Now, we will have to make sure that you behave yourself while you're out." He walked into the kitchen where the other man was sitting at the table playing solitaire. She could hear them whispering and her heart started racing as she looked at the door. Could she make it if she made a run for it? Every nerve in her body was sensitive at that very moment. At the moment that it felt like her body was going to make the leap and run for her life, a hand suddenly pressed down on her shoulder.

"Don't do anything stupid and you may get out of this unharmed." It was the man that had been sitting at the kitchen table. She sank back into the chair, almost relieved that she hadn't tried. Even if she had made it, they still had her parents to hold over her. The other man came walking out of the kitchen carrying a black leather briefcase and set it down on the coffee table. When he opened it up, she saw that it contained what appeared to be small lapel pins, each tucked neatly into foam indentations. Each indentation took on the shape of each particular pin. He pulled out a small blue pin that looked like a rose.

"Why don't you go get yourself ready for your dinner date. When you're ready, we'll put this on you so that we can listen in on your dinner conversation. After all, we wouldn't want you having a slip of the tongue, that might end up hurting your parents." Cats wanted to rip the man's heart out. She thought if ever there was a time she could kill someone, it would be now. She left the room, thankful that she was about to have some time out and away from them. As she left the room the man picked up the phone and made a call. They assured TNT that she had no idea what was going on. They told him about the bug they planted on her, but had no intention on using. He liked the thoroughness they were showing. He explained to them how he wanted it to be handled and told them that they were to pack up and head up to Newport. Once there, they were to wait for instructions from him. He had no intentions on having this go on any longer, it was time for it to end. There was far too much at stake.

When the doorbell rang, Cats almost screamed it startled her so.

"Easy now. Just act very casual. We don't want your company expecting anything. Have fun and remember, we will be listening." The man stood behind the door holding the gun across his chest. She had to stand still for a moment to control the anger and hatred that had swelled up inside her.

Pasting a smile on her face, she opened the door and greeted TNT with cheery voice. "Hi, how are you?"

"Not as good as you. You look stunning my dear." He always had a way of flirting with the ladies, Cats thought. She stood in the doorway and wondered how she was ever going to make it through the night, acting as if nothing was happening.

"May I come in, or would you rather just go. Laurie is waiting out in the car."

"Let's just go." She smiled, wanting to get away from there as quickly as possible. As the door closed behind her, she could feel the two men coming out from their hiding places and making themselves comfortable in her home. If this ever ended, she would have to sell her house and move a long way away from here. She climbed into the backseat of the car. Looking up at the window of her house, she noticed the curtains slightly pulled back on one side, as the men watched her. As the car pulled away Cats left them looking at her raised middle finger.

"So, how have you been my dear?" Laurie asked. She was like a mother to everyone, always concerned about everyone's well being and never having anything bad to say about anyone. She was shorter than her husband and had kept herself in good shape. Her white hair was long and she kept it in a bun mostly. On the odd occasion when she let it down, she made even some of the younger women envious.

"Not bad. Could always be better, but then I guess it could always be worse." She answered. Looking up she saw TNT's eyes looking at her in the rear view mirror, and an uneasy feeling washed over her.

"Yes, that is the truth isn't it? Besides, I have learnt in my many years of being alive, that it makes no sense to complain because nobody is going to listen to you anyway." Laurie joked.

They pulled up in front of the restaurant and TNT dropped the ladies off, then went and parked the car. They sat around talking mostly about the trip TNT and Laurie were going to take to the Cayman Islands. Laurie had never been there and was talking excitedly about all the information she had read and heard about the islands. TNT had been a couple of times, on business and talked about his favorite part of the islands. He had never been to Little Cayman or Cayman Brac, just the main island, Grand Cayman. He talked about the beautiful north side of the island and his favorite bar, The Driftwood. The more he talked about it, the more excited Laurie seemed to get. They told Cats that they were going to try and make it over to one of the other islands, so that there would be something new for both of them. As they waited for their after dinner coffees, Laurie excused herself to go to the washroom.

"Cats, Tony called me and asked me to check on you, he said he was afraid that you might be in some kind of trouble. Is there something wrong?" TNT was leaning over to her and talking in a quiet tone. His eyes were fixated on hers and her heart felt like it was going to rip from her chest. She wanted, and had to, tell him what was going on. God, she needed to tell someone, this couldn't go on like this. She started to feel lightheaded and took a large drink of water to try and calm herself.

Remembering the tiny microphone she replied, "No, nothing's wrong, I don't know why he would have said that." As she talked she reached into her purse and pulled out a pen and piece of paper. "How's Tony doing?" She asked trying to keep the conversation flowing for the benefit of those listening in.

"Seems to be doing ok. He told me that the story is going to be huge and that there is much more to it than anyone could imagine. Has he talked to you much about it?" He admired Cats and how she was handling the pressure she was under.

"Not too much, other than they found the lady and that there were other bodies found at the scene, that were never reported. That's a strange one, don't you think?"

How he wished Tony hadn't told her about the other bodies. Now there was no question as to whether Cats could be spared at the end of this. She now knew too much, she could not be spared. He watched her hand shaking, as she wrote on the paper then slid it across the table to him.

I need your help. Tony's life is in danger and my parents are also in danger. I have a microphone on me so be careful what you say.

He looked up at her, but said nothing. Taking the pen from her hand he began writing on the paper just as Laurie returned to the table.

"You know, for the prices they charge in this place, you would think they could afford to keep a supply of toilet paper in the washrooms. So, what have you two been talking about, newspaper jargon I would imagine."

"Cats had just asked me about Tony. I talked to him today, and to answer your question, he's doing fine. I was just going to go up to Newport to see him, but forgot to ask him where he was staying. You wouldn't know how I could find him, would you?" He looked at Cats as he asked the question and once again Cats had that uneasy feeling come over her.

"No, he didn't tell me where they went after leaving the motel." She could see that he wanted to get the piece of paper back over to her, but didn't want Laurie to notice. Cats dropped her napkin on the floor so that it landed between their chairs. As she bent over to pick it up, TNT offered to get it for her and placed the paper in the napkin, then handed it back to her. She excused herself and as she left the table, Laurie whispered to her, "Don't use the last stall, no paper in it."

Once inside the washroom, she unfolded the paper and read what TNT had written on it.

Ok, now you've got me worried. How can I help? Do you want me to arrange to have your parents brought here with you?

She sat down and wanted to cry. She was feeling so lost and confused, and didn't know what to do. She collected herself and the thought of having her parents here with her, seemed like a good idea. She was sure TNT would be able to arrange a safe place for them, and if she told him about what they had threatened her with, maybe he would be able to help them with that also. When she got back to the table, Laurie was sitting by herself.

"When he got the bill, I think it scared him off and he ran." Laurie said laughing and in spite of herself Cats also had to chuckle. "He will be right back. Just had to go make a phone call. So what's been happening in your life? Anything new on the romance front?"

Her mind thought of Tony. How she wished he would just realize, that what happened in his marriage, was not his fault and that it was ok to commit again. He must know how much she loved him. She recalled the night she told him how he deserved happiness and what a nice man he was. He had exploded in anger and frustration at the words nice man. Nice guys finish last, he yelled at her. He said he was tired of watching jerks and smooth talkers move on and get what ever they seemed to want, while so called nice guys just kept getting dumped by the wayside. She recalled how his eyes had swelled with tears, when he told her that if anyone told him one more time about what a nice guy he was, he was ready to commit suicide. The thought made her shudder and brought her back to the conversation.

"My, now that question had you thinking of someone." Laurie commented, noticing Cats faraway look in her eyes.

"Oh no. Nothing new yet in that department, but still keeping a watchful eye out."

"Well, hang in there my dear. Believe me, life has a way of working itself out."

Cats was almost as tired of hearing that, as Tony was hearing about what a nice guy he was. She smiled back at Laurie and wished TNT would get back to the table and maybe the topic would change. She saw him heading back to the table from the entrance door.

"Well, everything has been arranged." He said, looking over at Cats and grabbing Laurie's hand. "Cats and her parents are going to be spending some time with us at our place."

Cats looked at him in complete fear. She had made a huge mistake. They were listening and now knew what was going on and had probably figured out that she had talked. Her hands started to tremble and she clasped them together so no one would notice.

"It's all right Cats." He said reassuringly, knowing that the men that were supposedly listening in were long gone already. "Your parents will be here tonight."

"What's going on?" Laurie asked looking back and forth between the two of them.

"Nothing." Cats snapped, almost in a state of panic. She grabbed the tiny microphone and placed it in the palm of her hand.

"Cats needs our help. I will explain when we get home." He smiled at Laurie, as he tapped her hand. "Your parents will be here tonight. Everything is going to be ok, trust me." He was now looking at Cats, trying to get her to calm down. He had made the phone calls and was feeling better that he was soon going to have this situation back under control. He cleared the bill up and they left the restaurant. Cats was happy to be out of there, and yet, she also felt confused and afraid. To top it all off she couldn't seem to shake that uneasy feeling every time she looked into TNT's eyes. The fresh air outside seemed to give her space to breathe, she inhaled deeply and held it for a brief second.

"I wish I knew what was going on," Laurie said annoyingly. "What do you mean Cats needs our help? Are you in some kind of trouble dear?" Cats could see the genuine concern in Laurie's face, and it gave her a warm feeling inside.

Before she could answer TNT spoke up. "I'll explain everything when we get home. Please be patient my dear. Now let's get the car and head home." With that he promptly headed off into the parking lot and the women followed. Laurie had slung her arm through Cats' arm and held her close. What was she to do and how was this going to turn out? Cats felt her insides were being torn in two different directions, and yet this sweet lady walking beside her seemed to give her a strength that calmed her. Without hesitation, Cats squeezed Laurie's hand and said thank you. Laurie looked up and smiled quietly mouthing; "You're welcome."

As they approached the car, TNT was standing there holding the door open for the two ladies. Laurie whispered in her ear, "He has always been such a gentleman and romantic. Not many of them left in today's world, you know." She let Cats arm go and climbed into the car. Climbing into the backseat, Cats felt TNT place his hand on her shoulder. "Everything is going to work out. You'll see." He said.

Looking into his eyes, as he closed the door for her, she realized that they looked cold with no caring or warmth in them. That is silly, she thought to herself, and sat back in the leather seat, telling herself that everything was going to work out. As the car pulled out, Cats suddenly froze. How did he know where her parents lived? They had never talked about her family and why would he just take it upon himself to go get them without her permission. God, was she getting paranoid, or was there something more devious going on here? I'm going crazy, her brain yelled in the inside of her head. He has the connection and power to find out pretty much anything he wants about anybody. TNT has been a long time friend and is trying to help, she reassured herself. She tried hard to relax and calm down, but the feeling remained with her. It would be nice to be with her parents again. She would have to make a point of thanking TNT.

CHAPTER 14

❀

They sat around the house most of the morning, occasionally engaging in small talk, but mostly each were engrossed in their own personal thoughts. Tony couldn't help but notice that Paul and Sherri had started to form a tight relationship and he wondered if that was a good thing. Valerie and him were cuddled up close and just were feeling good, about being with each other. He sat and looked around. He couldn't help but think how it was all going to end. They looked like a band of fugitives, on the run. Shaken, but hanging on to each other for support and comfort. In all his years as a reporter, he had never been shot at. The ringing phone came as a small comfort and Valerie got up and answered it. As she talked, Tony gathered that it was a friend of hers and he got up to mix a drink. He was just finishing pouring the Crown Royal into his glass, when Sherri suddenly appeared next to him.

"Can I get you anything?" he asked.

"Whatever you're having." She replied.

Tony gave her a quick glance and shrugged his shoulders. "I'm not sure that you really want to have this. No mix in this drink and most people say that you have to acquire a taste for it."

"Please, don't baby me. I need something strong and shocking to help me right now, and by the sounds of things, this is exactly what I need." The tone in her voice told Tony to just pour and continue to, until she had enough. He handed her the glass and she took it affirmatively. Raising the glass in a toast, Sherri tipped it back and drained it in four gulps. Just watching her, made Tony's stomach take a nauseating flip. She took a deep breath and held her stomach. Even before Tony could say anything, Sherri was standing over the kitchen sink in preparation.

"How do you drink that shit?" she asked, between gasps.

"It wasn't meant to be drank like a glass of water. You're suppose to sip it and enjoy it."

"Well, you better pour me another one. Maybe I'll enjoy it."

Tony admired and at the same time felt sorry for her strong disposition. On one hand, she needed to feel the shock the whiskey gave her, to keep her mind off the horrifying recurring images, and yet she had to prove that she was strong enough to handle it and get through it. Tony grabbed the glass and poured another one for her.

"Listen, I have to make a phone call. I'll be right back." Sherri looked up at him and for the fist time he saw a genuine smile. As he headed out of the kitchen, Valerie was standing by the doorway smiling at him.

"You're something else, you know that?" she said, as she leaned over and brushed her lips across his cheek.

"Why do you say that?"

"It doesn't seem to matter how terrible things get, you at least try to make other people feel good. I don't know what happened between you and your ex-wife, but all I can say, is that she was a fool to let someone like you get away."

He felt his cheeks turn red, as he wasn't used to being complimented on a personal level. His heart once again began to race, as he looked at her beauty and realized how much strength and support he was drawing from her.

"Keep an eye on Sherri, I'm going to call Daikon. We're going to go out to the crime scene and have a look around."

"Not a problem, babe." Valerie headed into the kitchen and Tony could hear her voice as she talked to Sherri. He walked into the living room and sat down on the sofa beside Paul.

"How is she holding up?" he asked.

"Not bad, considering. She has moments when she just breaks down. I think she may have lost someone close there."

"Well, I'm going to call Daikon and then we're going out to the scene, so get your gear ready to go."

Paul's face lit up, with excitement. He had been sitting around for so long now, that he was itching to go do something. He was on his feet in a flash, leaving Tony still sitting on the sofa.

"When do we leave?"

"Well, let me call Daikon first and find out when and where we can meet him. In the mean time, why don't you make sure you got all your equipment ready to go."

Tony wasn't even sure Paul heard the end of his last statement, as he headed out of the living room. He had to admit that it did feel good to be doing something other than running and hiding. He went downstairs to Valerie's computer room and called Daikon.

"Hey there. So, what's the scoop, can we head up today and get some photos?

"Not a problem. Meet me at the usual place in about an hour, I have a few things to finish up, then I'll head out. Is the girl coming with us?"

Tony sat there and thought about Sherri upstairs pouring whiskey down her throat, and decided it would definitely not be a good idea. "No. I don't think that would be a good idea. She's not in a very good state today and going out there just might be way to much of an emotional strain on her."

"Ok, but I do need to talk to her soon. I can't keep this quiet forever, sooner or later they're going to find out, I'm back investigating this and just not being a tour guide for you."

"I know, just give me a couple more days. We'll see you in an hour then." Tony quickly hung the phone up.

Daikon headed downstairs through the maze of desks and stopped in front of a desk that looked like a war zone. Behind the clutter, sat a lady officer, who seemed almost lost in the pile of paper work around her. Officer Justine Hasker, was one of the best computer personnel on the force. If there was anything that needed to be researched over the net, she was the one most came to. What a lot of the other officers didn't seem to be aware of, was that she was one of the best and most trust worthy officers out in the field. She kept herself in shape and had a smile that seemed to just brighten up your day. It was on more than one occasion, that he had witnessed her take a violent situation, where most officers including himself would use force to take control, and with her smile and comforting personality, turn it into a peaceful resolve. He knew he needed help on this and even though there were other officers wanting to get answers, he knew without a shadow of a doubt, that he wanted her with him on this. Besides, her capabilities on the computer would be a great help.

"Hey DD. What's up?" She asked, keeping her attention locked onto the computer screen, totally engrossed in whatever she was working on. Right from the first time they had met, she had always called him DD.

"Not a hell of a lot. I was wondering if you had a chance to dig up anything on this Enviro Magna outfit and the holding company it's operating under?"

"Haven't had much time to work on it, but what I have found so far, I think you will find rather interesting. I'm still researching some other areas, if you can give me a bit more time, I'll have their whole life history for you."

Daikon smiled at her and knew that she meant it. "Listen, I'm heading up with that reporter that's in town, to the Whallington Valley where those killings took place. I would like it if you would join us. I would like you to meet him. We might be able to figure out what really happened up there, if we work with this guy."

Justine and him had sat down to a drink on many occasions, discussing why so much of what happened out there was being held back. At the end of each brainstorm session, they always came up with the same answer. There didn't seem to be an answer. She finally pulled her eyes away from the screen and looked up at him. She had intense brown eyes and he had always loved looking into them.

"When are we going?" she asked.

"Well, I'm suppose to meet them in about an hour. I just got a bit of paperwork to finish."

"Sounds good. I'll meet you in an hour then." Her eyes automatically went back to the screen and her fingers nimbly danced over the keyboard.

"If you get a chance, get as much as you can on that Enviro Magna group and bring it with you. If you don't mind."

"Working on it, even as we speak." She answered, not even glancing up. Daikon turned and headed off leaving Justine in her world.

When he walked out of the doors of the precinct, Justine was already standing there. They walked down the wide concrete steps and across the street to the car compound. Daikon went over the list of cars available and signed out an unmarked green sedan, and soon they were headed to meet Tony and Paul. The blue sedan parked halfway down the block, slowly pulled out from the curb and settled a few car lengths behind them. Silently, like a stalking cat, it followed their every move, hoping to get its prey.

"We're heading toward town on the highway. If my guess is right, I would say we're going to that restaurant where they met before." The tall man informed his partner. He had called him as soon as Daikon had emerged from the precinct.

"Ok, I'm on my way. Is everything still in the trunk?"

"No, I took it out for a cleaning. What do you think? I was right, they're turning in. You better hurry, because if they move, I'm not waiting around for you." He hung up the cell phone and drove past the restaurant and around the block, parking at the end of the street, so that his vision wasn't blocked. His attention was totally focused on both entrances. This was his realm. This is what he strived for. The adrenaline rush, the tenseness, the thrill of the kill. It wasn't long before his partner suddenly appeared at the passenger window, and climbed in.

"Anything?" he asked.

"Not yet. Where's that arrogant shit head Deric?"

"He's parked across the lot watching the back entrance."

The man let out a disgusted grunting noise and returned his attention to the restaurant.

As Daikon walked in, Tony looked up and saw Justine walking in behind him. A sudden panic gripped him for a moment, but he soon let it go. Daikon headed over and the two of them sat down.

"Tony, this is Officer Hasker. She's coming with us and has some interesting information on Enviro Magna and it's parent holding company."

Tony extended his hand and then introduced Paul. Looking over at Daikon, Tony gave him a questioning shrug.

"It's ok, she's one of the good guys and has been interested in finding out what the hell is going on with this, also."

"I've been doing some digging and found out that there are some very major players involved, from all over the world, in the holding company that operates Enviro Magna." Justine started. "Not only that, but it also handles major logging operations all over the world. Something I am finding very strange with all of this, is that quite a few of these people are also involved with companies that are working against each other. Now, I'm not just talking rival companies operating the same type of business. I'm talking about for example, logging and mining companies being owned by the same holding company that owns environmental companies, that are suppose to be opposed to the defamation of mother earth." She stopped and looked around at the three men sitting at the table staring at her. She enjoyed doing that, stepping in and taking over a conversation, showing that she was capable of doing her job and showing that she did it damn well. Especially, when it came to men. "Is there something wrong? Did I go too fast?" She was smiling now, and the three men looked at each other as if to ask, what do we do now?

"Told you she was good." Daikon laughed.

Tony returned his attention to Justine. "Have you got a list of these people and the companies they're involved with?" She reached down and pulled a folder out of the briefcase, she had brought in with her. Handing it over to Tony, she said, "I still have a few more things to look into, but I think you will find everything you need in there."

Tony took the folder and opened it up. It contained paper clipped together with notes attached, indicating what each selection of files was about. Taking a quick glance through it, he admired the organization, and the thoroughness of it.

"Well, maybe you could look at them later." Daikon suggested. "We really should get going. It's a bit of a drive and I don't want to have to explain where I've been all day."

"Since when have you ever explained where you've been?" Justine asked jokingly.

Walking out of the Restaurant, Tony walked over to Valerie's car and placed the folder in the trunk. His hand was shaking as he placed the folder down, for he had noticed a name, but wasn't perfectly sure if he had read it right, when he quickly glanced through the files. It looked like, but probably wasn't, Terrance Neil Tibbet. He closed the trunk lid and headed over to where Daikon had parked.

"Now, it would be interesting to see what that was." The shorter man commented.

"Well, we will just have to check it out later. Write that license plate number down. I think we should find out who owns that car and pay them a little visit. Right now, we don't want to lose them. If we can get our hands on that reporter, I'm sure we can convince him to tell us where that broad is, in no time." A smile spread over both their faces. They were known for aquiring information out of people, and it was something they enjoyed. They fell in behind the green sedan, dropping back a comfortable distance. Looking in the mirror, the tall man saw Deric behind them in an Explorer. If he did anything to blow this, he would take great pleasure in killing him, slowly. They were headed out of town into the mountains. A few small farms and acreages dotted the roadside, but for the most part the countryside was mainly dense cedar forests. There wasn't much land suitable for habitants, as it was extremely rocky and jagged due to the proximity of the mountains. The road wound its way through the valley they were in and at times climbing over large hills only to descend into another lush valley. It was getting harder to follow the green sedan, without being noticed, due to the fact that there was hardly any traffic on the road. Breaking over the crest of a hill, his heart stopped. The sedan was gone. Suddenly, the Explorer sped past him and then slowed down causing him to stop. Jumping from the car, the driver pulled his gun from its holster. Enough was enough, he was going to blow this asshole away. Even before he got to the driver's door, Deric poked his head out of the window smiling.

"You might want to put that away before someone drives by and sees it, or worse yet, it might go off and you could hurt yourself. They have turned up the logging road, heading up to where the killings took place."

The man stopped, realizing that he had to depend on this man, as they were now in unfamiliar territory, and the only person that knew it, was this smartass, whom he detested. Placing the gun back in its holster, he glared at Deric.

"Is there any other way out of there, other than that logging road?" the shorter man asked.

"No, this is it."

"Ok, then. What do you think would be the plan? We can either head up and try to surprise them, or we could lay an ambush for them when they head out." The short man was addressing his partner. It was now in their hands, any failure would come down on them. They had their target cornered and it was now just a matter of deciding how to achieve the end result.

"Any idea how far up they're headed?" the tall one asked Deric.

"Probably about eight or nine miles."

"Well, I say we get them there. They will be out of the car and we can surprise them when they come back to it. Besides, not much chance of anyone passing by up there. Deric can stay behind on the road and watch for anyone that tries to head up there."

Deric didn't mind that idea at all. The thought of killing a police officer and then the attention it was going to cause, still wasn't sitting very well with him. Besides, he thought, let them take care of the situation up there and he could take care of them, then collect the money for himself. They decided to drive half way, where Deric would park and then the other two would drive up closer, park and walk to where their intended victims would be. Deric warned them not to get too close with the car, as sound travels a long ways in the woods. When they got about halfway up, Deric pulled off on a side trail and parked the Explorer behind some alder bushes. As the blue sedan continued up the road, he watched it disappear from sight and found that his hands were sweaty and his heart was racing. This was it. There was no turning back now. The thought of pulling out and taking off crossed his mind, but he knew he would be looking over his shoulder for the rest of his life, wondering when they would find him. No, he was here and no matter how it ended, he would have to see it to the end.

The two men pulled the car over to the side of the road, as far as they could. Climbing out, neither man said a word. They had done this so many times before, they had the routine down pat. Opening the trunk, there was a small arsenal of weapons, available to them.

Each man selected two weapons of choice and ammunition to feed each weapon. With a disciplined quickness, silencers were placed on the barrels. Inspecting the guns and making sure everything was in good working order, they silently closed the trunk, looked at each other and with a nod headed off to locate and eliminate their quarry.

The first signs that they were getting close, was the yellow police tape, that had been strung across the crime scene to stop curiosity seekers from contaminating the scene. Pieces were lying here and there where the wind had distributed it. The winds this high up in the mountains, could be fierce at times. They didn't need to walk much further, when they spotted the green sedan. Crouching down, they surveyed the area for signs of anyone hanging around. Confident that the area was clear, they made their way to the car. Looking inside, nothing of interest caught their attention. The short man quickly went about the business of letting the air out of a tire, ensuring that there would be no chance of a quick flight. The sun had come out full now and the heat and bugs were making the job miserable. The men didn't complain, as they had spent time as mercenaries in the jungles of Guatemala, and had extensive experience with heat and bugs. The man with the scar signaled to the other one, that he was going to head into the forest and locate the group. He got the ok sign and a signal indicating that the short man would be hiding behind a hedge of brush across the road from the car. With that, the taller man turned and silently slipped into the dense forest.

For a man his size, he moved silently through the woods. Soon he could hear the sound of voices and what sounded like a camera shutter clicking. He headed in the direction of the sound and pulled his revolver out. Crouching low and stealthily making his way to the edge of the clearing, he could see the four in a small clearing. The detective, reporter and a female, were standing over a dark stained patch on the ground. Glancing over to his left, he watched as a man was engrossed in snapping photos of certain areas of the ground. He lifted the gun he held in his hand and set the sights on the detective's temple. Steady as a rock, the gun didn't waver, as he slowly wrapped his finger around the familiar feel of the trigger, a feeling of sensual gratification came over him. He stood there, in the all too familiar position, knowing he could take the detective's life at any time he chose. The bullet never left its resting place though. The detective wouldn't die here, not yet. It would cause panic and then there were too many places for the others to run and hide, which would make everything more difficult. No, out on the road, where they would be in the open, is where they would meet their final fate. Quietly he backed away and headed back to the road, where his partner was waiting and where they would finally finish the job they were sent to do.

CHAPTER 15

Tony was awestruck by the beauty of the country. They didn't talk much about the case, as both Tony and Paul watched the scenery of tall forests of fir, cedar and hemlock pass them by. At one point, they were so high that they could see several glacier-fed rivers, threading their way down the pristine mountain slopes, pouring into the wide estuary that awaited them at the bottom. Every where he looked, he could see small crystal clear waterfalls cascading over the edge of a cliff, sending a mist out, creating an abundance of small rainbows. It wasn't hard to see why logging companies cherished this land, for its abundance in a renewable natural resource and why the environmental groups fought to preserve it in its natural unaltered state. They had driven approximately an hour and a half, when they turned off the main road and headed into the forest on a dirt logging road. It was like something you would see in a nature magazine. Small streams trickled along side the road, in a joined chorus that seemed to fill the air with their music. Tony couldn't imagine anything, as horrific as they were about to investigate, happening in a setting such as this.

"Here we are." Daikon announced, as he pulled the car over to the side of the road. Stepping out of the car, Tony could hear Paul inhale deeply and hold it. The air was fresh, cool and crisp. It made the whole body suddenly jump to life. There was no exhaust smells from vehicles, or aromas from restaurant kitchens. It was just pure, crisp mountain air. What a life these men must have had, Tony thought, and to have it taken away, seemed almost as bad as the actual killing. Paul looked over at Tony and smiled.

"Wow," was all he said.

"Ok, the trail is a little rough and overgrown, but just stay close behind me." Daikon instructed.

Tony helped Paul with his equipment and they headed off, like explorers into the unknown. The going was tough. Paul made a comment about how the loggers must have been in incredible condition, to lug their saws and axes through this. They stumbled over the underbrush a few times, but soon came to the clearing where the horrors, of a few days past had taken place. On the ground could be seen dark patches of dried blood, some extremely large, where lives had been lost. A silence fell over them and the forest, as they gazed upon the ghastly sight. Tony's emotions were running rampant. One part of him wanted to cry out, another wanted him to scream in anger and yet another, wanted to be sick at the loss of human life in such a manner. The screams of pain and terror seemed to be resounding around him from everywhere. He could see that Paul, also was having a hard time with it. The talks with Sherri, as to what had happened, made it all too real. He could visualize Sherri, standing over the mashed body of the man she had killed. Blood dripping from the axe in her hand and from her body. His legs suddenly felt very weak and he had to start moving, otherwise he would have collapsed. There was a large dried patch across the clearing and Daikon was crouched over it as if searching for something. Tony walked over and stood behind him. Justine joined them and slowly circled the area, carefully concentrating on the ground around it. The sound of the camera shutter, made Tony's head snap around. Paul was on the other side, taking photos of the dark blotches of blood, that covered the ground and trees. The whole place gave Tony a very uneasy feeling and he didn't want to be there long. He wasn't sure what he thought he was going to see when they got there, but this was not what he had expected.

"Apparently, this is where they saw the lady standing." Daikon had stood, but his eyes remained fixed on the dried blood. "The men said they saw her standing over a body, with an axe in her hand, and two bodies laying in front of her."

"There is no way, she could have done all this by herself." Tony quickly jumped in. Glad to have his mind working on something else, other than the images that continued to enter his thoughts.

"We know that." Justine replied moving next to Tony. "That's why we really want to talk to her. The killings took place as soon as they entered the clearing and ended here. You see where the brush and grass has been knocked down and trampled in that area over there. Even though some of the grass has grown back up again, there are deep grooves in the earth where fighting took place. Also the majority of blood, is concentrated in that area. As you get closer to this spot, there is hardly any. Either everyone else was dead before this particular struggle happened, or they just separated themselves from the group. Either way, unless she could have magically split herself into three, there is no way she could have done all this."

"So why are they after her? If the public knew of the enormity of what happened out here, they would see that there had to have been more people involved. She was the only one that survived, when she wasn't suppose to, now they're making her a scapegoat." Tony blurted out, before he realized what he was saying. Both Daikon and Justine were looking at him now, knowing that he knew more than he had been telling them. He wished now, that he hadn't said a thing.

"What the hell do you mean she wasn't suppose to survive? And what the fuck are you talking about a scapegoat? You've been holding out on me. Shit man, how the hell do you expect me to help, if you're not going to fill me in on everything you know? And who the hell are they?" Daikon was standing with his hands on his hips and his face had taken on that familiar red glow, when he got angry. Paul had quit snapping pictures and was peering into the bush, to the side of him, as if looking for something. Tony knew that he had to tell them everything now, but he really wanted Sherri to be there.

"Ok, listen when we get back, I'll set a meeting up and she can fill you in on everything." Quickly, hoping to take some of the attention off him, he turned to Paul. "What's up? Something there?" Tony asked.

"No. Just had a feeling like there was something looking at me. Thought I saw some movement, but guess not." With a shrug, he started to move around the clearing snapping more photos.

"All right, no more bullshit! You screw me around anymore and I swear to God, I'll take you in for harboring a fugitive, with holding evidence in a murder investigation and any other goddamn thing I can throw at you. You're a real piece of work. No more bullshit you understand?" Daikon spun and stormed off to where Paul was.

"You definitely got on his wrong side with that move." Justine said to Tony, as they both watched him stomp away. "You have to understand, he is one of the few really good cops left and this whole thing is such a blatant cover up, that it has been eating his insides out. He wants to know why they aren't releasing the whole story, and quite frankly, so do I. To be able to keep this under wraps, the orders would have to come from way up there and the consequences for failure to do so, would have to be severe."

Tony was still staring off in the direction of Daikon and Paul, who were now talking and by the movement of their hands, were analyzing the order of events. "Well, I find it incredibly unbelievable that this has not leaked out. Is there anyway of getting a list of the officers who attended the crime scene?"

"Not officially. I have tried before and got shut down quickly. We were only permitted to come to the crime scene, after the lab crew had been out here and the bodies had been taken away."

They covered the area for a bit longer and Justine filled Tony in the best way she could, on how they surmised what had happened.

Tony asked a few questions, already knowing the answers from talking to Sherri, but he wanted to see if the police were even close. He was surprised at how close they were, to what had actually happened, except for the events leading up to the killings and what happened after. Soon, Daikon indicated that it was time to head back, as he had some other business to take care of at the precinct. Paul snapped a few last photos and everyone headed back down the trail towards the car, with Justine leading and Paul close behind her.

Daikon stopped and turned to Tony blocking him from advancing down the trail. "Tony, I am serious, you have to come clean with me on everything, or there isn't much I can do to help. I won't stand by and watch these people get away with whatever it is they're up to. That lady you're hiding, has the answers and I need to know them. I believe that this is a cover up, possibly leading high into the government, but at this point, I can't prove a thing." As Tony looked into his eyes, he could see the frustration and determination that held them locked on him.

"You have my word, that when we get back, I'll set a meeting up. Just don't push her too hard. We have only seen the aftermath. She was here watching it all unfold. I'm surprised she isn't in a mental ward right now."

Satisfied, Daikon nodded his head and turned up the path leading back to the car. Tony followed behind, with his mind racing over what he had just seen and envisioning the ghastly horror of that infamous day. His heart went out to Sherri and he made a point, that he would be more understanding and compassionate to her when they got back.

They were approaching the car and could see it sitting, waiting patiently for them. As they broke through the brush out into the open area of the road, Justine turned, to inform everyone of the flat tire. Later, she would come to realize, that it was that move, that saved her life. No one heard the shot being fired, but the dead sound of the bullet hitting her in the shoulder, was unmistakable. Neither was the scream of pain as she gripped at her shoulder. The force spun her around, spraying droplets of blood in an arc as she dropped to her knees. The next bullet found its intended target. Paul violently jerked back, as his head snapped backwards, as if from a blow to the forehead. Tony froze in terror, as he watched a hole explode out the back of Paul's head. Unable to move, he was thrown to the ground behind the car, with Daikon on top of him.

"Don't fucking move! Do you understand?" Daikon yelled at him. Even before he got an answer, Daikon scrambled over to Justine and helped her get to the safety of the car. "Are you all right?" He asked as he checked the bullet wound in her shoulder.

"Shit! Yeah, I'm ok. Did you see where it came from?" she asked pulling her revolver out.

"No. I would say those bushes over there across the road." He answered trying carefully to look around the corner of the car's fender. In response, a bullet shattered the taillight by his head.

"Fire some shots in their direction, to see if they'll return fire. Maybe I can get a fix on them." Justine nodded and cautiously turned, so as to have a better shooting stance. With effort, she raised her revolver and fired several shots across the road. Immediately a barrage of bullets came as a response. They had to cover their heads as glass from the side windows, being blown out, showered over them. The back window shattered and collapsed into the backseat. Daikon knew that whoever was out there, were professionals. They showered the car with bullets, to prevent anyone from taking stock of the situation. He hadn't been on the force for all these years, without learning a trick or two himself. Lying down in a prone position, he slid back into the ditch so he could have a better view under the car. Lying still he watched for any movement. It wasn't long until he saw the grass move at the base of some shrubs. Carefully, he took aim and fired. The exclamation that came from behind the brush, let him know that he had hit one of them, probably shattering his ankle. Immediately, there was a second shot and the sound as if someone had dropped a sack of potatoes to the ground. The shot had come from Justine. Her training had her prepared and when the hidden gunman jumped from being shot in the foot, she was able to place him in her sights and fired.

The scream from the short man made his partner turn, only to see the bullet rip through the side of his head. Watching the scene unfold, as if in slow motion, he watched as the short man fell hard to the ground. Without any emotion, he turned his attention back to the car. He had told him to wait until they were out from behind the car before the started shooting, but the short man had insisted on catching them by surprise, before they could get into the car. Well, you got your surprise, he thought, and have put me in one hell of a spot. Wrinkling his forehead, the scar above his eye seemed to create a fold that protruded. He could see movement from behind the car, but was unable to see what was happening. He had them pinned down fairly well and knew that the woman had taken a bullet. Just be patient he thought, sooner or later they will make a mistake.

Both Daikon and Justine were so intent with the situation at hand, that neither one of them noticed Tony, crawl back to where Paul lay. He was kneeling over him, with his hands shaking and tears pouring down his face and mixing with the blood on the ground. Numbly, going through Paul's pockets, he retrieved the rolls of film Paul had just taken minutes ago. Which now seemed like, the pictures had been taken an eternity ago. Lifting the limp torso up, he removed the cameras that hung from straps around Paul's neck. Blood drained down over his arm. Mindlessly, he continued to collect Paul's personal belongings. Suddenly, his body reacted violently and he turned, vomiting uncontrollably. The sound of him emptying his insides, made Justine and Daikon turn quickly, with their weapons raised ready to fire.

"Are you out of your goddamn mind?" Daikon screamed at him. "Get your ass back over here, or have you just become tired of living?"

Tony wiped the sweat from his face, clutched the cameras and film tight in his hands and crawled back over to where Justine and Daikon were huddled.

"You do something that stupid again and I'll shoot you myself." Daikon threatened him. Tony didn't even look up at Daikon. His eyes remained on his blood soaked arms. Soaked with Paul's blood.

"How are you holding up?" Daikon turned his attention to Justine. She was clutching at her shoulder and her face grimaced from the pain.

"Well, I'm not going to tell you I feel great, but not to worry I'll be all right. Any idea how many of them there are?"

"I think two, but I'm not positive. When I got the first one, there seemed to be a rustle over at the other end of that brush line, but again I'm not one hundred percent positive."

"Ok, now what? We can't stay here forever, and I really would like to see a doctor sometime today." They both looked up at the same time and shared a short laugh, which seemed to break the tension of the moment.

"Just give me a second to think." Daikon replied, looking out into the forest as if the answer lay out there somewhere. The answer came from the most unlikely source, Tony.

"What if you two were to keep them busy, by firing shots into the brush. I could drive the car into the brush line, which would force them out and then they would be all yours. Besides, I owe the bastards."

Justine looked at Daikon and shrugged. "It just might work." She said.

"Ok." Daikon agreed. "But you'll have to be damn careful. With that front tire being flat, you're going to have a hard time controlling the car. We'll stay behind the car for cover. As soon as the car drives into the brush you lay yourself flat on the seat."

Tony nodded and moved to the front door. Justine made her way to the back of the sedan, where Daikon waited, his gun raised and ready. Reaching up, Tony slowly opened the car door, expecting shots to be fired at any time. Keeping as low as possible, he slithered first onto the floor and then up onto the seat, like a snake. His heart was pounding and his mouth craved water. Placing the key in the ignition, he said a quick and silent prayer. Turning the ignition, the car jumped to life, and gun shots immediately shattered the silence. Tony jammed the gearshift into drive and stepped on the accelerator. The tires spun in the dirt and the car lurched forward. With tremendous force he turned the steering wheel and aimed it for their hidden enemy. He wasn't sure if it was the sound of the bullets hitting the car, or just the sound of the blood pumping through his veins, that he was hearing. At the moment the sedan was about to hit the brush, Tony gripped the steering wheel white knuckled and screamed from his very soul, totally forgetting about his instructions to lay flat. The car slammed hard into the brush sending branches and leaves exploding everywhere. It came to such a sudden stop, that it threw Tony forward, smashing his chest into the steering column. The wind exploded from his lungs and everything started to spin and waver around him. He rolled his head to one side and could see the form of a tall man, standing with a gun in each hand yelling. Tony couldn't hear him or the guns, but he could see the gun barrels jump with each bullet dislodged. Tony fought to keep his consciousness. Pulling at the door handle, he tried to open it, but found that it had been jammed against the branches that were pressed against it. Frantically, he checked on the gunman and watched as his body jerked with each bullet that entered him. It almost seemed like a new age dance, then there was stillness. The man's arms slowly settled down by his sides, the guns slipped from his hands and fell to the forest floor. His knees wavered, then collapsed as his body fell forward getting hung up in the branches. Tony laid back in the seat, gasping for air and fighting to keep control of his consciousness. Slowly, he calmed down and sat there staring out the cracked windshield. How peaceful the forest suddenly seemed. It was the sound of Daikon's voice, that broke the tranquility that he had enjoyed but for a moment.

"Tony, are you ok?" Daikon was tearing branches back, trying to get to the car, but to no avail. "The branches are too thick, I can't get to the door. You will have to climb out through the back window."

Tony slowly turned and hauled himself over the front seat and made for the opening, where the back window used to be. His chest was in pain and there was broken glass everywhere, cutting into his hands. Daikon was standing at the back, ready to assist him down from the trunk. Justine came over and gave him a smile and a nod.

"Not a bad idea at all." Justine credited him. "Looks like you'll be remembering this for a while." She indicated to his bleeding hands. Tony was sitting with his hand on his chest and his shoulders hunched forward. "Well, looks like we've got a bit of a hike in front of us. Can you make it?" she asked concerned.

"Yes, I think so." Tony answered, finding it ironic, that she would be asking him if he could make it, as she stood there with a hole in her shoulder.

Daikon was checking the two gunmen out, looking for identification, or some clue as to who they were and why they were there waiting for them. He came back shaking his head.

"Nothing. We will have to get the lab crew to do their thing with them. Damn, I can't believe we didn't notice we were being followed. That had to be the only way they knew we were here."

Daikon helped Tony to his feet and then went and collected Paul's equipment, that Tony had retrieved. Before heading down the road, Tony walked over and looked at the two men, that had tried so desperately, to kill him and were now lying lifeless on the ground. He recognized them as the men from the motel. Turning, he joined Justine and Daikon, who were already slowly making their way down the road. They stopped several times, giving Justine and Tony time to rest. When they came upon the blue sedan, Daikon let out a sigh of relief. He had been getting concerned about Justine, who was starting to look extremely tired and her pace had slowed down. Smashing out the side window, he gained access to the car and soon had the steering column dismantled, enabling him to hot-wire the ignition. The three of them sat quietly for a moment, reflecting on what had happened. With not a word spoken, Daikon put the car in drive and they were soon headed back down the mountain.

Deric had heard the shots and the revving of an engine, and it made him very nervous. He knew the two men would have silencers on their weapons, so the loud shots, could not have been theirs. He couldn't figure out why the cars engine would have been revved like that, and with all those shots being fired at the same time. He wanted to go up and see what was happening, but knew that would be foolish. He sat in his hiding place waiting to see who would be coming down the road. As the blue sedan approached, he started to climb out of the Explorer to greet it and find out what had happened. He was about to step out from his concealment, when he noticed that there were three heads in the car and it wasn't slowing down. Ducking back behind the brush, he watched as the sedan passed by him. Inside, he saw the lady with her head back and her hand holding her bloody shoulder. Behind the steering wheel was the detective, driving and talking to the person in the back seat. As the car came parallel to him, he saw the reporter sitting in the backseat, staring out the window. A vacancy was in his eyes, as though he was looking but not seeing. When he couldn't see the sedan anymore, he pulled out from behind the brush and headed up the logging road.

As they pulled into town. Daikon swung by and dropped Tony off at Valerie's car. He was going to take Justine to the hospital and make sure she was taken care of. Then he would have to go to the station and organize to have the crime scene unit go out to the scene. There would be two detectives assigned to investigate. They would check the corpses and the scene, then bombard him with questions. Not to mention that he would also have to try and explain this to his superiors, and he knew that wasn't going to be fun. At that particular moment, he was sure that what he had chosen for a career because he loved doing it, was about to come to an end.

They had decided that they would hook up with each other later that night. In the meantime, Tony had to try and figure out how to tell Valerie and Sherri what had happened. He was particularly worried about Sherri and how she was going to react to it. He sat there for a long time, staring at the world outside passing him by. The thought of Paul lying up in the mountains, cold and still with no one around to watch over him. Tears filled his eyes and the pain consumed his heart. Fighting to control the shaking in his hands he brought the car to life and pulled out of the restaurant's parking lot. He would call TNT when he got back to Valerie's place and make sure Cats was ok. Concentrating on his driving, he sped along the highway just wanting to get to Valerie and the comfort he knew he would find with her. As he pulled into the driveway, the urge to pull out again and just drive seemed to be overwhelming. Turning the ignition off, he climbed out of the car, and on shaky legs, he slowly made his way to the front door and the nauseating task that awaited him inside.

"My God, what happened to you?" Valerie exclaimed as she appeared at the top of the stairs and saw the condition he was in. "Where's Paul?" His eyes met hers and he could see she understood. Throwing her hand up to cover her mouth, she slumped down on the top step shaking her head.

"Where's Sherri?" he asked settling in beside her, wrapping his arm around her and laying his head on hers.

"Laying down. Oh God, what happened? I thought you were just going out to have a look at the crime scene." She said pulling herself away from him and looking over his body at all the cuts and scrapes. Her eyes seemed to freeze as they settled on the dried blood smeared on his arms.

"The two men from the motel, were waiting for us when we came out of the woods. It all happened so fast. They just started shooting at us."

She grabbed his arm and helped him up. "Come on, lets get you cleaned up and tend to those cuts." She helped him remove his shirt and let out a gasp. His chest was a dark purplish color, that turned a red hue as it expanded out around his sides. She ran a warm bath and helped him climb in. It felt so comforting, that he laid his head back and closed his eyes for a brief time. Valerie gently washed his hands and chest, quietly sobbing.

"I don't know how to tell Sherri. She's been through so much and now this." He said without opening his eyes.

Neither one spoke and time seemed to be suspended in the bathroom. The silence was peaceful and soothing with both of them deep in their own thoughts, fighting their own demons. Valerie stopped washing and grabbed a towel drying her hands. Looking over at Tony, she softly whispered, "I'm so sorry, but I just can't do this anymore."

Opening his eyes, he watched as she left the room and him to his world. He felt that he was now feeling, a small part of the pain and loneliness, that Sherri must feel every day, since witnessing those killings. He knew the sight of Paul, would haunt him from now and forever.

CHAPTER 16

✿

After making sure Justine was all right, and filling out the report at the hospital, Daikon made his way to the station. Finding the staff sergeant and filing his report, Daikon went to find, Captain Hal Harris. Captain Harris wasn't a tall man, but his build was often compared to that of a bulldog. His short solid body, often reminded Daikon of the mafia muscle men, in the movies. Daikon found Captain Harris sitting in his office, with two other men, that Daikon had never seen before. Seeing that he was busy, Daikon turned to leave, but it was too late, Harris had spotted him.

"Detective Daikon, would you come in here please?" The deep gravelly voice, made sure it was known that this was not a request, but rather an order. Daikon stopped and raised his eyebrows, thinking how close he had made it, to getting out. Turning, he walked into the office.

"This is quite a fortunate coincidence. These two men, have actually been waiting for you." Harris indicated to the two men seated against the wall. Daikon looked over at them and nodded a greeting, then looked back at Harris. "They are from the FBI and think that you might have some information, in regards to that lady everyone has been looking for. Now, I have informed them that that is impossible, as you haven't been working on that case. Isn't that so Detective Daikon?"

Daikon's legs suddenly felt very weak. It was only a matter of minutes, before Harris was going to find out what happened earlier that day, and now the FBI.

"Captain, can I talk to you for a minute, privately?"

"Why? Have you got something to hide?" one of the agents blurted out. Daikon didn't even respond, but kept his gaze focused on Harris.

"If you gentlemen would step outside for a moment, please. We will be right with you." Harris said to the two agents.

"Wait a minute if this has anything to do with this case, we will be in on the meeting." The one agent stood up defiantly.

"And you will be. But you are in my house now and I am not going to ask you again. Will you please, step outside for a minute, or I can arrange for you to step out of this station for a hell of a lot longer." Harris was keeping his voice calm, but the authority of it reverberated with every word he spoke.

The two agents glanced at each other, then slowly walked out. The one agent making a point of coming close enough to Daikon, so as to bump into him. After they left and closed the door behind them, Daikon collapsed his body in one of the chairs and let out a huge sigh.

"Ok, what the hell is going on?" Harris demanded.

Daikon sat there rubbing his sweating palms on his knees. He proceeded to tell the captain what had happened, without telling him everything. He felt it was best, that he didn't let anyone know that he was going to have a meeting with Sherri. As he told the story, at times he wasn't even sure Harris was listening. Harris just sat there, staring at Daikon and not showing any emotion. As Daikon finished his tale, both men sat there with their eyes locked on each other.

"Now, just so I know that I heard you right. You're telling me, that there is one of our cars parked in some bushes on a remote mountain logging road, one of my officers is in the hospital with a bullet in her and there are three dead bodies laying out in the woods, in an area where a murder investigation has been going on?" Harris's voice was so calm, that it sounded eerie, causing goose bumps to form on Daikon's arms.

"Yes sir, that pretty much sums it up."

"That sums it up? He sits there and all he can say is, that sums it up. Are you out of your fucking mind?" Harris's voice was no longer calm. The veins in his neck were starting to protrude and his eyes took on a dark glare. "Is Hasker going to be ok, or am I going to be dealing with another corpse here?"

"She's going to be fine. It was only a shoulder wound."

"Lucky for you." Daikon felt like melting into the chair. "What the hell were you thinking, going out there? Were you not told to leave this alone? Christ, this isn't your investigation, now there is going to be all kinds of assholes, like those two, sticking their noses into this. You'll be lucky if you're still on the force after this, and there isn't much I can do to help."

Daikon could feel his face turn red. He was a good cop and wasn't going to have his job threatened for doing something that he felt was right.

"I'm just trying to find some answers myself." He retorted. "Like, why are we holding back so much information on those killings? If anyone wants to threaten me with my job, then I'm sure the public would be interested in the whole story." In what seemed like a blink of an eye, Harris was standing over him, with his face just inches from Daikon's.

"Don't you ever, think about doing something that stupid. This is not our concern anymore and it's out of our hands. If this leaks out and I have any kind of suspicion that you had anything to do with it, I will wipe my hands clean of you, and you will face the consequences on your own. That is not a threat, but a promise." Before Daikon could say anything further, Harris went and opened the door inviting the two agents back in the office.

"Detective Daikon, this is Agent Reid and I'm, Agent Williams." One of the agents said. As he looked at them, he wasn't sure if he was going to be able to tell them apart. They both wore the same black suit and black skinny tie. Their shoes were polished and their hair was cut short and slicked back on their skulls.

"What can I do for you gentlemen?" Daikon asked, letting the contempt roll off his tongue. The local police never did like the FBI, or any other government agency, sticking their arrogant noses into their affairs.

"We have reason to believe, that you may have information as to where our suspect might be hiding."

"Well nice try, but wrong guy, gentlemen. I don't have a clue." He wasn't lying, as Tony had never revealed where he was keeping Sherri, and for the first time he was glad that he didn't know.

"Do you deny, that you've been having meetings with a reporter by the name of Tony Parkins?"

"No, I don't deny it. He is doing an article on the logger's murders and I am giving him background information. Nothing out of the ordinary."

"And he has never mentioned that he knows where the lady is hiding?"

How did they know that Tony knew where she was? Alarms went off in his head. "Not that I can recall." He answered looking straight into the eyes of the questioning agent.

"We have it on good authority, that he is keeping her hidden somewhere. Are you sure he has never mentioned her where abouts?"

"Like I said before, not that I can recall."

The agents looked at each other than back at him. "If he does, or the next time you have a meeting with him, we would like to be informed."

"Yeah, you bet. Anything to help out a fellow law enforcement officer."

"Would it be possible to talk to the shot detective." Agent Reid asked.

Daikon immediately jumped in. "She needs her rest cap. She's pretty weak. By the time we got her to the hospital, she had lost quite a bit of blood. Now, I want to know how you know about her being there?"

"Everyone in the station is talking about it. You did file a report."

He turned back to Harris. "I'll check with the doctor and let you know." The two agents seemed satisfied with that, then briskly left the office.

As Tony dried himself off, after climbing out of the bath, he stood naked and motionless for quite some time. He felt as though he was exposed to the world, alone and he didn't care. How life could change so fast. The feeling that things had taken a sudden and unbelievable turn between Valerie and him, gripped at his stomach. One second there seemed to be love and support, now only to be replaced with loneliness. He thought about his failed marriage, his up and down career and the sight of Paul, laying still and calm on a bed of leaves. Without warning, he vomited into the bathroom sink. The memory was just too much for him and he knew that it would be for awhile. He needed a Crown Royal, and he needed it now. It was time to call TNT, and make sure Cats was all right. He also had to break the news to them, about Paul. He headed for the stairs to go and use the phone. Walking out into the living room, he suddenly felt very awkward and out of place being there. Valerie was sitting at the kitchen table and didn't look up.

"Is it all right if I use the phone?" he asked.

"Yes, of course." She answered, now looking at him, and he could see the shine was gone from her eyes. He felt his stomach start to turn and he headed down the stairs, in an attempt to focus on the task at hand. As the phone rang on the other end, he sat there numb waiting for a voice to answer.

"Hello?" it was TNT.

"Hi, it's Tony. How's Cats?"

"She is here with her parents." He reassured him.

That was a relief, at least something worked out. "Terrence, I have some bad news."

"It truly must be. You haven't called me Terrence in, God, I can't even recall. What's happening?"

"Damn, I don't know how to say this but, Paul's dead." He fought the sickening feeling that was returning to his stomach.

"What! How in the hell did it happen?"

"When we went out to the crime scene, to get photos and have a look around. We were with a couple of police officers and when we came out onto the road, these two men started shooting at us. The one officer got shot in the shoulder and Paul got shot in the head. We had no warning, whatsoever."

"Did they catch them? The ones that were shooting at you? Did they get any information from them, as to why they did or who they are?"

"Yeah, they got them all right. But they aren't going to be answering any questions. Killed both the bastards." If Tony didn't know better, he would have swore he heard TNT let out a sigh of relief on the other end. "Is Cats there? I need to talk to her?"

"You bet. Do you want me to break the news to her?"

He wanted so badly to say yes, but knew it was him who had to do it. "No, that's all right, I'll do it. But thanks, all the same."

He could hear the phone being placed down and TNT's footsteps fading away. Moments later Cats voice came on and he just felt like sitting there, listening to it.

"Hi you. Long time no hear. What's been going on up there? Tony, you wouldn't believe what's been happening here. It's a nightmare. I couldn't talk to you on the phone before, because I had two men in my apartment monitoring my calls. I'm so sorry, I wanted to warn you. Are you and Paul all right? I've been so worried."

His mouth felt dry and stagnant. He could feel his pulse racing and his hands started to shake. Gripping the phone tight, to help himself keep control, he took a deep breath.

"My God, Cats, I don't know how to tell you this. Paul is dead. He was shot this afternoon."

"Oh my God! Please tell me you're lying. This can't be true." The room was spinning around her. Dropping to her knees, she fought the vertigo, so as not to pass out. She was having trouble catching her breath and her mind suddenly seemed unable to grasp and hang onto any thought.

"I'm so sorry Cats. Are you going to be ok?"

"How?"

Tony went over the events, yet once again. He tried his best to avoid going into too much detail, trying not to expose her to all the horror, of that afternoon. He wanted to be there for her more than anything, right at that point. Not only for her, but for himself also. As he finished filling her in, the phone line was quiet, except for the sound of Cats, sobbing. He could hear TNT softly talking to her, as he helped her up off the floor and onto a chair.

"Tony it's me." TNT was back on the line. "Listen, I'm coming up there this evening, I'll be at the same hotel, you were staying at."

Tony was going to say no, but the support would be very much appreciated. He was feeling extremely alone and knew that there was a lot of work ahead of him.

"Ok, sounds good to me. Would be nice to see a familiar face. Make sure Cats is ok, I think this has hit her real hard."

"You know I will. You take care of yourself and I'll get there as soon as I can."

Tony hung the receiver up and sat in quiet. He had one more person to tell and that was going to be the hardest one of all. Sherri had developed a bond with Paul, and Tony was extremely worried about what this news was going to do to her. As he sat there contemplating how to proceed, he suddenly remembered the folder he had gotten from Justine. With a new focus, he jumped up and quickly made his way out to the car. He went to the kitchen table and sat down opening the retrieved folder. He went over the organized files. She categorized each bundle of files, under headings such as environmental groups, logging operations and one called common thread. This last one seemed to interest him the most. He went directly for it and began reading. On the papers in this folder, she had the names of the individuals and the companies or organizations they belonged to and in what capacity. There were the names of major business people and politicians. After reading the page on one of the local politicians, he turned the page and there in bold print was the name of Terrence Tibbet. He began reading the information under his heading. As his eyes slowly scrolled down the page, it fought to absorb what was printed on them. But the confusion and disbelief wouldn't allow it to happen. It seemed as if TNT, was in some way directly involved with environmental organizations or else in a CEO position with different logging groups. This wasn't making any sense to him. He closed the folder and tried to sort out what he had just read. He was seriously thinking of calling TNT again, to see what this was all about. That would have to wait though, as Sherri walked into the kitchen rubbing her eyes, Valerie close behind her. Tony's stomach did a quick flip and his hands began to sweat.

"Oh, did I ever need that nap." She said, pulling out a chair at the table and sitting down. Tony glanced up at Valerie and saw her shaking her head in a no motion. "So, how did things go up there today?" she asked, looking at Tony. He noticed she was clutching her hands together and moving them in a ringing motion. His hands once again started shaking and suddenly he had to jump up and dash to the sink as he got sick. Sherri stared at him and then at Valerie.

"What's wrong? What's going on?" Sherri frantically asked, starting to rise out of her chair.

Tony rinsed his mouth out and splashed cold water on his face. He let the water run for a few seconds, to wash the inside of the sink clean. Slowly, he turned around and leaned on the kitchen counter for support. Inhaling as much air as he could, he stared at Valerie, who had moved over to be beside Sherri, and then he placed his eyes on Sherri's.

"I have some very bad news." He started slowly. "There is no easy way to put this, so I'm just going to say it, because I won't lie to you. Paul got killed this afternoon." Even as the words were leaving his mouth, he could feel his stomach turn once again. Still staring into Sherri's eyes, he could see the disbelief in them. She quickly glanced over to Valerie then back at Tony. In a surprisingly calm voice she quietly asked him how. Tony made his way over to the table and sat down beside her, as once again he relived the story. When he finished, Sherri sat there quietly, staring down at the floor. Slowly, she lifted her head and peered into Tony's eyes. He saw the pain and hurt that was in them. She reached over and grabbed his hand, giving it a gentle squeeze. Then wrapping their arms around each other, both allowed the tears to flow as if to wash the pain away. After the tears stopped, nothing was said as the three of them sat there, in the kitchen in total silence. After a while Valerie got up and went to the sink and stared out the kitchen window. Tony got up and poured himself a Crown Royal on the rocks. Grabbing the folder from the table, he decided to wait until he saw TNT that night, to ask him to make sense of all of this. He left the two women in the kitchen and found himself a place in the living room to be with his own thoughts.

H e wasn't sure when he had slipped into sleep, or for how long, but he woke with a start. Picking himself up off the sofa, he walked out to the kitchen where Sherri was still seated, gazing at the small television.

"How long have I been snoozing?" he asked, rubbing his hand over his face, trying to wake up.

"Not sure, I haven't been paying much attention."

"Is Valerie around?" he asked, looking down the hall.

"No, she got a phone call and said she had to go see a friend. She told me she would be back in a couple of hours."

Tony checked the time and saw that it had been a few hours, since he had talked to TNT. He picked up the phone in the kitchen and dialed the Travelers Eight Motel, to see if TNT had checked in yet. He was told that reservations had been made, but that they hadn't checked in as of yet.

"They? Who else is checked in with him?"

"There was a room reserved for Mr. Tibbet and one for a Catherine Montgomery."

Tony hung the phone up, not believing that TNT would bring Cats up to this. Feeling angry, he slammed his hand against the wall and heard Sherri jump behind him.

"I'm sorry." He said, spinning around to see her standing by the table, looking at him with big round eyes. "It's ok. Really, just getting very frustrated." He reassured her. She slowly lowered herself back into the chair and placed her attention once more on the television.

"So, how are you doing?" he softly asked her.

She just shrugged her shoulders and continued staring at the screen, not even looking up. There was some kind of game show on, that tested your knowledge on trivia.

"Ok, I guess. Things sure have gotten out of hand, haven't they. I am so, so sorry about Paul. I can't help but feel that it's my fault. I still don't know why this is happening and why to me? I have always lived my life with the attitude of respecting everybody and everything. Joining, Nature's Select, was my way of getting involved and trying to help the world in a small way. Is that something to be punished for? Because I sure do feel like I'm punished for something. I mean, I have been trying and trying to figure out what brought this on. Was it something I said or did? All I keep coming up with is a total blank. Who would want to kill people, just because they don't agree with you? That's not what it was all about. If anything, it was about preserving life, not ending it."

Tony sat silently and listened. He knew that she was finally letting out a lot of built up frustration out and it was good for her to talk it out. Besides, he needed to just listen for a change, as he didn't seem to have much to say anymore. He had retold the story of Paul's death so many times now, that he didn't care if he talked to anyone at all for awhile.

"I remember when I first joined Nature's Select. There was a road being built to connect the highway to a planned acreage subdivision. There was an alternate route that could have been used, but would have cost the developer more money in construction and government fees. The only problem with the intended route, was that it would have destroyed a creek that was used by fish for spawning. We protested and fought them every inch of the way, until they decided that to continue fighting was going to cost them more money, than if they were to change the direction of the road. That creek is still being used by the fish today and the people are getting to their homes in the subdivision. Not to mention that they have a beautiful creek to enjoy. That got me started and I have never looked back. Now it just all seems like a dream. What happened along the way?"

Tony wished he had answer for that. If he had the answers, maybe he could have stopped all this senseless killing, saved his marriage and he might even still be on top of his career. No, he didn't have any of the answers, just the questions.

"I don't know. I really don't know." He answered quietly and help-lessly.

They both sat there quiet and returned their attention to the game show. One of the contestants was answering the bonus question and had wagered all the winnings he had made up to that point. As Tony watched the man wait in anticipation to see if his answer was correct, his mind continued to rummage through the information he had read in the folder. He was feeling very uncomfortable, with the conclusion he was coming up with. The loud cheer from the crowd on the television brought his attention back to the screen. He watched as the man jumped up and down in one spot, with a smile that spread from one side of his face to the other. It felt good to see someone have something happen nice to them. After all the pain he had witnessed over the last couple of days, he needed to see something positive again. They sat and watched till the end of the show, neither one of them saying anything. When it was over, Tony got up and decided to give Daikon a call to see how Justine was doing.

He wasn't able to reach him at the precinct, so decided to try him at home. After a couple of tries, he figured Daikon must have gone up to the hospital to see Justine. He would try again later, but in the mean time he felt as though he should stay close to Sherri, until Valerie got back. He had to talk to TNT and he had to talk to Daikon. Something wasn't fitting together and he didn't like it. The answers were out there, close, and he felt that they lay with TNT. Heading back into the kitchen, he noticed that Sherri was no longer at the table and a twinge of panic snapped at his stomach. He walked swiftly down the hall and checked in both the bathroom and bedrooms. When he didn't locate her in any of the rooms, he ran for the door to see if he could catch her before she got too far. As he reached the top of the stairs leading to the front door, he saw her lying on the sofa. Stopping hard, he looked over at her and dropped his head. He was feeling relieved and silly at the same time.

"What's the matter with you?" Sherri asked. "You think you're the only one around here that is allowed to lay down on the sofa?" With that she rolled over so that her back was facing him and snuggled up close to the back of the sofa. Relieved, Tony walked into the kitchen and poured himself another drink. Things were going to get even crazier than they already were and he just hoped he was ready for the outcome. As the backdoor flung open, he almost lost his grip on the glass. Regaining his composure, he looked up and saw Valerie place two grocery bags on the kitchen counter. She looked exhausted and he knew that sooner or later they were going to have to talk about this.

CHAPTER 17

"Yes, they checked in about half an hour ago." The receptionist informed Tony. "I'll transfer you to Mr. Tibbet's room now."

The word, they, still ate at Tony. Cats should not be here, he didn't need to worry about another person.

"Finally made it." TNT sounded tired. "Traffic was incredibly busy out there. And slow!"

"Why did you bring Cats up here? I've got enough worries on my head right now." Tony cut in. He didn't have the time or patience for pleasantries right now.

"Well, I'm glad to talk to you to. If anybody should know her, you should. She wouldn't take no for an answer and what was I suppose to do, tie her up? You know how stubborn she can get. When she sets her mind to something, she is gonna do it."

Tony did know that, all too well. If TNT hadn't have brought her, she would have probably come up on her own. As soon as he had a chance to see her, he would convince her it wasn't safe and get her to leave.

"Listen, why don't you give us a bit to settle in, then I'll buy dinner. We can talk about what's been going on. I want to check with the police to see what they've got on those murdering bastards that killed Paul. So, how are you holding up?"

"I'm ok. Is Cats there?"

"No, she's in her room. Room two thirteen. If you want to give her a call she would love to hear from you."

"Yes, I probably will."

"Is the lady doing ok?"

"It has been real rough on her, but she seems to be one tough lady. I better go, so I'll call you in a few hours then?"

"Perfect. Talk to you then."

Tony hung the phone up and walked into the living room where Valerie and Sherri were sitting on the sofa, engaged in conversation. He sat down in a recliner, the type with the big pillowy arms and cushions. It exhumed comfort. The two women stopped talking and turned to him with expectant faces.

"Well, we will soon have answers and hopefully some kind of an end to this." He said watching them.

"I am so sorry about everything." Sherri said as her eyes once again began to fill with tears. "I should have just turned myself in to the police and maybe Paul would still be alive." Valerie put her arm around her as she broke down in tears.

"You wouldn't have been safe doing that. Until we find out exactly what's going on here, I think you did the right thing. It wasn't your fault Paul got killed. I think we were in the wrong place, at the wrong time. Now, it's up to us to make sure he didn't die for nothing." Tony knew it wasn't just a matter of being in the wrong place, but he didn't want Sherri to beat herself up over it.

As he sat there looking at the two women, he shook his head at how things had taken them on an uncontrollable rollercoaster ride. This was supposed to be just another assignment, but turned out to be a struggle to stay alive. Looking at Valerie, he wondered how he could have been so wrong about her. He was so sure that after the night they had been chased and with everything else they had been through, that what they felt for each other would have become stronger. Yet, with her it seemed to turn her in a different direction and in a quick way, as if everything before didn't even matter. He picked himself up out from the chair and headed downstairs to try Daikon and Cats.

"Detective Daikon here. How can I help?" Tony picked up on the irritated tone in his voice immediately.

"Hi there. I have been trying to get in touch with you, but figured you might have been up at the hospital. How is Justine doing? Is she going to be ok?"

"Yeah, she's going to be fine. There are a couple of FBI puppets here, snooping around now and they want to plug her with questions. I think I've managed to hold them off for awhile, anyway. So, what are the chances of me seeing this lady now?"

"I'll set something up for tomorrow."

"Good. Listen, I need you to come in and file a report on what happened out there. Maybe you could do that this afternoon, if you don't mind? My captain is some pissed at me right now, so we're going to have to do things by the book for a bit."

"Not a problem. I'll be there in a couple of hours. I read that file Justine gave me and there is something I want to go over with you. If my suspicions are even close to being correct, this whole thing is like something out of a Hollywood conspiracy thriller. I don't believe it myself and yet everything seems to be pointing in that direction. I'll have to fill you in later."

The phone was quiet for awhile before Daikon slowly answered. "I think we may be heading in the same direction, with our thinking. See you in a couple of hours then."

Hanging up the phone, Tony dialed the Travellers Eight Motel and asked for room two thirteen. After a couple of rings, Cats answered sounding very fatigued.

"Tony, how are you?" her tone picking up immediately upon hearing his voice.

"I'm ok. What are you doing here?" he started on her right away. "It's not safe right now. I sure wish you would go back, so that I wouldn't have to worry about you on top of everything else."

"And do what, sit around waiting, maybe getting another phone call informing me that this time you were the one that got shot? Not on your life."

He knew it was pointless arguing with her. He had heard that tone far too many times before. He did want to see her very much though, just to be around someone he could be comfortable with and draw support from. She had always done that for him.

"Listen, I have to head over to the police station in a couple of hours to file a report. Interested in joining me? After we can go somewhere and have a drink."

"Would love to. TNT was talking about stopping by there, want me to see if he wants to join us?"

"Sure, why not. He did offer to buy us dinner, so it would be the least we could do. I'll swing by and pick you up in front of the motel. I'll call you just before I leave here."

"All right, sounds good. Thanks for not pushing too hard, about me leaving."

"Would it have done any good?"

"No." Was her only answer except for the hanging up of the phone.

Tony headed upstairs and asked Valerie if he could use her car once more. Handing him the keys, she stopped short of placing them in his hand and looked up into his eyes.

"Tony, I am truly sorry about this. It's just that I can't go on like this. I used to have a normal life and that's pretty much all I ever wanted. I guess I got caught up in the excitement of the cloak and dagger fantasy you provided. But this is no fantasy. You know, I would do anything for you that I could, but I would really appreciate it if you and Sherri could leave as soon as possible."

Tony reached out and took the keys that were still in her shaking hand. Grasping the keys in his hand and studying her face, he knew that he couldn't, or wouldn't be upset with her. After all, how could anyone expect to put up with this? People were being killed around her at a regular pace and nobody seemed any closer to knowing why, or by whose hands.

"Just give me till the end of tomorrow, then we'll be out of here." He assured her with a smile. Stepping closer, he gave her a kiss and held her tight whispering in her ear, "Thank you, for everything. I'll never forget you. You are and always will be very special to me."

Quickly, he turned and made his way out the front door to the waiting car. As he pulled up to the motel, he smiled at the sight of Cats and TNT. Seeing familiar friendly faces, gave his spirit a boost. Cats started waving and smiling as soon as she recognized him in a car. He couldn't seem to get out of the car fast enough, wanting to be near her.

"God, I am so glad you're ok." She exclaimed, as they parted after holding on to each other for awhile.

"And that goes for me to." TNT said holding out his hand. Tony took it in his and shook it so hard that TNT asked him to at least leave his elbow connected. After a few excited and hurried questions and answers they climbed in the car and headed for the police station.

"I guess the FBI have gotten involved with this now." Tony informed them.

"Well, it's about time." TNT snorted. "The local police haven't been doing much from what I can see."

"Now that seems to be the strange thing. It's like their hands are being tied and for some unknown reason, they are not allowing the whole story to come out."

"So, no one else other than the local authorities, those few that were out there and you, really know what happened out there?" TNT asked slowly, making the hairs on the back of Tony's neck rise.

Looking in the rearview mirror he could see TNT's eyes boring into the back of his head. "That's right, that is the strange part of this. You wouldn't have any idea who would have that much authority, or power to silence the police, would you?" Tony asked him.

"I wouldn't think anyone would." TNT answered.

Soon they were pulling up in front of the station. Walking in, Tony asked to see Daikon. He was pointed down a short hall formed by cubicles, and told he could find him in the third one on the left. They found him with the telephone receiver squeezed between his cheek and his shoulder, with his two index fingers slowly seeking and pecking at the keys on his computer. When Daikon saw them standing there, he immediately informed whoever was on the other end that an emergency had just come up and that he would have to transfer them to another officer. Pressing a button on his telephone, he informed another officer there was a call waiting for him on line two.

"Glad you made it." He said standing and shaking Tony's hand, while his eyes never left Cats. Smiling, Tony introduced everyone.

"So, I hear the FBI are investigating these grizzly murders also." TNT asked immediately, after the small talk was over.

"Yeah, they're here sticking their noses in, bothering everyone." Daikon answered nonchalantly.

"Well, personally I think it's a good thing; them getting involved. Perhaps we'll find out what's going on around here." Tony looked quickly at Daikon and gave him an apologetic look along with a shrug of his shoulders.

"If you want, I can arrange for you to talk to your super heroes and see just what they have found out."

"I would appreciate that."

"All right then." Daikon turned to Cats and Tony; "I'll be right back in just a few minutes. Please have a seat." Turning, he asked TNT to follow him and they headed off.

"What's up with TNT?" Cats asked. "He just doesn't seem to be himself and I can't help but get this, this…oh, I don't know how to explain it. It's like an uneasy feeling when he looks at me sometimes. I've never felt uncomfortable around him before."

"I know what you're saying, but there is something I want you and Daikon to look at later. I think it will explain a lot. I'm not really sure, but things are definitely not the way they look around here."

"What do you mean?" Before Tony could answer, Daikon appeared back at the cubicle.

"Quite the jovial one that one." He said, raising his eyebrows in TNT's direction. "He's in the captain's office with the FBI agents. What does he do? It was strange, but the way they greeted each other, it seemed like they knew one another."

"I guess you could say, he's semi retired. Don't think the old boy will ever actually retire." Tony said. "He was the man who founded the *Garibaldi Daily Newspaper.*"

"Guess he must meet a lot of different people." Daikon shrugged. "Well come on and follow me, we'll get that report filed, then get out of here so we can talk."

It sounded like a good idea to Tony and soon him and Cats were following Daikon down a hallway passing by small offices. The sound of phones ringing and keyboards being pecked away on, made him long for the comfort of the newsroom again. They came around a corner and he could see a glass window, where TNT and two other men were in conversation, with all three of them shaking their heads in agreement. As they approached closer to the window, Cats froze and gripped Tony's arm, spinning him so hard he almost fell to the floor.

"What the hell?" he said as he regained his balance. A few people looked up to see what the fuss about, but no one took much notice. Cats face was white and her fingernails were cutting into his arm.

"What's wrong? Jesus, ease up on the arm." Tony could see the fear in her eyes.

"That's them." Was all she said.

Daikon had stopped ahead blocking the view from the office window out to where Tony and Cats were standing.

"Who's them?" Daikon demanded.

"The men, that were holding me and threatening my parents."

Both men turned and looked at the scene behind the glass window. One man had both hands thrown up and was walking away. TNT seemed agitated and was shaking his finger at him. Then he turned and jammed his finger into the chest of the other agent, who seemed to be very submissive.

"Are you absolutely positive?" Daikon asked.

"Yes." She snapped, as she tried to conceal herself behind Tony.

Tony's mind was racing. He wanted to charge into the office and demand answers. The tugging on his arm from Cats kept him aware that they had to make a move out of there. Daikon had already turned and was pushing them back. Tony could see the movement in the office and realized that they had been spotted. Quickly, he spun on his heels and grabbed Cats, hurrying her down the hall. Passing by the desks and bodies that occupied them, he could see the exit door. As they reached it, he shot a quick glance behind him to see how close they were, but there was no sign of anyone pursuing them. He could see Daikon, TNT and Captain Harris standing at the end of the hall and it looked like Daikon was getting a royal butt chewing. What bothered Tony, was that the two agents were nowhere to be seen.

Tony and Cats ran to the car and sped out of the parking lot. He dodged in and out of traffic, racing to get to Valerie's place. Cats sat there, just looking out the window showing no emotion.

"We've got to get Sherri and get her out of town." Tony exclaimed.

"Tell me this isn't happening." Cats pleaded. "Do you really think TNT is involved with these people? I'm so confused."

"I wish I could tell you it isn't, but it is. I was going to talk to TNT, but I guess I don't have to anymore. I was given a file on the Enviro Magna company and the holding company that it operates under. Along with that, it had all the subsidiary companies and their main people. There is a group of very powerful people from all over the world, that are either directly or indirectly connected, not only to it, but also to the governing body for the logging industry here. Now, what doesn't make sense is, why would you finance and run a group that is trying hard to prevent logging, and yet run and finance a group that makes its living from logging? And what do people from other parts of the world and from totally different walks of life, be doing involved with logging or environmental groups. I'll let you have a look at the file when we get back to the house. Right now, the main thing is to get everyone safe." He only wished he knew where that place would be. He slowed the car down as he pulled onto Valerie's street and calmly turned into her driveway, so as not to arouse any curiosity from the neighbors.

He did a quick introduction with Cats and gave a shortened explanation of what happened and emphasized the necessity of them leaving immediately. With the ladies behind him, he quickly moved down the stairs and opened the door. The three women stopped suddenly. Tony stepped out into the doorway, only to see a man with a gun pointed at them and stepping into the house. It was one of the agents from the police station.

"Going somewhere?" The agent asked, as he closed the door behind him. "I think we'll all just stay here for awhile and wait. I do believe some people want to come over and visit. They have a lot of questions, so let's just go back upstairs and make ourselves comfortable." He motioned upwardly with the gun, his eyes constantly scanning the four people standing in front of him. Once they were all in the living room, he had them sit down on the sofa and he sat in the recliner, never taking the barrel of the raised gun off of them.

"Who are you people and what is it you want?" demanded Tony.

"Your questions will be answered soon enough and so will ours. Now, why don't you just sit back, shut up and make yourself comfortable. Nice to see you again Cats. How's your parents?" he asked mockingly.

"Why don't you put the gun down dirtbag and we'll discuss how her parents are doing." Tony snarled, his blood feeling like it was boiling.

"You obviously don't listen very well. I said sit back and shut up. You are of no interest to us, so it really wouldn't bother me to take care of you right here and now." He said moving forward in the recliner and bringing the gun to Tony's eye level.

Cats grabbed Tony's arm and pulled him back. "Please." She pleaded him.

"It's me you want, isn't it?" Sherri cut in. "Well, you've got me now, let these people go. They know nothing and quite frankly, neither do I."

"A little late to let anyone go now, my dear. I must say you have been an illusive one."

They heard the door open and a voice called out, "Reid?"

"Yeah, come on in. We're up here, all cozy." He called back.

All eyes were on the stairs as the footsteps made their way to the top. First came the other agent that Tony and Cats had seen in the captain's office, then slowly the silver gray crown of TNT's head, rose above the banister. As he reached the top, TNT looked over the four sitting on the sofa, then without any recognition to either Tony or Cats, turned his attention to the agent he had come in with.

"Well done Williams. It's about time something started to go right around here. Has our man here been notified?"

"Yes sir. I called him on my way back to pick you up."

"Terrence, what the hell is going on?" Tony yelled at him.

"Relax my friend. We'll have our chance to talk soon enough. Right now, I would seriously recommend that you sit there and not say anything. It will truly benefit your well being." TNT's eyes were cold and hard as he looked at Tony.

"You prick." Tony breathed.

"I guess, I've been called worse." He said without looking at Tony, as he made his way over to the recliner. "Would you mind?" TNT was standing over Reid, who was still seated in the recliner.

"Sorry." Reid replied and hurriedly climbed out of the comfortable chair allowing TNT to replace him.

"Well my dear, you have certainly caused us some serious problems. I must commend you on your ability to evade my obviously over paid people." He smiled at Sherri.

"Now who are you?" he asked as his gaze fell upon Valerie.

"This is my house." She timidly answered. "Please don't hurt us. I won't say anything to anyone. Plea…"

TNT raised a hand and she cut her voice off short, as she sank back into the sofa in fear.

"My dear, some things in life are just too enormous for any of us to control. Sometimes sacrifices must be made, to obtain an ultimate goal." TNT calmly said in his sonorous voice.

"What goddamn goal is worth all these lives that have been lost?" Tony wasn't sitting back in the sofa anymore, but rather on the edge, challengingly with Reid and Williams closely watching him.

"It is a goal that has been pursued over the centuries and only a very select few, are allowed the privilege to obtain it. Some come close, but in the end they are not willing to commit wholly, to obtain it. It is those few that do acquire it, that are willing to give all of themselves, to obtain the final goal."

"What? There is nothing that is worth the sacrifice of human life. Especially, the life of someone who considered you a friend." Cats yelled at him, her face had turned a bright red with anger.

"You are referring to Paul. Yes, that was most tragic and definitely not the direction in which I would have liked to see it go." TNT hesitated for a moment, as if to reflect. "What goal you ask? What is the one thing man strives for more than money? Immortality you might say. Even though that is a contemplative thought, I really don't think that anyone wants to live forever, putting up with all of this world's crap. Not to mention that it is unobtainable. No, the ultimate goal for any man, or ladies, is ultimate power. The power to decide the fate of how the world will be. To form and mold it into a perfect, living environment with everything operating in a controlled balance."

He stopped for awhile and let what he had said settle into the thoughts of those seated in front of him. Their faces reflected exactly what was running through their minds.

"Mad? Yes maybe, but none the less, still a goal that has been and will be strived for until it is achieved."

"My God." Was all that came out of Cats.

"How the hell can killing some loggers and trying to kill us acquire world power for you and your insane group?" Tony snapped at him. "Those killings were done in total waste!"

"Oh, this is such a small part of the whole scene Tony." TNT answered as he settled back into the recliner, like a professor about to engage some eager students. "In the big scheme of things, this will go unnoticed. What happened here was but a small balance struggle that we had to take care of. Our struggle has gone on for centuries and will, for a few more before we acquire our final goal. You see, we have most of the control on the world's events already. We decide if there is going to be a fuel shortage, who will be at war at any one time, if there will be a deadly outbreak of some virus somewhere. It is up to us to keep the world appearing as if it is running on it's own destiny, until we are in position to take complete and total control of it. This was but one more show that we had to put on. Logging versus those who try to protect our beautiful forests. You see, it gives people something to stand behind and keeps them occupied believing they are making a difference, while we can carry on virtually unnoticed. People pay in support of both groups and we reap the benefits, it all goes in the same pocket. Those loggers were to die and our little friend here was to die with them. When the police found her dead, along with the loggers, the public would be horrified at the environmentalist groups. The police would have reported it to the public in such a way, as to make it look as though the environmentalists had committed the murders, and the outcry would have started. You see the public opinion has swayed too far in the direction of the environmental groups and it's my job to balance it out. Unfortunately we allowed some incompetent people to handle the situation and it got all out of hand. If the public had been leaning too far toward the logging industry, I would have had it balanced out the other way."

He stopped there and asked Reid if he would get him a glass of water. Turning back to his captive audience, he looked at each one as if to emphasize what he had just told them.

"Why did you argue with Jason so hard to have me come up and do the story on this? I would have exposed the whole thing. This isn't making any sense." Tony was staring at TNT in disbelief at what he had just heard.

"Oh, Jason didn't want you to do the story, that is true, but that's not what we were arguing about. We were arguing, because I know you are the best reporter they have and I figured you were my best bet in finding our friend here. I told Jason that the story would not go to print until I had a chance to review your findings first. He took extreme offense to that. Said I was stepping on his toes and making him look bad to everyone. After all, he his the chief editor."

"And what was to become of me once I found Sherri?"

"Well my friend, all I can say is we're back to that sacrifice thing I was talking about." Tony could feel his face turning red with anger, at the pompous nonchalant attitude of TNT. Turning his attention to Cats, TNT continued, "Catherine, I truly did hope that you could have been spared, but you were so persistent in coming. Don't worry about your parents. They will be well taken care of. I will provide well for them and they will look upon me as a close friend and savior."

"You bastard!" she screamed, as she leapt from the sofa, only to be met with a blow to the side of the head from one of the men standing over them. Tony immediately started to rise, but sat back as the barrel of the gun pressed hard against his forehead.

"Help her back up." TNT ordered Williams. Reid stood guard over the three on the sofa, while Williams helped her back onto the sofa. A small trickle of blood ran down the side of her face.

Once again, the door opened and Deric appeared at the top of the stairs. Tony felt his stomach flip and all the blood drain from his face.

"I do believe you two know each other." TNT said, looking first at Deric then at Tony. An uncomfortable silence followed. "Well, no matter, we're all here now."

"How did you find us here?" Tony finally asked.

"Very simple. When Cats said you were coming to pick us up at the motel, I phoned and had Mr. Reid here wait for you. He did a run on the license plate of the car you were driving and got the address. I knew sooner or later you would be returning to wherever this lovely was." He indicated towards Sherri. "Then you showed up at the station, all they had to do was to follow you. Well, unfortunately our time together is almost over. Normally, I would leave at this point, but so many things have gone wrong lately, that this time I believe I will stay to make sure it is finished right."

TNT and Tony locked onto each other's eyes and for the first time in all the years Tony had known this man, he was seeing someone he had never seen before. Even his facial features seemed to have changed, as Tony looked at him differently now. Maybe understanding what was going on through Tony's mind, TNT smiled and gave him a nod, then turned and quickly whispered something to Williams.

CHAPTER 18

"**A**re you sure you're up to this?" Daikon asked, as they sped down the highway.

"Just drive." Justine answered, short and to the point.

Valerie and Sherri were holding each other's hands tight. Sherri just stared off across the room, not believing this was the way it was going to end, after everything she had been through. She thought of Frank and how happy they had been together that night. She knew deep inside, that he had felt it too. At least it was going to end, she thought to herself. It gave her a sense of calm. Valerie sobbed uncontrollably, and pleaded for her life. At times, she had even offered herself to the men, if they would spare her life. It just fell on deaf ears. Now she hung onto the hand that was gripping hers and silently prayed. Cats sat straight on the sofa and kept looking around the room. Her eyes following the men and the preparations they were making. Valerie and Sherri were to be killed in the house. It was to look like a burglary and murder. One of the men had jokingly suggested that they get a little something from the women and make it look like a rape. TNT exploded at this suggestion, telling him to start acting like the professional he was hired as and not a third rate hoodlum. As for Tony and Cats, they were going to meet in a tragic car accident on the highway. The brakes would fail and they would plunge over an embankment, into the ocean. Tony sat with every muscle in his body tense, just wanting an opening to attack one of these scum. TNT more than any of them. He figured that if he were going to die anyway, he would love to at least inflict some pain on one of them. His main focus remained on TNT. He could not believe the way TNT had sat there and so calmly explained everyone's fate, as if instructing actors as to how a scene was to be played out. How, over all these years, did he not see even a hint of this side of him?

"Ok ladies, it's time to break up your little huddle." Williams headed toward Valerie and Sherri. Valerie started screaming and grabbed Sherri's arm with all the strength she could muster. Quickly, Williams placed the gun to her head and told her to shut up. Sherri wrapped her arm around Valerie and they hung on to each other. Even as Williams and Deric grabbed the two to separate them, TNT tried to convince them, that there was no sense in fighting the inevitable.

"Come now, don't make this harder on yourselves than it already is. Either way, the end result is going to be the same." TNT said in a calm, fatherly tone.

As the men started tearing the two women apart, from each other's grip, Tony twitched but was met with Reid's gun barrel in his face. A plead escaped Valerie's mouth, as the grip her and Sherri had on each other, was finally broken. Crying and pleading, she was dragged into the kitchen by Deric. Sherri was numbly led into the dining room that joined the kitchen. She appeared to be void of any emotion, as if she finally had given up. As Williams cocked his gun and raised it to Sherri's temple, Cats buried her face in Tony's chest. Tony was crying at the sight of Sherri. After all she had been through, and the strength and courage she had shown, to have it end in such a cowardly act.

"You may want to close your eyes and make ready." TNT instructed Sherri.

Slowly she turned her head, looking hard into his eyes, making him realize that she had no fear of him, or death.

"You can go to hell," she said defiantly.

"There is no doubt in my mind, that that is exactly where I'll end up. But then there is always a price to pay, for what a person strives for in life. Enough, let's get this over with and get out of here. It has been a pleasure. Goodbye." He said giving her a smile.

Tony watched in horror, as Williams took a firm grip and steadied the gun, expecting to see the bullet put an end to Sherri's life. With the sound of Valerie's hysterical screams filling the house, the sound of the glass breaking, as the bullet passed through it, wasn't even heard. Instead of Sherri collapsing to the floor, Williams's head violently jerked to one side. What seemed like a slow motion scene from a movie, his body fell sideways, sending the bullet intended for Sherri, hammering into the glass china cabinet that was against the wall behind Sherri. Every bewildered eye in the house, was on the lifeless form lying on the dust rose carpet, with blood flowing out into a puddle. An eerie silence fell over the scene, as everyone stood in shock and confusion at what they had just seen. The crashing of the back door being forcibly opened, made everyone turn in unison as Daikon emptied a round into Deric, dropping him even before he had a chance to aim his gun. TNT turned and made an attempt to pick the gun up off the floor, where it had landed when Williams had hit the floor. Seeing what his intentions were, Tony dove from the sofa to intercept him. Reid came charging out of the hallway aiming a spray of bullets into the kitchen where Daikon was. As he turned the corner, Daikon lay flat on the floor and fired up from the prone position. The bullet hit hard into Reid's forearm. Suddenly, another bullet slammed into Reid's chest sending him stumbling backwards as he fell into the hallway. Daikon rolled over to see Justine standing there holding her shoulder and heading into the hallway where Valerie was curled up on the floor, screaming and crying.

Tony was surprised at the strength and agility that TNT had for his age. TNT had the gun in his hand and was trying desperately to force it around to Tony's direction. As they wrestled, a shot was fired but missed both men. Daikon tried to get an aim on TNT but couldn't do it as the two men continually rolled. Tony saw an opportunity and rolled TNT over onto his stomach with the arm holding the gun under the weight of his body. Not being able to pull his arm out, TNT finally gave up the struggle and lay still on the floor.

"It's over. Do you hear me, it's over." Tony breathed in his ear, as he kneeled on his back holding him down. Daikon was heading over with the handcuffs ready, when the gun under TNT went off. The bullet rushed by Tony's cheek, spraying him with blood. Tony jumped off him scrambling to get away. When there was no movement from TNT, Tony cautiously went and rolled him over. There was blood trickling from his mouth and his eyes were already taking on a glazed look. A hole in his chest showed where the bullet had entered.

TNT grabbed at Tony and pulled him down close. "It will never be over." He said, barely audible.

"You bastard. Why? I'm going to make sure the world knows what's going on out there."

Coughing and doubling over in pain, TNT shook his head. "You'll never be able to prove it. No one will believe anything like that would be possible."

TNT fell back on the floor again coughing, as more blood spewed from his mouth. Reaching into his pocket, Tony pulled out a small tape recorder he always carried with him.

"Remember? You taught me to never go anywhere without it. Never know when you may need proof for a story, you told me. Well, I guess you were right. I have the proof I need right here."

As the look of comprehension sunk into TNT's eyes, he desperately reached for the recorder in Tony's hand, but his hand fell limply to the floor. As TNT's eyes slowly started to show that he was about to meet death, he smiled softly and said, "Just the ramblings of a crazy old man." Grabbing Tony one more time, he struggled to maintain consciousness. "Tell Laurie, I'm sorry and I love her very much. Take her to the Caymans." As the last word left his lips, his eyes froze into a glassy stare and his chest no longer rose and fell. Tony stood up and looked down at the man, that he had for the most part of life, considered a friend and a mentor. Cats slid up beside him and wrapped her arms around his neck, crying softly. Holding her, he stood and looked around to see what had transpired.

"How the hell did you know where we were?" Tony asked, now facing Daikon.

"I didn't. I had this feeling that something was coming down, but damned if I could figure out what it was. The other day when I met these two, so called FBI agents, I was convinced that whatever it was, was going to happen soon. When I went to see Justine, we checked her out of the hospital."

"As if I was going to miss this." Justine cut in, leading a wide eyed but much calmer Valerie into the living room, where everyone had gathered.

"Anyways, Justine has been watching these two the whole time. She came up with the very brilliant idea, of putting a bug in their car. I guess they never thought some small town cops would be smart enough to do something like that. So, when they followed you here form the station, she knew exactly where you were, and called me. By the time the captain was done reading me the riot act and threatening to have me removed from the force, everyone had left. On the way over, we were just hoping that we were going to get here in time."

"Well, I'm damn glad you did. But do you think you could have cut it any closer." Tony said holding out his hand. Daikon took it and they exchanged a mutual respective smile.

"Is it really over?" Sherri's voice startled everyone. She had sat down at the dining room table and was staring up at everyone. Her face was white and still had an emotionless expression.

"Sherri, this is Detective Daikon. He has wanted to meet you for quite a while now. He was out there and knows the truth. You can trust him. And this is his amazing partner, Justine Hasker." Justine looked at Tony and smiled.

"You're too kind. Pleased to meet you Sherri. You have been an incredibly brave lady." She said, smiling at Sherri.

"You saw what they did?" Sherri asked Daikon. "You know?"

"Yes I do, and it is pretty much over now." Daikon reassured her. "We'll still have to go to the station and fill out reports, but from what I've learned and am going to learn from you, not to mention what we can get from the tape, I think not too much is going to come from it, as far as you're concerned."

Daikon got on the phone and made arrangements for a crime scene unit to come out. Tony and Cats took Sherri and left the house with Justine, helping Valerie out. A small crowd had gathered on the sidewalk, craning their necks to see if they could catch a glimpse of what had gone on inside. As Tony led the small group, out of the house, they could hear the crowds gasps and quiet whispers, asking each other what had happened. Did anyone see anything, was anyone killed, the questions seemed to ripple through the whole crowd. There would be lots to gossip about over coffee, for quite sometime now. After getting Valerie settled, Justine headed off to deal with the inquisitive group that had gathered. She would give them the usual line. Nothing here for them to see, they could all go home and read about it in the paper in the morning. Even as she said it, the irony of it hit her and she shook her head.

Tony, Cats and Sherri headed over to Valerie's car, where Valerie sat on the curb, staring at her house. It seemed like a strange place to her now. The warmth and welcoming feeling it once possessed, was lost forever. Each one of them stared at the house, deep in their own thoughts. Cats had her head on Tony's shoulder and he held her close, while Sherri sat on the curb beside Valerie, holding her hand. Soon their quiet contemplative mood was interupted by the screams of the ambulance and police sirens approaching. The sound of the sirens made Sherri tense up. Tony walked over and placed a hand on her shoulder and gave her a smile.

"Don't worry, we're here to the end with you." He said.

"Thank you." She replied, as she reached up and grabbed his hand, letting the tears of gratitude and relief flow freely. Tony stood there looking over at Cats, who had tears of her own running down her cheeks and a smile on her lips. Tony reached out a hand inviting her to join them.

Daikon and Justine approached the small group, but kept their distance allowing them to share a well needed moment of release together. After a few minutes, they separated stepping back and looking over towards the two detectives.

"Well, what say we get the hell out of here." Daikon said, smiling at the four of them.

"You know, out of everything I have heard today, that has to sound like the best idea I have heard yet." Tony replied. There was a murmur of approval from everyone.

Valerie stood back a bit from the other three. "Mind if I tag along? I don't think I'm much into going back in there again." She asked.

"We would never mind. I think it would do us all good just to be together for awhile." Tony said, as he stepped toward her and gave her a kiss. They both stared at each other for a moment and smiled, knowing that they had gotten through it.

"Justine and me have got to head back to the station to fill out these annoying reports, but there's a nice neighborhood pub just around the corner. We'll meet you there just as soon as we're done. We'll make arrangements for each of you to come in and fill out your reports." Daikon instructed.

"I'll buy the first round." Tony offered.

"Good thing, because I'm broke." Sherri said. It seemed to hit them all at the same time and they shared in a laugh that came from the heart and was well overdue.

"Come on, the least I can do than is the driving." Valerie said, as she started to climb into the car.

When everyone had climbed in, Cats leaned over and kissed Tony, squeezing his hand.

"Have you ever been to the Cayman Islands?" he asked her.

"No." She looked at him, thinking of the dinner conversation she had had with TNT and Laurie.

"Want to go? I hear it's a great place to have fun and escape the ordinary."

"When does the flight leave?" she asked, leaning over and kissing him again deeply. Looking in the mirror, he saw Valerie's eyes and the nod of her head. The car pulled away from the house, leaving the growing crowd of curiosity seekers and the busy uniformed police officers, who were scurrying around trying to secure the crime scene, from the curious crowd.

Men may pursue power, Tony thought to himself, as they turned a corner and the house disappeared, but very few knew how to handle it when they have it. As for him, all he wanted was to pursue happiness. He had seen enough sadness to last him a lifetime, it was time to live again. Settling back in the car seat, he let his mind wander to a sandy beach, surf and the lady sitting beside him, who he now knew without a shadow of doubt, he loved.

0-595-26400-X

Printed in the United Kingdom
by Lightning Source UK Ltd.
9403200001B